Private
Family Business

A WAVERLY CONSULTANTS NOVEL

D.L. Gollnitz

Cover Design by Jill Zee Graphic Design
Cover photo Unsplash.com Carolina Pimenta

ISBN: 979-8-9985232-1-2

For my parents.

Stories originate in recesses of the mind.
No one can account for strange plot development when a writer allows a character to lead the way.

TABLE OF CONTENTS

CHARACTERS

The Walker Family

Albert & Charlene Walker	Founders of Shore Industries
Philip Walker	Eldest Son
Albert Walker, Jr.	Grandfather's Namesake
Charlene Walker	Grandmother's Namesake
Raymond Walker	Younger Son (m. Joyce Walker)
Carl Walker	Aunt's Namesake (m. Holly Walker)
	Two Young Sons
Carla Walker	Daughter (Deceased at Three Months)

Shore Industries Staff

C-Suite:	
Phil Walker	Chief Executive Officer
Ray Walker	Chief Operating Officer
Adam Barnes	Chief Financial Officer
Katie	Administrative Assistant
Christine	C-Suite Secretary
Procurement Department:	
Carl Walker	Executive Director
Sharon	Department Secretary

Waverly Consultants

Dominick Pierce	Managing Director
Melanie Sullivan	Business Consultant & Coach
Carl Walker	Former Business Consultant & Coach

CHAPTER 1

Melanie Sullivan walked down the hallway, stepped on the elevator, and let the tears fall. The C-suite team at Shore Industries had started out to be jovial, back-slapping buddies. They ended in a snarl. Their business would be dissolved, and she was to blame.

One level down, the elevator stopped. She dragged her wrist across her cheeks to dry them before the doors opened. When she saw the perfectly creased suit pants and brilliant polish on Italian leather shoes, she knew it was him. Carl Walker.

"What brings you to Shore, Melanie?" His voice was deep but upbeat, professional but inviting.

"Business." Her heart rate bumped up a beat or two like it did when she avoided a car wreck on the city streets of Boston. She could think of nothing more to say.

The elevator stopped on the third floor. "I'm making another visit here. Good to see you!"

"Are you sure?" His voice was urgent, but he did not stop the door from closing.

Melanie was not sure it was good to see him, but she was sure she needed to get off that elevator. She stepped into a barren space filled with storage lockers. The elevator door closed and blocked his voice.

Melanie dropped her briefcase and purse at her feet and pulled her cell phone from her blazer pocket. No phone signal. No opportunity to phone a friend for moral support. Rather than risk the elevator, she decided to take the stairs to the garage four flights down. She slung her purse and briefcase across her body and descended the stairs, mentally preparing for her own decline.

It was not easy to walk downstairs in heels anymore. She was not sure if it was her age, or if she had become accustomed to comfortable shoes. But it did not matter by the time she reached the street level entrance. She had had enough exercise and decided it was safe to return to the elevator to the below-ground parking structure.

Melanie pulled out her cell and saw that service was back. Just to confirm where her car was parked, she searched for the photo she had taken of the garage placard, a habit developed when leaving her car in long-term parking structures.

That trick saved her more than once from wandering through garages, lost and disoriented. She recalled losing sight of her mother in a store when she was four years old. Fear had squeezed her body and finally pushed her to the cold tile where she lay hugging her doll until her mother found her.

When the elevator door opened to an empty car she stepped in and confidently tapped the button labeled *Parking*.

The drive from Shore Industries to her hotel was long enough for Melanie to put her personal feelings about Carl back into the box where she kept them. Right now, she needed to focus on the next steps for the team at Shore. It was not going to be easy to walk them through a shutdown process. Internal communications, starting with upper management through hourly production line staff, would take careful crafting and patience. Each person was important, and each would be devastated to learn their company was folding.

The hardest part of the day was seeing Carl before she was ready. She took the evening to hunker down and hash out the project timeline. Tomorrow was going to be another distressing day.

****

She awoke to light rain tapping on the hotel room windows. It had been a late night of work, and sleep was fitful. The anxiety of knowing what was to come propelled her out of bed. The coaching sessions had wrapped up days ago, but the next phase was always more difficult. The action planning would be a bear, especially since this was Carl's family business. The process had started with remote meetings between Detroit and her Boston office. Yesterday was the in-person session where she delivered unwelcome news about the company's long-term financial health.

Phil and Ray Walker were not happy, and the guilt of destroying the brothers' pride for a lifetime of work weighed heavily on her. The Walkers compromised the planned timeline of events by asking her to audit the records of the Procurement Department, which was directed by Carl Walker.

Melanie knew there was nothing she could do with a business plan, corporate restructuring, downsizing, or debt acquisition that would change the landscape. She was the right person to shift things in a better direction, but she would feel more confident with one specific person working at her side.

After all, they were the best team on the Waverly Consultants staff and everyone knew it. Independently, Melanie was a good turnaround specialist, but she did her best work when she collaborated with Carl.

Attention to detail would be important today. Details about her hair, her makeup, her clothing. It would be important to look like an expert with a soft touch. Much of what she learned in market and financial analysis came easily to her. But her personal presentation took the expert work of a pro. For several years, Melanie worked with a personal stylist and shopper. As a result, she had packed three suitcases of varying sizes with everything needed for each stage of this process. There was a time when her mother would have been the right person to shop for her. They would pick out school clothes and church clothes, each with their own place in her closet. Her mother's death nearly twenty years ago still caused her heart to ache when she selected an outfit for an important meeting.

Yesterday was a day for school clothes, now better known as her work wardrobe. Nothing over the top. Simple brown slacks, a white blouse open at the neck under a tweed blazer. All the signs of a professional digging in with shirt sleeves rolled up to deliver difficult news. She had worn heels to maintain the impression of a youthful style.

Today she reached for the plum-colored sheath dress, multi-colored scarf, and black jacket that gave her a business-with-a-heart look. Her stylist described this look as one that portrayed Melanie as a flexible person, open to discussing options yet serious about her work.

She curled the ends of her shoulder-length auburn hair with a curling iron and spritzed it with hair spray. Just enough makeup accented her cheekbones, eyelashes, brows, and lips. Flat black leather shoes were simple, polished, and functional. The mirror reflected the look she ordered.

Day two was about to begin. Melanie checked the clock. Five-ten. Too early for breakfast in the lobby restaurant. She laid her briefcase and crossbody on the bed and dialed room service. While she waited, she contemplated the shiny black leather strewn across the white bed linen. Years of traveling with consulting teams had taught her black leather reeked of the old boys' network, a crowd she had clawed her way into long ago. But even after thirty-five years in her career, the company she kept was no less forgiving. Women still had to prove themselves above the capabilities of their male counterparts.

CHAPTER 2

Carl stepped off the elevator on the second floor and took the next available ride up one level, which was supposed to be blocked from elevator access. The door slid open. He stepped out of the car and looked in all directions. No sign of her. Listening for movement, he walked with soft steps through the rows of storage lockers, but the space was still. His dress shoes caused an echo in the open rafters, and memories of why this huge space was converted to a concrete locker room splashed around his brain. An exercise facility for staff, a way to treat them a little better. Something about that story had never seemed quite right, but he had trusted his father's explanation.

The same nervous twitch from a year ago struck him when he touched Locker Eleven, his personal storage. It was the day he signed his employment contract and stashed related documents here. He later added personal possessions.

He knew he should be more attentive to the contents, but there was no reason to assume anyone would have a need to know what was stored for safekeeping. When he thought about all these things, he dizzied as if sitting at the top of a roller coaster that was about to inflict undeserved whiplash.

Right now, there was no time to worry about it. He needed to find Melanie.

****

Carl returned to his office in a daze. His cell phone buzzed with a text message. Sharon, his department secretary, was at the purchasing agents meeting and was looking for him. Bumping into Melanie was a huge distraction, and the detour to the lockers threw him off his game. He texted back.

On my way

No one would ask questions about his tardiness as he was Executive Director of Procurement for all of Shore Industries. Carl was sure of that.

By the time he entered the conference room, everyone who needed to be in the meeting was present. That was a bit unusual. The staff usually found an excuse whenever possible to skip a monthly lecture on how badly the company was performing. Forty purchasing agents and assistants worked with diligence day in and day out to find the best pricing and avoid price fixing and collusion. No matter what they did, costs stayed the same for materials and components that were the largest expense in the manufacture of safety grab bars for bathrooms and home entrances.

He heard Phil's drone across the room. "The industry is mature, but somehow suppliers don't seem to see that it's time to cut the per-unit price for raw materials that haven't changed since the dinosaur age. Well, maybe the 1970s. The point is there is no R & D premium left to cover. If they'd improved the mounting brackets or the thickness of the stainless steel in the tubes used, we might understand. Or maybe our customers would understand. But none of us gets it. Money hungry corporations need to back down."

Words bounced from Phil Walker's mouth off the tops of heads lowered in front of him. These employees looked like they were praying for forgiveness when all they had done was fight and scrape to keep raw material inventory levels where they needed to be. Carl never understood why Phil could not see the people in front of him. Instead, he saw paupers groveling for handouts from the company.

"If we're not able to find other resources, then no one at Shore Industries will see a pay raise in the coming year. And that's not a threat. It's a promise that includes every single employee all the way up to the chief officers. So find a way!"

There was silence in the room when Mr. Phil, as employees called him to differentiate him from his brother Ray, stepped back from the podium and marched out of the room. Not one person moved.

Sharon looked sheepish. She eyed Carl and nodded slightly to the podium telling him to get up there and do something, say something, to save the moment.

"Well!" Carl called out from the doorway where he had paused before entering the meeting. "We all know that Mr. Phil is very enthusiastic about his company, as are all of you." He made his way through the group to take the podium as he spoke.

"We all understand the challenges of our work, and each one of you has done an incredible job of keeping our buys as cost-effective as possible. We also all understand the way inventory backups create space issues for production. It is not just our department finding ourselves in a circular pattern, the same is true in sales. You all know the story. Raw materials inventory is costly, production costs are high when there are short production runs, sales drop when prices go up, inventory builds up again, we need to make smaller buys at higher costs, and on and on."

A middle-aged woman at the back of the room stood up. "If I may interrupt, Mr. Carl, do you think this company is going to make it? You know, stay in business?"

The question came from so far out of left field that Carl could only shake his head with a scowl on his brow. "What are you asking? Do you think that Shore Industries is going bankrupt or something?"

"I'm just asking. Mr. Phil seemed upset. I don't remember that kind of demand from him in the fifteen years that I've worked here."

She was right. Phil was out of character. Sure, he was always brusque with the employees and never really showed his human side. But underneath, workers generally knew that he did care about them and their work. Not today. Maybe there was something Carl did not know, especially since Melanie Sullivan was in the building.

He paused to find the words.

"I can stand here today and honestly say that I am not aware of any financial situations with Shore Industries that indicate this family business is on a path to failure."

"Thank you for that." The lady returned to her seat and others in the room clapped.

There was a lump in Carl's chest. Why was Melanie, a nationally known executive coach and turnaround consultant, at his family business without his knowing? What was Uncle Phil hiding?

The drive home was harsh. Rain was pouring on the Motor City, and headlights created glare making the highway difficult to navigate. The windshield wipers were ineffective in the deluge. When Carl reached the underpass just before the exit from I94 to I75, the trail of red taillights let him know the road was flooded. Again. He would be stuck for a while. He pulled over and called home.

His wife picked up on the first ring. "Hi, honey. The road's flooded and I'm going to sit and wait for it to drain. How are the kids?"

"We're all home safe and sound," Holly said.

"I expect to be there soon. It looks to me like the rain is slowing. If I sit tight, my guess is that I can drive through in about twenty minutes."

"Yeah. Okay. Food will be in the oven."

Carl chuckled. "Good. I appreciate that. Hug the boys for me."

The call disconnected. Nothing felt right. Not even with Holly. Married for eight years, two years together before that, two great little boys, and yet the spark was already gone from her voice.

The rapping on the roof of the car got more intense before it finally slowed down, sounding like a soundtrack to his life. His relationship with Holly had started off like gentle rain, calm and soothing when they first fell in love. Her presence was a lifeline for him, always taking away the stressors of even the worst day. Their marriage had been a big celebration, like lightning bursting in the sky. Then babies arrived less than two years apart. Things were intense with late nights of work and little uninterrupted sleep. They lost their spontaneity and the joy of one another's company. When the pounding rain had begun to subside in their relationship, the mundane drizzle of daily living was enough to keep the fire from reigniting.

A car horn blew behind him, and Carl pulled the car ahead. He drove slowly through the shallowest part of the flood, always on the very edge of the right lane. When he drove out of the underpass, he saw rays streaming down from the dark clouds. It was like Lord Jesus was going to descend at any second. Carl wondered what would happen to him if he met his maker right now.

Holly pulled the door open when she heard Carl coming through the garage. "You have to call your mother." The urgency and tension in her voice spoke louder than her words. "We just hung up. Your uncle Phil collapsed."

Carl got to the hospital as quickly as he could and spent a long night of waiting. It was early morning, and his uncle Phil was beginning to speak in short spurts. Words that did not quite make sense were strung together in unintelligible combinations.

"Make…ness...biz. Nie…mel. Deal. No. Sell. No. Things." Phil struggled.

"Make business? Nie Mel? Melanie? Business deal?" Carl wondered if Phil was talking about Melanie Sullivan. "Did you talk to her yesterday?"

Phil blinked three times and tried to nod.

"Uncle Phil, you should just rest."

This was probably why Phil collapsed. Melanie Sullivan was at Shore Industries. Now he started to see the connection.

"Sleep. Ever… for. Later. Lockers. Fix."

"Uncle Phil, it's okay. We'll get the lockers finished. That's not important right now. You need to recover."

"Impor…Im…Tant. Move."

A monitor beeped and a nurse appeared at the door. "Mr. Walker? Are you okay?"

Phil's head fell to the side, his eyes closed, and his breathing was labored.

"Please step out of the room for a minute," the nurse ordered as she began checking Phil's vital signs.

Carl walked into the hall and pulled out his cell. The chances of getting an answer at five-thirty in the morning at his parents' house were very slim. The phone was usually unplugged in the bedroom every night at eleven and not restored to service until eight in the morning. It was his mother's wish to never have her beauty sleep interrupted. His father Ray went along with anything his dear Joyce requested. Carl's opinion was that Joyce was a princess, the likes of which he would never marry. But under her domineering persona, Carl knew she loved him and that he could count on her to support his every decision. Holly was nothing like his mother.

As Carl expected, his call went to voicemail, or in this case recording. His parents still used an answering device. It was an older digital recorder, so his message would be difficult to understand. He left it anyway. "Dad, you probably should come to the hospital now. Uncle Phil is trying to tell me something, but I can't understand him. Something about Melanie Sullivan, I think. You can call my cell if you get this message. Okay. Bye."

He ended the call and headed to the hospital cafeteria for something to eat. Soon enough, Holly would be up, and he could call to talk with the kids before school. One was in first grade and the other in kindergarten. He felt guilty about the amount of time that Shore Industries had taken away from them. On the other hand, Holly was on a flexible work schedule, so she could pick up the slack. That was probably the root cause of the growing chasm he felt with her. But then there was Melanie, a connection he just could not snap. He sometimes wondered if he was cheating Holly by holding a place for Melanie in his soul.

No call from his parents, no word from the nurse. After a light breakfast, he returned to the waiting room, and when seven o'clock rolled around, he called home.

"Hello." Holly sounded groggy.

"Good morning to you! Are you awake?"

"What do you think? I've been awake for two hours. The boys were up in the night. They were both coughing and sneezing. I might need to take the day off and keep them home from school."

"Oh, I'm so sorry, Holly."

"I know. You can't be here because your uncle and father need you. I get it. Family first, right?"

Her comment struck a nerve. "Well, I guess. Are two colds worse than a pending death?"

No response.

"Holly?"

"Of course not! I've got it. Talk to you later." Holly hung up.

The nurse was standing in front of him. "You can go back in, but don't stay too long. He's on medication to keep him sedated."

All Carl thought about was the imposition placed on him. Where were Phil's kids who should be here? Albert and Charlene only wanted the riches. Neither of them worked at Shore. They had no idea what was about to happen. If their father died, and the company was on the precipice of failure, their inheritance would plummet. They had better keep their hands out of the till.

The buzz of his phone in his pocket pulled Carl back to his responsibilities.

"Hello?"

"Oh, Carl. I'm so glad I reached you. Your father isn't ready to come to the phone. You know he needs his morning coffee first. Is everything going okay with Phil? Are you able to manage things on your own? I feel so bad that we were just too tired to stay at the hospital longer but—"

"It's okay, Mom. But Dad needs to tell me what's going on. And he needs to get here as soon as he can."

"Well, that might be a while. You know he likes to read the morning paper and then take his shower and then go for a short walk in the garden. How is Phil?"

"He's sedated. There might be something I need to know from Dad. Can he talk to me?"

"He's indisposed."

"Of course he is. The morning constitutional."

"Stop that! Your father—"

"Somebody needs to be with Uncle Phil. Bye, Mom." Carl disconnected the call.

There was an oxygen mask on Phil's face. The passage of air hissed and monitors beeped with every heartbeat that seemed to be in rhythm with Phil's breathing. The white skin around his eyes made him look like a ghost, maybe the one that was trying to move into his body.

"Phil, can you hear me?"

Nothing.

"Lift a finger if you hear me."

He may have imagined it, but Carl took it as a signal. The middle finger of Phil's right hand lifted just a fraction of an inch off the bed sheet.

"Same to you!" Carl walked out of the room to calm himself. This would not be the only confrontation of the day.

It was late morning by the time Ray arrived at Ford Hospital. Carl was passing near the nurses' station when he arrived. "Who the hell's running the purchasing department if you're hanging around here?"

"Good morning to you, too, Dad." The tone in Carl's voice carried just enough disdain for Ray to know his son was not happy with him.

"Well, not the best morning, I suppose."

Carl closed his eyes and exhaled slowly before he answered his father. "No. It's not."

A pause was filled with the clatter of lunch trays being delivered to patient rooms. Beeps of monitors set a syncopated cadence that reflected patterns of the family. Ray and Phil Walker, both on different wavelengths, both vying for power at Shore, and neither hearing the beat of the other. No one at Shore Industries knew who to follow, leaving staff in constant flux.

"So what happened yesterday, Dad? Phil gave a rough talk at the monthly purchasing meeting. People were baffled. He yelled at them."

Ray rubbed his chin and considered his reply. "Hm. I suppose it was warranted."

"What?! Those people don't deserve to be slapped in the face. They work hard to do what's right, and you know that's true."

"Maybe that's not enough. This isn't the place or time. Let's visit Phil."

Carl abandoned hope of leaving the hospital and fell behind his father who led the way into a room filled with machines.

"He's sleeping," Ray said.

"I'll go to the office and leave you with him."

Ray nodded his approval and Carl walked out.

CHAPTER 3

A breakfast tray was delivered to Melanie's room. The waiter was at the end of his shift. The food was crammed on the tray in no arrangement that made sense, the flatware was wrapped but on top of the covered plate, cream and butter were missing, and the pancake syrup was dripping on the outside of the stainless-steel container. All telltale signs that he was tired and ready to get off duty.

"I'm okay without butter, but I really do need cream for my coffee. Would it be too much trouble for you to bring me some cream?" Melanie smiled to soften her request. She knew the overnight shift could be tough for the staff. They probably had no way of predicting the needs of travelers who came and went at all hours of the day and night.

The waiter flushed. "I'm sorry. Of course not. I'll be right back."

He exited the room as if he needed to save a damsel in distress. A vision of long golden strands of hair hanging down the side of a castle spire made Melanie laugh. She could hear the soft voice of her mother reading bedtime stories as she drifted off to dreamland. It felt like yesterday. "If only I were living in a fairy tale," she said aloud.

She sat at the table where the tray was placed, an impressive view of the skyline ahead of her. The Detroit River was smooth, and the sunrise shone on the glassy surface. In the distance, she watched the fade of twinkling lights in Windsor, Ontario. The early morning local news channel was broadcasting a similar view on their 4Warn weather report.

The day was shaping up to be chilly but sunny with overnight showers clearing out of the area. Melanie hoped her day would go from glum to bright, but she needed to turn the tides with Phil and Ray Walker before everything was lost to a chaotic roll-out of bad news.

She pulled a notepad from the center of the table and made some bullets to fill in with talking points for her next meeting with Dominick Pierce, one of the Waverly directors. She had been considering retirement or at least taking a different direction with her work. Dominick was open to discussion, so she noted to inquire about a consulting agreement that was less arduous. Maybe accepting selected projects. Shore might be her last onsite assignment.

She tore the notepaper from its pad and crumpled it in a ball, putting the idea on hold until she landed the plane successfully at Shore.

The knock on the door brought a welcome sight. The waiter was returning with not only cream, but a carafe of fresh hot coffee. "I thought maybe your coffee would be cold by the time I returned, so here you go."

"Now that's the kind of service that deserves reward." Melanie retrieved her purse and produced a twenty-dollar bill. "Use it wisely."

The brightest smile she had seen in days glowed on the young man's face. "You just made my day!" He gave her a slight bow.

"No, you made mine. Now, go. Have a wonderful day!"

"Yes, ma'am!" He exited the room with a lift in his step.

As she poured a hot cup of coffee, Melanie thought maybe she could do something to make it a good day for the Walker family. There had to be a positive spin on the future. These men were proud, and she could not bear to hurt Carl's father and uncle.

When she got to Shore Industries, Melanie wasted no time getting to work in the conference room on the fifth floor. Her requests for financial documents and access to active contracts were provided. Moving boxes from chair to table to floor, pulling folders, removing and flagging key documents, and returning everything to its original box produced more paper cuts than answers. For such a large company, many archaic systems were in place, which was not unusual for family-run businesses. It was often the third generation of a family that started to push current practice a little harder, and Carl was the only third-generation family member working at Shore.

Carl's shared stories of his grandparents, Albert and Charlene Walker, had impressed Melanie. Their business had been developed around their empathy for aging people who wanted to live long, productive, and happy lives in the comfort of their own homes. She had researched Shore Industries and created a digital scrapbook of news articles about the Walkers. They had expanded into a major manufacturing business that specialized in grab bars, entrance ramps, and handrails for multiple purposes. They partnered with builders and architects to produce assistance equipment designed to accommodate specific needs. Melanie had been saddened by the obituaries written for this admirable couple. The company continued successfully, but Melanie wondered if the business decline had not correlated to the loss of a true patriarch of a family, the community, and a private family business. The Walkers had been predeceased by a daughter named Carla, the youngest of their three children, who died from what was called crib death when she was just three months old.

Phil and Ray Walker had honored their parents and sister when naming the grandchildren. Phil was the older brother, and his children were named after company founders, Albert and Charlene, but neither of his offspring cared about Shore Industries. Carl was his aunt Carla's namesake. The cousins were in their fifties and sixties, and none of them had spent any time working at Shore.

When he prepared for his departure from Waverly Consulting, Carl had explained his sense of obligation to take a role in the family business. His cousins were not getting involved and aging owners had no one else to carry their legacy into the future. When Shore Industries started declining under the leadership of Phil and Ray, Carl accepted his father's invitation and left his career in Boston.

Melanie and Dominick had believed that Carl's heart was not aligned with his logic. His justification included obligation, pride in his family, and the benefits of shorter workdays with less travel. Sure, Chinese food in cardboard boxes was getting old, but the fire in Carl's belly stayed at Waverly when he left Boston. His uncle Phil, CEO, appointed Carl to the position of Director of Procurement, where he would learn about the home grab bar industry. It had been only one year, and Melanie was sorry to witness the mistake her colleague had made. Beyond that, her heart still ached for the relationship she once had with him.

The legal documents adding Carl to the organization seemed to be in order with nothing jumping out as suspicious or unusual. She questioned if Albert and Charlene were still in line to receive the profits of any buy-out. Keeping the company afloat long enough for Carl to inherit the sinking ship was illogical, but she knew he could turn a profit if given the chance.

Phil and Ray refused to bring Carl into the company as a chief officer because he needed to earn his place at the Shore table. But he had a place waiting for him at any table in the Boston C-suite club.

If the company was sold or liquidated, payouts to Carl's cousins, Albert and Charlene, would be interpreted as an inheritance, but because Carl worked for the firm, Melanie thought Carl should receive a greater share. His cousins would receive something from their other employment. They might have commissions, retirement accounts, or stock options. None of these were part of Carl's employment package until a review on his five-year employment anniversary. It was not her business, but she did wonder how Carl felt about it. Or if he even knew all the details that involved his cousins.

Melanie wanted nothing more than to invite Carl to collaborate with her. She knew that would be a conflict of interest. The Walkers did not know her personally, they only knew that Carl had a great partner at Waverly Consulting, a firm known nationally for its efficient operations and strong results with turnaround management. She was sure she could keep personal and professional relationships separate. That was before she saw the full picture.

A thorough review of documents had not revealed any problems, but she was puzzled that Carl would agree to the conditions of his employment contract.

Melanie jumped and looked up when someone rapped on the door. It was him. What should she say? “Come in.”

“What's going on? Does Waverly actually have a contract with our company?”

“Hello, Carl. How are you?”

Her hands tremored, so she lowered them to her lap under the table. She was conscious of the twitch that pushed at the corner of her mouth. Carl would see how nervous she had become when he entered the room.

"I'm fine. I was shocked to see you yesterday. I didn't think your assignment would have you looking through Shore Industry documents."

"Well, it does." That came out sounding a little too curt. She lowered her eyes before continuing. "I guess your uncle and father failed to notify you that Waverly was called in for consultation."

"They didn't tell me. That's a slap."

"I'm sorry, Carl. How could I have known?" She hated appearing desperate, but she was. Desperate for him, his input, his business savvy. And him.

"Of course you couldn't know. We don't seem to communicate these days. Well, good luck."

Carl left the conference room.

Melanie lifted the thick curly hair from her neck to let some air circulate. Why did his family not tell him what was going on? There had to be something in the accounts that she was missing.

A walk down the hall for a coffee was enough to bring her mind back to the research needed to answer her doubts. She must have missed a financial or legal issue. Surely, Ray was trying to protect Carl, his only child. Or maybe Ray knew something about Phil's work that would become transparent with a keen eye on purchase orders. It was time to dig deeper.

It was nearly six o'clock when Melanie packed up her things and left Shore Industries for the day. All her research pointed to one last possibility. She wanted to talk with Adam

Barnes, Chief Financial Officer, about some cash accounts with a regular flow of funds through electronic transactions.

She stepped into the elevator and pressed the button for the garage level. The cool night air was rolling in with a breeze that funneled into the elevator when the door slid open. She tipped her head down to avoid the unpleasant odor of carbon monoxide and noticed a hard hat in someone's hand. Before stepping out onto the cement landing, Melanie's briefcase caught the edge of the door frame, pushing the hat out of a man's hand.

"I'm so sorry. The wind caught me off—"

"No big deal," the man answered. His voice was gruff and threatening.

He was wearing overalls and work boots and carried a collapsed tool bag under his arm. Melanie walked to her car a little faster than usual, got in, and locked the doors immediately.

On the drive back to the hotel, she pulled into a Coney Island restaurant. There was nothing better than a Coney dog to add to her pending heartburn. But why not? She would have indigestion with or without splurging on local food, so she may as well enjoy a good hot dog topped with chili and all the fixings.

A cup of coffee complemented the gastric disaster and energized Melanie's thinking. She wondered why neither Phil nor Ray came to the office all day. She pulled out her phone and emailed Phil to let him know she did more research today and planned to be in the office at eight o'clock in the morning. She copied Ray. Surely one of them would respond.

She ate slowly, hoping to minimize the stomach upset. Detroit was a place she had visited only a few times for business, and once with Carl. Their short romantic relationship had to end, and he had gone on to find a wife. Now he had a life in the 'burbs, the kids, everything he wanted that Melanie could not give him. She still could not shake the wave of regret that washed over her when she thought of those times together.

Melanie pushed a napkin back and forth on the table, staring into the half-full cup of coffee. It was like endless work, keeping a table clean or building relationships in her career. When a tabletop was shiny and inviting, someone would sit and drop food on it. Coffee would splatter, and someone needed to clean again.

It had taken multiple attempts to get the accounts payable records for review, as Adam only assigned an administrative assistant, Katie, to help. Melanie received what she requested, but the reports were summaries, not detailed transactions. With some cagey wooing in the form of frothing lattes and healthy snacks, she forged a relationship with Katie that allowed her access to the information.

The data would be documented all the way through the cash flow chain. If these accounts were clean, then she would move to the next phase and outline the schedule to shut down Shore Industries.

With one last sweep of the table, she crumpled the napkin into the now empty coffee cup. "Goodbye, Shore," she said to no one. Maybe she should not have taken this assignment.

CHAPTER 4

Carl made it back to the hospital in time to walk in on a one-way conversation. Medical equipment continued to pump and beep and swish. Phil still lay pale against the propped bed, but he was awake.

Ray was preaching to his older brother. “If you hadn’t gotten so worked up about Melanie’s report, none of this would have happened. Maybe it is time to let Shore fade away, Phil. We’ve worked as hard as we can, and we’re still bleeding green.”

Carl decided to be a wallflower and listened. He stayed behind the drawn privacy drape that surrounded Phil’s bed, back far enough that his feet could not be seen under the curtain. He leaned on the wall and listened.

“Mom and Dad had a good vision. But we both know that the market is saturated with home aid products. We can’t compete anymore. Our process is ancient, and nobody wants to pay our prices.”

“Mm.” Phil was trying to speak.

“Is that agreement, Phil?”

“Ahh.” He coughed and choked enough to set off an alarm on one of the monitors. A nurse appeared and gave away Carl’s presence on the way to Phil’s bedside.

“Move out of the way, please.”

When the curtain was pushed back for two nurses to pass, Ray spotted Carl. “Oh, son! I didn’t know you were here.” The blush on Ray’s cheeks told Carl that he did indeed hear something he should not have, but he put that thought away.

"Looks like they took the oxygen tube away. That's a good sign."

"Yeah, blood oxygen level is better. Why did you come back?" Ray's inquiry trumped any concern about Phil's health.

"I talked to Melanie Sullivan. At our office. In our conference room. She's working on something. For Shore! What's going on?"

Ray pulled Carl's sleeve and led him down the hall to an alcove. They sat on a bench, too close together for Carl's liking. Ray spoke first.

"Look, son. Phil and I, well, got into a little financial bind. It's nothing we can't fix."

"So why is Waverly here? Why Melanie?"

Ray gave the reasoning. Waverly was the best fit for their current situation, and they requested Carl's former team to do the analysis.

"And you think I don't know how to do these things? I helped build Waverly's reputation! Why not just ask me? If you're having financial problems, why spend more money to have someone do what I've done for years? Very successfully, I might add. Didn't you trust your own son?"

"It's not that."

"No? So what is it, *Dad*?"

The emphasis caused Ray to pull back.

"Calm down. Let's try to talk like two businessmen for a minute."

"It might be too late for that. But go ahead."

Carl leaned back against the wall and propped himself for an avalanche that would need boots.

Ray tried to explain. Materials purchases seemed to be the core problem. Too much cash was going out at a faster rate than it should be. Asking Carl to do a full analysis of his own department did not seem smart to Phil or Ray. With high material costs, they had trouble getting contracts. Phil was pulling a little weight to bring in work, which caused a greater cash flow problem.

Carl stood up. “In other words, there’s some wheeling and dealing going on that you don’t want me to know about. Great! I’ve built a reputation on ethical practices, and Phil’s pulling down the business with kickbacks. Is that what you mean by ‘pulling a little weight,’ and you let it go? Or are you trying to put the company’s failures on me?”

“Wait, no one said that.”

“You don’t need to name it, Dad. I made a huge mistake coming to work for you.”

Carl walked away.

****

While the day had been challenging, his evening got even worse. After hearing that his uncle Phil was doing something to bring in more business, all kinds of illegal possibilities came to mind. Carl had nightmares about Holly and the boys being put in some kind of danger because the business was failing and Phil owed money to criminals. Thoughts of the horrible scenarios he and Melanie uncovered in Chicago, Boston, and New York years ago ate at him. The mafia was not kind when underhanded deals got out of control. People disappeared and reappeared in trunks of cars, under overpasses, and on beaches.

He crawled out of bed with dread for the day he had to face. If Phil and his father were both in on something, there was a good chance that Melanie knew what it was. He would need to confront his family first and worry about Melanie later.

She would think he left the team at Waverly to take part in shady business deals. After all, the two of them knew every trick out there for corporations to be successfully on the take without getting caught. But he had no knowledge of illegal business at Shore, and he could not risk hurting Melanie's impression of him.

The first thing on his to-do list for the day was to visit his uncle Phil before his father went to the hospital. He scheduled time in Shore's shared online calendar to be out of the office. Emails were sent to Sharon asking her to get other procurement managers to attend meetings in his absence. To maintain a level of security, he left a voicemail for her as well. "Watch for requests from Mr. Phil to get pricing for work on the lockers on Floor Three."

He thought about what Phil had tried to tell him when he was first admitted. It sounded like it had something to do with business, but the words came out like his tongue had been scrambled in a cement mixer. Not a good image given the reputation of infamous mafia families.

Ray was trying to convince Phil to let go of Shore, and Carl needed to know if the two brothers were on the same page. They had never agreed on things in the past, so Carl would be surprised if they were working together on anything, legal or illegal.

Phil was propped up in the hospital bed. Fewer devices were attached, and he seemed much more lucid.

"Uncle Phil, you look great! Are you feeling better?" Carl plastered on a smile to bury the skepticism.

"Bet... Bett...er."

This did not look good to Carl. "Are they taking good care of you here?"

"No. No foo…d. Hung…ry."

"What?! Are you saying no food? Well, I'll order your favorite filet from Ruth's Chris Steakhouse and have it delivered." Carl chuckled to keep the tone light.

There was a smile that appeared a little lopsided on one side of Phil's face. Stroke. "Are you moving around more today?"

Phil lifted both hands and let them drop. Then he wiggled his toes under the sheets. "That's great! You'll be out of here in no time."

A nurse came into the room just as Carl was about to ask the next question. "Sorry, but this handsome man is heading to the lab for a photo shoot! You'll need to come back this afternoon."

"Just one more minute?"

"No, sorry. The Imaging Department is looking for us. They have scans scheduled back-to-back today. Can't miss our time slot."

Carl patted his uncle's shoulder as the orderlies moved Phil out of the room. He left the hospital and stopped for breakfast before going to the office.

When he pulled into the parking garage, a blue rental car was parked in the reserved space again. Just how long was Melanie's project going to continue and exactly when did she start?

His jaw clenched when he thought of all the possibilities. She could be there to find inefficiencies in purchasing, as his father claimed. She could be doing a Sigma Six quality and efficiency review. That would have required notification to at least the executive directors, but no one informed him. Melanie and Carl had trained in the Sigma Six process and protocols together, and they made a dynamite team. No one could wrap up the details of those visits faster or more effectively than the two of them. But what if she discovers that Phil's efforts to bring in more lucrative business involve kickbacks?

Carl slammed the car door harder than necessary, and he kicked the front tire with his shiny black shoe. He was exploding with negativity about why she could be working in his family's business.

He picked up his pace and jogged to the elevator, pushed the button, and paced while he waited for the car to labor down to the garage level.

CHAPTER 5

The alarm sounded at six-thirty. Melanie desperately needed coffee and a shower but opted for the latter. She wanted to get to Shore Industries before the staff started to arrive. One last investigation of cash transactions had to be finished, and then she could move on to a timeline for announcements to staff.

More than anything, she hoped there were no dirty transactions. She would have to open that trapdoor carefully and just hope that Carl was not privy to any such activity. He could not be. After all, he had always abided by the law and would not be caught dead doing anything out of line. But what if he is implicated in some way?

Today was a roll-up-the-sleeves-and-get-into-the-work kind of day.

She was surprised to see the parking garage heavily occupied at seven-thirty when she pulled in. Aside from prime parking real estate, this project was anything but a cream puff. And the visit with Adam Barnes would let her figure out if there was even any cream in the mix. She was anxious to get back to Boston.

The glass wall of the conference room let everyone who walked from offices or the bullpen to the restrooms, coffee room, or elevators take a good look at who was there and what they might be doing. Was that the point? Did Ray and Phil want everyone to know she was a consultant?

Absorbed with her own little drama, Melanie was oblivious to Ray who was walking down the hall from the coffee room, porcelain mug in one hand and a Danish pastry in the other.

"Good morning, Melanie! I'd shake your hand, but well. . ." He lifted both hands for her.

"I understand. How are you today? I haven't seen or heard from you in a couple of days. Is everything okay?"

"Yes and no." Ray paused, and Melanie tipped her head in question.

"I guess you don't know. My brother Phil is in the hospital. Seems he had a little stroke or something. Right after the monthly meeting with our purchasing agents in the Procurement Department."

Melanie expressed all the right concerns, asked all the right questions to show her empathy. Ray just shrugged his shoulders, gave a tight smile and a quick shake of his head. Not the kind of reaction she would have expected. The brothers had just met with her about dismantling their entire family empire, and Ray was brushing off what sounded like a life-threatening event.

"Well, these things happen. We'll all get through it and come out better on the other side. Now, do you have the timeline ready?"

A middle-management looking guy in a dark gray pin-stripe suit stepped off the elevator. She noted a tasteful red tie that contrasted with his distinguished graying hair. The suit nodded at Ray and turned his head to see Melanie's face but kept walking toward the coffee bar. Although their eyes did not connect, Melanie shivered. His gait was confident with enough swagger for her to classify him as a suave gentleman. If she did not know better, she thought perhaps she was blushing.

"Maybe we should go talk in my office." Ray led Melanie to the farthest possible room down the hall and out of view of anyone else who may happen down the corridor.

Melanie twisted her fingers in her gold necklace and listened to Ray Walker tell her how important it was to move as fast as possible to liquidate Shore Industries. He carried on about timing for the market, competitors who would love to buy Shore's great machinery and inventory, and general coordination for how to achieve the goal he was outlining.

"We should act as fast as we can, of course. I don't want Phil to have to handle any of this. The stress would be bad for him. He'll be in rehab for—"

The door burst open. Carl walked in and planted fists on his hips. "What are you trying to do behind Phil's back?"

Melanie recognized a burn in Carl's voice. She had heard it more than once when they confronted dirty businesspeople. What did he know that she still needed to uncover? Her heartbeat picked up at the thought of missing something important. The hold on her necklace tightened and one hard twist pinched her fingers. She dropped her hands to her lap and just stared at Carl.

"Answer me, Dad. What does Melanie know that I don't know?"

"Nothing!" Melanie's spontaneous response sounded like a cover-up. "I really don't know anything, Carl. I've not completed my review."

"What do you mean?" Ray stood up and walked around to the front of his desk. "I thought you produced one alternative for Shore Industries. And now you tell me you haven't finished your review? What's holding up the timeline we talked about?"

Carl looked back and forth between Melanie's pale face and Ray's red cheeks. Melanie cleared her throat and wiped a wisp of auburn hair away from her brow. "It's not that the review is unfinished. But, when you and Phil were not exactly happy with the recommendation, I was hoping to find another way or another avenue. And, well, I did see a place where maybe some cash funds could be recovered if maybe there's. . . um—"

"Carl, you can leave the room." Ray's deep and steady voice told Carl and Melanie that he had less-than-pleasant words to share in private with his hired consultant.

"Maybe I should stay. I think Phil tried to warn me twice about Melanie's work. I know what's happening here. Melanie, can I have a word with you?" Carl exited the room.

"Not now!" Ray shouted.

Melanie felt the stickiness in her armpits, her sweater just warm enough to feel prickly. She pulled at the neckline, careful to avoid twisting her necklace again.

Ray plopped back into his chair. His head hung down for a moment before he lifted his face with a full smile. "I'm sorry. Sometimes family business can get a little emotional. Carl isn't aware of the conversations we've had."

"As I've gathered. Why not?"

"I don't know if that's any of your business, Ms. Sullivan. Let's say we reconvene mid-afternoon. You take on the next bit of review you wanted to perform, and I expect you'll be ready to set the communication timeline as we discussed."

There was nothing to say. Melanie made a slight nod and left the room. It was clear that this was condescension and not a serious intention on Ray's part to consider any added research.

****

Ray left the office to spend his lunchtime at the hospital. He wanted to be with Phil when they moved him to the rehab unit. When he got there, Charlene was visiting her father.

"Well, look who's arrived! Good to see you, Charlene."

"And you, Uncle Ray." Charlene stood and gave her uncle the requisite peck on the cheek.

Phil's eyes locked on Ray's face with brows knitted together, accentuating the creases in his forehead. Ray studied Phil before he spoke. "Are you doing okay today, big brother?"

Phil did not try to talk but kept his brows pinched. A slight shake of his head was hard to read. Was that a twitch or a negative response to his question? "No?" The shake again, this time a little more pronounced.

"Charlene, has your dad been able to eat anything today?"

"It's not about food or feeling ill. I need to know what you're planning to do that has him so upset. He had a nurse text me with his phone last night requesting I visit today."

Charlene's drive in from Chicago was not difficult, and Ray wondered why she had not made the trip two days ago. This was her father suffering a stroke, her father who lived alone and had only Charlene within reasonable distance to help him. Her brother Al was living in Florida and would only visit if there was something in it for him. Of course, there was enough money in the family to hire any services that were needed, but that was not the point. His own kids should be with him. Everyone knew a daughter's presence in a time like this is usually expected, even welcomed. Exception noted with Charlene.

Ray sat beside Phil's bed. "Look, Phil. You don't need to worry about anything at Shore. I've got it under control. If Adam takes care of everything on his end, the business will be sold in no time."

"Sold? You're selling Shore?" Charlene gave Ray a look telling him she wanted more information.

Phil shook his head, but Ray responded. “Yes, but we haven’t announced anything yet. We have a consultant working out the details.”

“Well, maybe I’ll have that new house by the end of the year after all!”

Phil coughed and wheezed. He shook his head and struggled to speak. “N-n-n-not.”

Ray sank back into the chair. He really would have a fight on his hands.

A knock on the doorframe announced medical staff. “Well, good morning, Mr. Walker. What’s going on with you today? I see you had some Jello and sipped some water. That’s great news.”

Ray pushed himself up. Charlene led him away, not letting Ray hear the doctor’s comments. “We’ll talk in a minute. Why don’t you go out in the hall?”

He followed her suggestion and went to the sitting area in the alcove where he could see Detroit in all its glory. Good and bad. The city looked okay today. There were buses making stops, people getting on and off, everyone going about their day as usual. Whatever that meant.

He sat on the same bench he shared with his son Carl two nights ago. His chest expanded with a deep breath when he thought about that dialogue. He exhaled but felt no relief from the stress that was building in his muscles. The doctor left Phil’s room and walked past Ray who leaned his head back on the wall and closed his eyes for a moment. What was Charlene saying to Phil? He needed to get back there to control the story. He mustered the determination to impose on a father-daughter moment and returned to Phil.

When Ray stepped back into the room, Phil was smiling at Charlene. His squinted eyes and a lopsided smile told Ray that Phil had found a renewed spirit. "What did the doc have to say?" Ray kept his voice upbeat and cheerful.

"Well, they've decided not to keep him in the hospital for rehab. Just a day to work with him. Then he can have the therapy he needs at home."

Phil nodded. Ray did the same.

It was only an hour later when Phil was moved to a new wing where he would receive physical and speech therapy. Ray learned that Phil had walked the hallway with a walker, fed himself a small amount of food, and was showing all signs of full recovery. He was being treated for a concussion suffered when he fell during the ministroke. Brain scans and other tests showed minor swelling that was expected to decrease on its own. A shadow in one image would need to be followed carefully. The medical staff were ruling out possible causes for the episode. The prognosis was good, better news than Ray had expected.

When Ray and Charlene walked to their cars, he decided to probe into what Phil may have shared with her. "Is there anything you want to talk to me about? About Shore?"

"No. I don't think so. I figured out from Dad that he doesn't think the business will sell anyway. At least not now. Maybe in another ten years. Too bad. I would love a little extra money to buy a house in the Chicago suburbs. I've been eyeing a great neighborhood."

Ray was unsure how to respond and chose to remain neutral. "Did he talk to you? I haven't seen much more than a few nods."

"Oh, yeah. That was all an act. When no one's around, his speech is fine."

Ray stopped and Charlene continued to walk ahead. When she realized she was alone, she turned around. "Come on, Uncle Ray! Don't read too much into things. You know my father. He's just buying time. Nurses are starting to notice his act."

"Maybe I don't know him as well as I thought I did."

"Unless Dad needs something specific that can't be handled by an aide or someone else, then we should be good. I'll be out of here tomorrow."

Ray hoped his own son would never be so uncaring. He left the hospital ready to hear Melanie Sullivan's timeline for the big news.

CHAPTER 6

Carl waited for Melanie to find him in his office. His temples drummed and the tempo was not his favorite, like music at the New Year's Mummers' Parade in Philadelphia. He had never seen the likes of the group with their colorful and vivacious movement. It was fun at the time, but he did not know what to think about the cadence they kept. They were on an assignment that started on January second, the last project he and Melanie managed when they were still a couple nearly a dozen years ago. Eleven years, nine months, and two weeks, to be exact.

More than an hour had passed. Carl would have to go to Melanie. Not that he wanted to be the one seeking her out, but she had never catered to his wishes. The glass conference room was not the best place to have the conversation he needed to have with her. It was clear that his father and Melanie were not at all in agreement with whatever was going on.

Melanie was not there when he arrived. File boxes were packed up in a corner. She could not possibly have finished her work that fast unless she already had answers about cash recovery.

Carl called security to see if Melanie's car was still in the parking garage. It was. While Carl was mulling over every possible next step he would take if he were in Melanie's shoes, Katie walked by and waved at him through the clear glass. The smirk on her face was a tip-off.

Adrenaline roiled through his body with the realization that Melanie really had found something bad. She must have worked with Adam's departments and did more than a review of purchasing records. Why had she not contacted him during the audit of his own department? He used the pounding in his temples as a marching rhythm and made his way to the C-suite.

Carl was not surprised to find Melanie sitting in the armchair in front of Adam's mahogany desk. The tapestry seat and dark wood of the chair wrapped around Melanie's body in a way that caused the drumbeat to slow down. His shoulders lowered and his voice was calm.

"May I come in?"

"Carl, of course. My door is always open. You know Ms. Sullivan."

Melanie smiled. "No need for the formalities. Carl and I go way back."

"So what can I do for you?" Adam directed his question to both.

Carl chose to sit without being asked. The matching armchair was the perfect place. He and Melanie were at the same level, facing the same potential fountain of knowledge, and they could be back in the game together.

It was Melanie who spoke first. "Would you like me to return a little later?"

"No!" Carl's voice was a little more robust than he had intended. "No, I was looking for you. But since you're here with Adam, we might both have the same questions for him."

Melanie looked Carl directly in the eye. "I'm not sure I understand."

****

Melanie caught Carl shifting his gaze between her and Adam. She had to admit they were both very appealing men. Bright, articulate, and competitive. The gray suit that had caught her attention in the hallway that morning fit Adam impeccably. At first, she did not classify him as a chief executive kind of person. After spending more time with him, she imagined his broad shoulders standing in front of a sea of customers at a major conference. A keynote speaker delivering the statistical analysis of why pricing was a challenge for home aid manufacturers. He would be lying, of course. It was a challenge for Shore. Other businesses were doing fine.

Melanie was alerted by specific words that Adam was saying to Carl. Common language, like *layered accounts* and *separate transaction purposes*, instead of describing subsidiary accounts and categorical expenses.

"Adam, you don't need to use laymen's language with either of us. And I'm not sure why you feel the need to do that. Unless, of course, there is something else you really want to say and don't have the right words." Melanie was being as direct as possible but knew she must be insulting Adam.

Adam shifted in his leather chair and picked up his gold Cross pen. It was a long classic writing implement, the type used for showy document signing. There was no document in front of him, and he tapped the pen on the glass that protected the dark wood desktop. Melanie detected a slight flush on his cheeks and decided he was trying hard to minimize her concern.

Carl stood up. "Let me close the door."

Adam swiveled to the left and right, looking for something. Melanie could not imagine this composed keynote speaker feeling uncomfortable with just a single confrontation. She decided to take a different approach. "Would it help if I am a bit more direct with what I'm wondering about?"

Adam adjusted his shirt cuff. "It feels like you're accusing me of something, and I have no idea what that could be. So to answer your question, yes. Let's get to the real matter. And, before we continue, does it require Carl's presence?"

"You tell me," Carl said.

Melanie's legs quivered, and she crossed them to hide her discomfort. The last time she became this tense in a client meeting she was also with Carl. They had uncovered misappropriation of funds in a law firm when one of its attorneys was being sued by the prosecutor's office. The junior partner had been caught red-handed with fingers in the till of several contractors and using the money for private expenses. Waverly had taken on the unlucky task of divulging that information to the named partners. It had been an ugly day, and Carl had been by her side through all of it. There was an instinct for shady dealings that she and Carl developed together. Without him at her side in this line of work, she wondered how many times illegal transactions had gone undetected in the past year.

Adam put his pen down. "You both sound like there's something wrong here. Shore Industries has done nothing out of bounds."

"How about if we look at the liquid asset accounts together, then?" Melanie was ready to move on. "And to answer your question, I have no problem with Carl in the room. If everything is in order, you should be fine with that too."

Adam picked up the desk phone and ordered Katie to run hard copies of the most recent account balances for specific cash flow accounts that Melanie requested.

Before Adam placed the handset back on the phone, Melanie called for more information. "We need more than account balances. I already have that information, but I need to see the subsidiary, or as you call them *layered,* transaction details for the past two years."

"Why?"

"Because that's my job. And that detail should include the names of any payees, as well as the details of related cash receipts, including where they originated."

"That might take a little while. She'll need to run a query and then—"

"I have a little bit of time," Melanie interrupted. "Database queries really don't take that long. You can deliver the results to me in the conference room. And Adam, Ray will be asking to meet with me around two o'clock. So don't procrastinate."

Melanie stood up and faced Carl. "It's good to see you again, Carl."

****

Carl waited for Melanie to close the door. "Adam, we don't have to do this the hard way. I just have no idea what's been going on lately."

"Neither do I!"

Carl furrowed his brow, squinting an inquiry back at Adam. "How can that be?"

"I oversee things, which means I trust your father and the experts he hired before my time here to do their jobs. I work on the big picture, and my due diligence hasn't pointed to anything untoward. So I don't know what is going on."

Carl played into what he considered a false statement by asking questions to get Adam to divulge more information. Adam joined in by expanding on his ideas that there was a hidden agenda in having an audit performed.

"Did Ray or Phil specifically name Melanie to come onsite? Did they think they would have leverage over her so she would skew the final reports?" Adam asked.

"Maybe that's it!" Carl stood up and paced the room. "If they want to hide something, they might have thought that she would give a pass because of our work history. Then they could do whatever was needed to present a positive position to overcome the sales slump."

"If they wanted to improve the bottom line, why did they start with your department?" Adam asked.

"You knew that?"

"No." Adam pulled on his cuffs and touched his nose before he continued. "I've asked people who retrieved documents for Melanie. She wanted the purchasing records. Phil told me staff needed to give the Waverly consultant anything she asked for, and that was all they gave her."

"I'll be back." Carl walked out on the cue that Adam had something to hide when he posed questions about Phil and Ray specifically asking for Melanie as a pushover consultant.

****

Melanie was glad she was wearing comfortable shoes and clothes when a queasy stomach pressed on her abdomen. The ache reminded her of getting hit by a dodgeball in middle school gym class. Rather than return to the conference room, she paused at the restroom and sat in the lounge area of the ladies' room. A full-length mirror reflected her overall state of being. Dark circles under her eyes and pale cheeks only confirmed her heart's message. She really did not want to take down the Walker family business.

Options were not presenting themselves, but she needed to excavate the things that were holding her back from doing her job. Carl Walker and his family would not be held to a different moral standard than anyone else.

With a few minutes of isolation and time collecting herself, her mind was in a better place to move forward. The first step was putting on the right look.

She applied some lipstick and stared at herself in the mirror. The lighting in the ladies' lounge was not designed for makeup, but she did not want bright lights. She looked solemnly at the subdued face in front of her. The crow's feet were beginning to show, and her lip color had bled into the fine lines around her upper lip. She shrugged, smirked at herself, reached up to smooth the makeup, and grabbed a tissue to wipe the mess off her finger before she exited the lounge.

She was in the fishbowl conference room for only a few minutes when Carl paid her a visit.

"Mind if I join you, maybe have a conversation?"

"I think that might be a good idea."

Carl started by apologizing for his family's asking her to do this work.

"Why? You know I'm good at this stuff."

Carl chuckled. "Yeah. They didn't know how good."

Melanie shifted her eyes away from Carl's face to the table surface and focused on the portfolio that lay open to the list of questions she had jotted down last night. None were answered, but she had a clear path to what would happen next.

"Do you have something to tell me, Carl?"

Carl's face fell. All his smart aleck shine vanished. "Melanie, I'm completely in the dark. You don't think for a minute that I would be doing something that you need to investigate, do you?"

The visceral response to his pleading tone was an ache in her chest. The same response she'd had the day Carl Walker left

Waverly. “No.” It was more of a whisper than a definitive response.

Katie appeared in the doorway. “Would you like these documents now, Ms. Sullivan?” It was the same person who already had produced only clean records.

“I would, thank you. And let me ask you, is anyone else helping you retrieve all the documents I’ve needed?”

“No, ma’am. Just me.”

Melanie reached for the papers extended in front of her by a hand accessorized by a beautiful gold Rolex watch.

“Thank you.”

Melanie watched Katie as she walked back down the hall like she belonged on a fashion runway wearing little more than a thong and a bra. She wondered if Adam saw his cute little report in a manner other than a professional assistant.

“Melanie?” Carl drew her back to the moment.

“You don’t think that attractive girl is up to something, do you? With Adam? She’s the only one who has given information to me.”

“Melanie, don’t go there.”

“You do think that’s possible. You saw the Rolex, too.” When Carl’s eyes averted hers, she said, “It’s good to know I can still read you.”

“Look, I didn’t come here to talk about office fraternizing. I want to set the record straight. I have no idea why my father and uncle contacted you instead of just asking me to do the review. Or why the purchasing group is under scrutiny when no one else is. And, yes, I still function with my ethics intact.”

Melanie put on her mischievous smile. “And I’m not accusing you of anything. But why would you even have to tell me these things?”

Carl sat down across the table from Melanie and gave her a straight response. "Something Adam said earlier. And, like you, I feel like the Walker ship is sinking under shady dealings. Why don't we work together?"

"Because your uncle and father contracted me, not an in-house employee. And I, too, continue to engage my ethical standards, regardless of the relationships I have." Melanie's gut clenched again, another dodgeball hitting her hard. The resulting knot caused her to put a hand on her stomach and take a deep breath.

"Still feeling that gut punch when you're in a tough spot?"

Melanie closed her eyes and made a slight head nod. "You know me too well, Carl."

"Yeah. Your body tells you when something's wrong, and it's wrong. Let's pick this up later."

He left the conference room without saying another word.

Melanie forced deep breaths in and out. She could feel her lungs burn and her stomach tighten. She closed her eyes and tried a visualization exercise, one where she was on a beach somewhere. Instead, she saw Carl behind bars and had no idea why.

CHAPTER 7

It was nearly two-fifteen when Ray returned to Shore Industries offices. He parked in his reserved space and took the elevator directly to the C-suite. It was strange not to see his brother sitting at the desk. He was always in his office at this time of day.

He gave a wave to Adam who was on the phone in his office where the door was left open as usual. The aromatherapy Adam enjoyed was wafting into the hallway. Ray detected the woodsy note that highlighted Adam's love of the outdoors and understated manliness. It was almost like clockwork that Adam would use aromas in the early afternoon. He sniffed and shook his head, a response to his dislike of what he considered uncharacteristic of a man's office. Maybe that's what kept Adam going after lunch. The Lord knew Ray needed a boost on many afternoons. Usually in the form of bourbon or coffee, sometimes both.

When he reached the sanctum of his office, he pulled off his suitcoat, tucked his necktie in the pocket, and hung it behind the door. Ray could count the number of times he had allowed himself to dress down in the office. Today was an exception when he would not need an energy boost. The starched white shirt contrasted with his tanned face. He rolled the sleeves to his elbows and pulled a cold bottle of water from the mini fridge under the bar behind his desk. He unscrewed the cap and chugged the refreshment without a crystal glass as he usually preferred. He needed to clear his brain and get Melanie Sullivan in his office with her plan. Now.

Before he could dial the phone for his secretary, Carl was standing in the doorway. “Ready for a fight? You look like you’re prepared for it.”

“Good afternoon, Carl. Have a seat.”

“I’ll stand. What’s going on?”

“That’s a pretty broad question.”

“Look, Dad. It’s time to talk. What’s happening in the Finance Department and who’s behind it?”

Ray’s lips pinched together as he cocked his head. He sniffed loudly and stared into Carl’s eyes. He detected fireworks behind the deep blue orbs and thought of his wife who had the same coloring and disposition. Maybe that’s what made Carl the upright man he was, his mother’s gene pool.

Not a single thing could be out of line with Joyce and that was a sticking point in Ray’s marriage. He could bend the rules under tough circumstances. Joyce and Carl called him out every time his toe slipped over the yellow line in the middle of the straight and narrow road, even with something as innocent as trying to get Carl into a theater at the children’s rate when he was a teenager.

“What do I need to know, Dad?”

Ray sat down at his desk and grabbed the arms of his leather chair. “Why do you think there’s something I need to tell you?”

“Oh, just a few little tidbits that have fallen my way. How many do you want me to name?”

Carl continued to list the evidence pointing to things that were out of line. At the top of the list was Phil’s harsh pep talk to the purchasing staff, followed by Phil’s collapse and attempt to talk about Melanie and keeping something. He ended with the question of why Melanie was working at Shore Industries when he could have done the work at no added cost, especially if there were no problems to be exposed.

Ray leaned his head against the high back of the chair. Beads of moisture at his temples tickled him. He touched his fingertips to his graying hair to hide his disjointed reaction. There was no need to tell Carl anything. But, then again, there was a need to tell him everything. He struggled with the choices. He could trust his own son or protect Phil. Other options were to let Carl badger him about improprieties or get out of business to keep a clean reputation for Carl's sake.

"It's always more complex than we think, Carl."

"Bringing Melanie here? You can at least admit that's not too complex. You brought in my old firm, and you must know how intimately I know their work and why companies like Shore call them in for coaching and consultation. It's all obvious."

He was trapped. Another deep sniff and Ray propelled himself forward to lean on his elbows. The glass-topped desk offered the sense of a cool, smooth skate through this interaction just the way life had always been for the Walker family. The business was founded on strong ideals by pillars of the community. The Walkers were respected for the way they treated their employees. But that would have been in his parents' days. Ray and Phil were the next generation and things were different.

"And by the way, what's the deal with the third floor? Phil tried to say something about lockers too, I think."

Ray's head snapped with the shock of what he just heard. The lockers were a secret. No one was supposed to talk about that renovation. He sniffed and sat back again. "I don't know. What did Phil say?" The heat in his cheeks was building and the beads of moisture returned to his temples.

With Carl's keen focus on him, Ray dared not reach up to wipe the sweat away. He sat waiting for more information or for the phone to save him. Neither happened. When the silence lingered, Ray knew Carl was playing a game. He was waiting for Ray to break.

"Son, you know the story of the locker installation. The construction got put on hold when our cash flow was hurting."

"Why is the elevator stopping there when no one in the elevator tries to push that button? And when there is no one on the third floor waiting for the elevator? Strange, don't you think?"

Ray's embarrassment soaked his armpits and the middle of his back. Fear gripped his lungs, and he was sure Carl could see his struggle to stay calm.

"It's like I said. There's been a hold on construction. We'll have to check the elevator."

His secretary, Christine, buzzed the intercom, and Ray stepped out to meet Melanie.

Ray watched Carl shaking his head when he left the office, and he knew the answers he gave his son did not pass the test.

****

Carl walked into Phil's hospital room before he was escorted back from therapy. A cell phone was vibrating on the tray table, and Carl wasted no time in retrieving it. Habits like that are not easily put aside. There was a text message from Adam Barnes. The banner notification was truncated, but there was enough information there to set Carl reeling.

> They're on to me.
> When can I come see . . .

Carl heard Phil's attempted chuckle in the hall and dropped the phone on the bed. He had been right about Adam.

His hands tightened and shook, making it difficult to get a grip on the device that had a slippery leather cover. When he reached to retrieve the device a second time, Phil caught him in the act. An aide steadied Phil as he walked, but a shove of the cane let everyone know that Carl had startled his uncle. "C-C-Carl?"

"Uncle Phil. I, ah, just heard your phone. Thought maybe it was important."

"L-l-leave it. No. I'll t-t-take."

The aide guided Phil to the chair that sat beside his bed and told Carl that dinner was being served soon. When the aide left, Phil yanked the service table closer, staring at Carl who set the phone in front of him. With slow, precise movements, Phil navigated his way to the text message from Adam.

"Do you need help, Uncle Phil?"

"No. I'm fine."

Carl's eyebrows shot up and the corners of his mouth curved downward into an exaggerated frown. "I see you've had a miraculous recovery." He paused and slowed his speech to add an *aha* signal to his words. "Or was there no recovery needed?"

When Phil did not answer, Carl continued. "Who did you pay off so you could be here under the guise of some physical condition?" His speech quickened, his anger bubbled into his reddened face and his eyes narrowed. "And why did you want to stay longer than you need to?"

Carl could feel Phil's eyes boring through his torso. The sting of acid bubbled up and stung the back of his throat.

"What's your concern, Carl?"

"You don't need speech therapy, do you?" He watched Phil lift his chin, open his eyes wider, and focus on his phone. There was no response.

"Right now, Phil, I have more questions than I can even begin to ask!"

Phil nodded in response and Carl knew his questions were just given validity.

"Fire away."

Carl started with the most pressing matter. "Have I been set up?"

Phil squeezed his brows together without answering. He focused on his nephew but said nothing.

"It seems like something big is going on, Phil. When you were first brought here, you had trouble speaking and you tried to talk about Melanie and about keeping something. I thought you were mentioning the lockers. What was that about?"

"I was scared. Concussion."

"Temporary. Now you're just a bluff." Carl put his hands on his hips and stared at Phil. He gritted his teeth and breathed in with an exaggerated rise of his shoulders and release of air.

Phil stayed silent, so Carl pushed on. Phil had no choice but to admit that Melanie delivered some news that he did not want to hear.

Phil's eyes darted around the room. That was one of his weaknesses. Lousy poker face and worse liar, at least about Christmas secrets and surprise parties. Carl was not sure how he handled business dealings, but it was likely the twitches followed him in all aspects of his life. Phil was lying.

"Why didn't you ask me to do the work Melanie's doing? Can't trust me? Or are you hiding something from me?"

The dinner cart arrived. Phil pulled his stunt. "Th-th-thank."

"Bye, Phil." Carl shook his head and left the room. His hands were balling up into fists, so he stuck them in his pants pockets.

Next stop. Melanie.

CHAPTER 8

Melanie reviewed the subsidiary accounts. The two years' worth of accounts payable detail included multiple cash payouts under an expense item titled Business Development. There were electronic transfers totaling tens of thousands of dollars each quarter, and some were checks for smaller amounts written to suppliers. The smaller amounts were probably valid.

Luxury Home Supply, Chicagoland Design, Percy Residential, Miami Grab Bars, and Stainless Safety received regular transfers. None were raw materials suppliers.

She ruled out possibilities, including purchasing specific hardware for unique installations and outsourcing. Shore had plenty of production capacity and a solid workforce, an unusual phenomenon on the Detroit factory scene. It was a cycle that Melanie could not unwrap. Inside this mystery package was something other than straight-up business processes.

Based on all the data she had, her review showed material purchases were draining the company, the same conclusion that Phil Walker had come to. The puzzling piece was a lack of unnecessary acquisitions. Besides, costs were aligned with the industry.

The flip side, of course, was the lack of sales. Or too much waste in the production process. Melanie saw no way of turning things around by restructuring the supply chain process or with debt acquisition. Her recommendation to liquidate or sell was an easy decision if the Walkers would not open the review to other departments.

Melanie looked at the summary she had prepared. She had no proposal for communicating the shutdown. She only had more questions, and Ray wanted a concrete timeline.

She needed to dig deeper into the cash flow imbalance, even if it meant uncovering painful results for the Walkers.

She doodled on the sheet where she had listed her questions. Nothing settled her mind, so she sent a text to Liz, her most trusted friend.

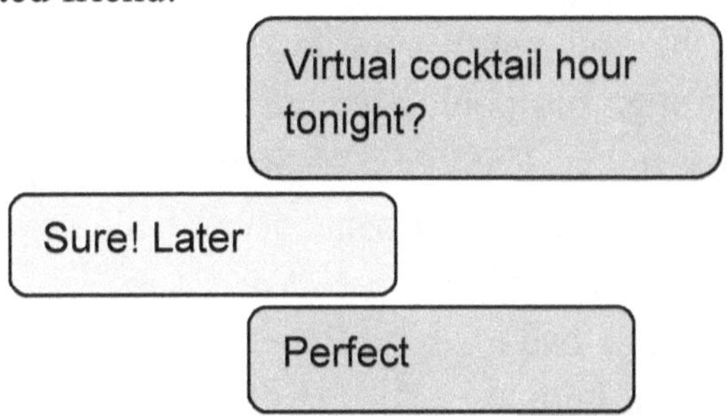

She felt a twinge of guilt about arranging a venting session with Liz, but knowing she could consult with a friend was a relief. She tapped her pen tip on the question that most puzzled her and wondered why Carl's department was being investigated. Family trust and confidence was questionable among the Walkers.

Ray came to the door and pulled her out of her thoughts. "Time to show me the timeline."

"Well, that might not be possible." Her voice quivered, and she coughed to cover her embarrassment.

Ray gestured for her to follow him. "Let's go to my office. We don't need to give a show right here where everyone will hear us." The response suggested Ray had not expected difficult conversations to arise when he set her up in a glass-walled conference room.

She followed him, but her knees did not want to function. Humidity lined the inside of her sweater. She lagged, scanning the offices every step of the way looking for a friendly face. In her mind's eye she was staring at cougars. The fight-or-flight instinct was kicking her gut, and she dug deep to detach from thoughts about hurting Carl Walker.

****

After telling Ray she had more work to do, and essentially bluffing her way through postponing the inevitable, she wished to see her hometown lights. The world of Shore Industries was crushing her spirit, and no amount of wine or hot bathing would take away the guilt she was feeling.

Waverly Consultants had a large office on Boylston Street in the Prudential Center, known as The Pru. The iconic location offered the best of the city. People came for the view from the observation deck, a definite tourist haven perched fifty-two stories above Boston with panoramic scenery on all four sides. Melanie had been enjoying that attraction since she was a child and knew she was living her dream when the Waverly job came through for her. On late workdays, she sometimes took the last elevator up to see the city lights that outlined a whole landscape to conquer.

After she and Carl had ended their romantic relationship, the panoramic view brought different sentiments. The vastness started reminding her of her insignificance and how minor her work was in the grand scheme of life. Carl remained important to her, and they worked as a team for a dozen more years. But their last assignment and his departure left her feeling empty. She had decided that people are more important than bottom line revenue, and she needed him to know they still shared the same moral and ethical compass.

The FaceTime cocktail hour with Liz was exactly what she needed.

"Hey there, girlfriend!" Liz's bright face and genuine smile welcomed Melanie into their virtual space. Her living room was displayed in the background with its pristine decor of white-on-white furniture poised on a gray area rug surrounded by shiny dark hardwood. Contemporary pendant lights cast a cozy yellow hue that blended with a Boston sunset on the harbor. Liz was curled in the corner of a cozy sofa with a gray knitted throw over her legs, her long fingers holding a glass of red wine.

"Oh, it's so good to see you, Liz."

"What's going on in Detroit?"

"This conversation stays in the closet, right?"

"Ooooh, you have good dirt, huh?"

"Stop it. This is serious."

The two shared an understood laugh. She and Liz had been friends since middle school. Their giddy late-night phone calls about boyfriends and girl arguments taught them how to share and keep secrets.

The night Liz described her first kiss with Gary Frye was their first secret. Melanie learned never to share girlfriend secrets with her mother again when Liz was grounded for a week. Tonight reflected the bonding that grew out of that experience.

"There are things going on at Shore that I really don't want to know. My main concern is that I'm going to ruin any chance I have of mending things with Carl."

She explained how she saw two choices. She could either dismantle the family corporation if the chief executives agreed or do a deeper analysis and find ways for them to continue operating.

"And where is the problem? I thought you decided liquidation was the only answer."

"I'm afraid some illegal practices, like bribery, will be exposed if I keep looking."

"What does your gut say, Melanie?"

"You mean the one that cramps and sends me to the restroom?"

Liz laughed. "Yeah, that one."

"It tells me this is the same dilemma that caused friction between me and Carl on our final project a year ago. I've had no chance of regaining his respect."

"I suspect he knows you well enough and doesn't even think about that assignment."

"Your vote of confidence is not working this time. If I don't uncover what's happening at Shore, if I close my eyes and help them liquidate, I will be playing into the same situation I wanted to avoid with the last case. It was Carl who insisted that we uncover the bribery in that company."

"He was right."

"Yes, and I told him that at the time. It just doesn't feel like enough. I have to prove to him that I play within the law, always."

"So what's stopping you?"

Melanie let out an audible sigh. "How can you ask that?! This is the Walker family. That includes Carl!"

"You think he's involved." It was a statement, not a question.

"I don't know. No. Could he be?"

"You know your momma always said—"

"Your instincts are usually right," Melanie finished Liz's words.

"Exactly. He would report his own parents to the authorities if he had to."

****

Even with relaxation exercises before bed, she had a fitful night that took Melanie down a dark path. In a nightmare Carl was at the far end of an alley lined with a clap-in committee. Ray, Adam, and Phil were active in cheering. She hesitated in her jog down the dark path, pausing from time to time. The claps were louder and louder. Carl was shaking his head to warn her off. Devil horns grew on Ray and Phil. Adam smiled and cheered her on. Her chest pounded, her ears rang, and that's when she woke up. Wet and shivering.

Liz was right. Carl was a good person. There was no reason to suspect him. Planning a conversation with him would be the best thing she could do.

She needed to be kind to herself, and breakfast with Carl would be a step in the right direction.

There was no sense trying to sleep after she awoke at four-thirty with anxiety about what she would be forced to do today. A surge of purpose and working through the weekend would give her a better chance of success on Monday. The alarm on her phone rang an hour after she had showered and dressed.

The words of her critical friend reverberated in her head and echoed in her heartbeat. "Carl would report his own parents . . . if he had to." Liz had told her, without sugar coating, exactly what Melanie expected to hear. And even worse, Melanie had no way of refuting the truth that would destroy Shore and Carl.

To save her relationship with Carl, it was time to bring him into the project as he requested. Presenting a potentially ruinous discovery to Carl might shred any remaining threads of the deep friendship she enjoyed with him. If he were the one to discover what she suspected, they could decide together how to face his family.

Before inviting Carl into the circle, she knew she should talk with her managing partner at Waverly but would not bother him over the weekend. She would move ahead with her plan, knowing that forgiveness would come easier than permission.

When it seemed like a reasonable hour to leave a text for Carl, she did. Her hands trembled when she started the text.

Meet for coffee b4 office on Monday?

Starbucks 3 blocks from your hotel. 8?

See you there

Melanie heard herself exhaling as the drumming of her heart ended with the quick reply she received. She was going to bring Carl back. They would be a team again. Maybe not exactly Liz's suggestion, but close enough. His immediate response let her know they would be able to work through this dilemma together.

Two solid days of focus and strategizing alone called for afternoon walks in the city. She enjoyed the autumn air, found lovely restaurants along the river to grab light meals, and returned to her hotel suite only to go down a deep dark hole. The notes she had taken from physical files kept leading to more questions with no definitive answers. Waverly's goal was to help

Shore exit their business with a strong reputation intact. Instead, she would have to release the skeletons of bribery.

CHAPTER 9

Today's attire was simple and more powerful than a sweater and slacks. A dark green two-piece suit accentuated Melanie's well-proportioned body. The pencil skirt hugged thin legs defined by calf muscles, shapely without being athletic. The heels on her business pumps slenderized and added height to her stance, and the short, skirted jacket added curve where it should be. A rounded neckline on a peach-colored silk blouse gave her face perfect color and softened the contours of her chin. The natural pearls that fell at mid-chest typified her sophistication.

Melanie could hear her mother's advice about wearing the best outfit for a day's purpose. Early in her career, it was that advice that led to a wardrobe as varied as the Boston weather. Today she felt confident in her professional work attire.

Melanie requested a valet to drive her car to the front and went to the lobby to wait. Coffee brewing in the hotel lobby put her olfactory senses in motion, and she salivated at the aroma of fresh baked pastries. A five-minute wait for the car felt like an hour. She resisted a cup of coffee, saving the ritual to share with Carl.

On the ride to Starbucks, she prepared for the conversation. It would be important to acknowledge the wisdom of Carl's suggestion to work with her and to be empathetic when explaining the mysteries she was trying to uncover at Shore.

****

Carl hugged his wife Holly and added a soft lingering kiss on the cheek. When she turned away without responding to his affection, his throat hardened. He coughed and pushed air out of his lungs to shake the panic away.

"Holly?"

"What is it?"

"Is everything okay?"

"I've got to shower and get the kids up for a school field trip today." Her words were called out over her shoulder as she disappeared down the hall leading out of the kitchen.

Before Carl could say anything more, the door to their bedroom was shut, just like Holly's heart. He didn't know about the day's plans, a field trip he could be helping to chaperone. With Holly.

For several days she had avoided talking to him. His schedule was rough with Phil's hospitalization and trying to support the family business he committed to, but his days were ruined by the discord with Holly.

He looked at a photo of the boys on the wall in the entry. Their beautiful smiles in the sunshine, a day at the park that Carl remembered well. He closed his eyes when the sense of guilt made his skin itchy. The picture was taken in Boston, and Melanie was with them. He focused on the table where his car keys lay. A fast shake of his head pulled him to the present, and he hurried down the hall. The bedroom door was locked.

The minutes were ticking away. There would be time for the marital stuff later. Or was that what he always told himself—they would be around for a board game on the weekend, they would understand when he needed just one more hour in the office, Holly would keep dinner warm, and the kids would have a bedtime snack while he ate? Days and weeks had been ticking away in this cadence of assumptions, life passing in slow motion without him.

He stepped into the morning air and took a deep breath. Melanie had been the one to contact him for this morning's meeting. She unknowingly had saved him from going to her with the truth about Phil's real physical condition. Maybe she, too, had learned something suspicious, just as he had.

He pulled the car out of the garage and drove to his favorite coffee shop on autopilot. This Starbucks was not frequented by the staff at Shore, and it was a comfortable place to be alone, to think without Phil or his father giving criticisms of his work.

His assigned department at Shore Industries was more of a prison than a thriving workspace for Carl. Family and staff picked at him constantly, like pigeons on the hat of a street lady sitting on a park bench. It was his unlucky draw to be the son of a father who did not believe a reputation outside of the company called for respect and a position of influence in the family business. Now with the threat of illegal activity in the family, Carl needed Melanie more than ever.

With a screech and a long honk from a truck horn, Carl hit the brakes. He squeezed the steering wheel and swerved toward the sidewalk, now populated with pedestrians.

By a miracle, the car stopped sideways in the street without incident. No collision, no airbag deployment. The truck driver had his window down and blurted out an expletive that Carl did not hear. But a digital gesture was prominently shared. Carl screamed out, "Sorry," to no one in particular.

He loosened his grip and took a three-point turn to get the car headed in the right direction.

The three remaining blocks took all of Carl's attention and energy. The fear and anger spent on the near-crash moment was more taxing than it should have been.

Melanie was standing inside the door checking her phone when Carl arrived. She greeted him with alarm.

"What happened? You look like the devil just made a proposition to you."

Carl reached up to touch his sweaty hair. Without thinking, he at once told her everything about Holly, including her rejection of his attempt to kiss or hug her.

Melanie steadied herself against a table and eased herself into a chair. Carl saw something unusual in her response, as if he had dismantled her entire focus for their meeting.

Carl sat across from her. "Sorry, Mel. I didn't mean to do that. To vent about Holly."

She looked straight ahead and answered with a quiet, "It's okay." Her eyes locked on his with a distant stare, and he wished he could rewind his entrance.

"Let me get the coffees. Water on the side?"

She gave a nod, and he left her alone at the table for two.

Carl returned with two coffees, two waters, and a bag of pastries. He sat down and pushed Melanie's favorite latte toward her and sniffed his black regular brew before tasting it. The task of serving the morning selection was enough to get Holly and the boys out of his mind and to focus on Melanie's agenda.

"I'm really sorry, Mel. I shouldn't have dumped my heartache on you like that."

He noticed how she moved her focus across the room, then to her nails, and eventually to her coffee. When she finally landed her eyes on him with a weak smile, he knew she didn't want to talk about Holly and moved on with his questions.

"Why a clandestine meeting? Did you discover something at Shore?"

Melanie pursed her lips and lifted her chin to stretch her neck. Carl noted the deliberate and exaggerated movements. He'd seen them more than once. Melanie was preparing to tell him something he might not want to hear. He shifted his weight around in the seat and straightened his shoulders.

"Well, what is it?" Carl knew she was working up the guts to spill the news, however negative it might be. Guilt of betraying his family swirled in a stomach gurgle. He put his hand on his abdomen. "Sorry. Hungry."

Melanie was gracious and did not acknowledge the gastric sounds. Instead, she wiggled in her chair, a habit he knew signaled her discomfort in what she was about to say.

"I think Phil has been ordering payments, large payments, to builders so they'll give orders to Shore Industries. Bribery or kickbacks maybe. Less notable property developers get small checks every now and then. Major project developers, the ones developing upscale home communities, are on the take."

Carl swallowed hard. Payback. To builders of upscale homes. This discovery could ruin him.

He watched Melanie's face for a wiggle of the eyebrows, a one-sided grin, or scrunched nose. Even roving eyes. Each meant something different, and it was the scrunched nose that told Carl something at Shore stank like old meat. Melanie kept a straight face with clients but always added the personal quirks when she talked with Carl. At least she did in the good old days, as Carl now saw their past. But now he was her client, and that felt awkward at best.

He had to steer the conversation away from his personal interest in what Melanie had uncovered. "I haven't seen procurement managers processing requisitions that are unusual. That tells me orders must not be any greater than usual."

"Maybe not, Carl, but how many times did we uncover crazy things? It looks like Adam is supporting Phil, and Ray is ignoring them both. They're running payouts through Accounts Payable, so it looks normal. These things are buried in subsidiary accounts with odd titles, like Business Development. We both know that's usually for vastly different activities, not bribes!"

Carl just listened. His brain was in overdrive. What did Phil try to tell him about Melanie? And something about keeping or fixing the lockers?

Melanie was still talking. "Carl, your father wants to unload Shore. Phil can't let go of his life's prize, and Adam might be caught in the middle."

Carl looked at her and did not reply. Melanie's high cheekbones and deep-set green eyes captured him. Her words about the biggest company collapse they discovered a half dozen years ago reverberated in his head. She had badgered him about having thieves in C-suite offices and no whistleblowers brave enough to step up. She had reminded him everyone could go to jail. Including the two of them if they uncovered something without acting on it.

That sermon Melanie gave him was hitting harder now. The focused energy he had mustered at the start of his day was waning. His family were the criminals. He had to be the whistleblower or go down with them.

"You're awfully quiet, Carl."

"Sorry. I just heard every word of your sermon about thieves in C-suites."

"I can understand why. When it's your family, it must hurt like heck."

"More like it's me, not just my family." Carl looked at the table and sipped his coffee. His success was wrapped up in meeting a sales target that he could not impact. Based on what Melanie had just said, bribes were connected to that goal.

Melanie reached across the table and touched his wrist. "We're both in a dirty mess. I've never had such a difficult assignment."

"Seriously? You haven't found things like this before? You haven't beat the sinner with your sermon on the end of a big stick?" Carl's voice cracked.

"Only with you by my side, Carl, not from across the negotiating table."

Carl managed a small smile of appreciation. "Thanks, Mel. That means something to me." And he meant it. But he also knew there was more to the story.

****

Melanie struggled with what had to come next. She paused to nibble on a thick Danish pastry filled with cheese and fruit. The savory, sweet food helped calm her frazzled brain. The latte was creamy and rich, and paired perfectly with the flaky pastry. She wondered if this treat would be as delectable if Carl were not present.

She noticed that he may have been having similar thoughts when he savored his coffee. A strong black brew usually brought him back to his senses and made him calm and rational at the most difficult points in their work. Like the day they uncovered fraud, and she delivered her C-suite thievery speech, the one he referred to as a sermon from that day on. The cards fell hard, but they were the heroes. It could happen again with a different outcome if she were not careful.

"Let's not get sappy. We've got some serious plans to make. Are you in, Carl?"

"That depends. What are your plans?"

Melanie had to get Carl to share everything, including details of conversations he had had over the past few days. Her first day with Ray and Phil was the start of a barrage of suspicious activities. She also knew Carl was in a difficult place. Although Ray was not being straight with her, she wasn't sure Carl could ever cross his family. He also would be cautious of joining forces with his ex-partner. On top of everything, there was Phil's health. From where she sat, things did not look good for Carl.

They developed a plan that would cause someone to report possible bogus transactions in the Accounts Payable department. They left Starbucks ready to begin.

Melanie pulled into the Shore Industries parking garage. She arrived first and went up to the conference room. Carl was to join her within twenty minutes, after settling into his office and visiting the coffee bar down the hall from Melanie's war room.

Before occupying her workspace, she visited the ladies' lounge, touched up her makeup, and made sure her hair was in order. She fussed with unruly curls around her face and spritzed the hairspray supplied in the lounge for moments like this. She used a roller to remove pieces of white lint that had gathered on her skirt. After straightening the collar of her jacket, she gave herself an approving nod in the mirror and plastered on a smile, thinking how smart it would be to have her own bathroom so conveniently organized. She walked down the hallway with confidence, her swing calculated to energize and inspire anyone in her path.

Adam approached from a distance, on his way to his office. Now was not a suitable time to engage him. She needed to be ready to collaborate with Carl without added noise in her head. Adam's swagger matched Melanie's swing. Her imagination put them on a dance floor. She was the lead, and Adam followed her every step. Another couple spun next to them, and the lead changed. Melanie swooned in Adam's arms and followed him wherever he led her.

"Good morning, Melanie!"

That beautiful hair and fitted suit made her blood percolate. She felt her chest beating but managed to keep her level of pride and confidence at its peak. "Hi there! Beautiful day."

"Yes, it is. Let's hope it stays that way."

He did not stop and neither did she.

She noted the odd response.

Her step quickened with a resolve to get the answers she needed.

CHAPTER 10

Carl left his office door open according to their plan. Sharon would bring mail from the mailroom and place it on his desk, a normal morning routine. She was known to tidy any papers left lying around and generally snoop for things to gossip about.

He made his desk look in need of her housekeeping. He placed in clear view a draft email requesting Adam Barnes to produce transaction reports for Luxury Home Supply, a customer of major importance to Carl. While he had access to some of this information, Melanie had found transactions that were not available with Carl's level of user rights in company databases. She selected customers for her focus of research, with Luxury at the top of her list. Carl did his best to hide his fears from Melanie since his financial future was resting on higher sales volume from her number one pick for investigation.

If the secretary reacted in her typical way, they would have a volunteer whistleblower. He looked at his handiwork, swiped his palms against one another to clear off the deceitfulness of his act, and walked away with a tight-lipped smile.

Before nine o'clock Carl and Melanie were reviewing the revised timeline for the shutdown of Shore Industries. At nine-thirty they would meet with Ray who would be shocked to see Carl shoulder to shoulder with Melanie.

"If we start by talking to Adam around noon today, do you think our whistleblower will have already acted?"

Melanie was seated facing away from the glass wall. Carl sat on the same side of the table with one chair between them. Anyone walking down the hallway would not be able to read lips or see facial expressions. The tabletop between them was strewn with documents. It was meant to look like they were deep in conversation on the task she was originally assigned, a review of records related to all materials acquisitions.

"She will at least have tried to get the reports from her confidante in Accounts Payable. The two of them are close, and he'll balk when she asks. She'll tell him she's not supposed to know, or something like that. In the end, she'll say something to get what she wants. Always does!"

Melanie put both palms on the tabletop and looked at the wall straight in front of her. "What if our planted email backfires?"

"It can't. In the year I've been here, there's never been a purchase order written to Luxury, I'm sure of that. I did my homework. Sharon won't be able to let that go without asking her buddies." He kept a close eye on that account activity. They placed occasional orders for grab bars, but Shore never bought anything from them.

"Correction, you did not do the research. I did it for you. You didn't have time between Starbucks and here to do anything."

"We did it together over coffee."

Melanie turned to Carl and grinned. "It's good to have you with me, Carl."

"I know. I feel it, too. Just not sure Dad will be happy to see me in the game."

His shoulders relaxed with relief that she had not figured out his keen interest in Luxury Home Supply. His research was ongoing and included tracking orders from three customers.

Adam appeared in the room. "Hey! What's going on here? I thought Melanie and I had a meeting with Ray later this morning, and I expected she would be drilling me about something by now. No?"

Carl looked from Melanie to Adam and back again. He remembered Adam's text message to Phil. The one where he all but admitted to guilt in a scheme of some kind. But Carl could not remember if he had told Melanie what he had seen.

"Good morning, Adam. I think I'm good to go. Did you have something you needed to tell me?" Melanie turned the question.

Adam gave a quick shake of his head and looked directly at Carl. "Not me. Maybe Carl does?"

Melanie was quick to respond. "No. I've asked Carl to join us in the meeting since my work focused on his department."

Carl settled back in the chair. She had him covered. "Yeah. Melanie was pleased with the work of my department, so I'll be there just to hear if my father has any other questions for me."

"I thought we were past that part of the work."

"We?" Melanie looked straight at Adam. Carl detected a spark in her eye. Was she flirting with Adam? He brushed away those thoughts, filled with pride that he had been her lover, and a smile covered his face.

"Well, you, I guess." Adam shifted his weight from foot to foot. Melanie had him on the defensive. Good for her.

"I'll let you know when Ray is ready."

Carl was proud of Melanie's ability to maintain control.

Adam nodded at Carl with a clenched jaw and left the room.

Melanie gave an audible sigh of relief, and Carl's eyes danced with adoration. "You haven't lost your edge at all."

"Thanks to you." She tugged at her skirt and wiggled in her seat.

****

Melanie noticed the wall clock, a reminder that time was ticking away. She had managed to stay calm and sharp with her responses, but what did Adam mean when he said Carl might have something to share? Her hands were tingling the way they did when she tried to lie. She remembered lying to her mother about spending the night at Liz's house once when she was in high school. That did not go well. When her thoughts scrambled and her hands and feet were stabbed with pins and needles, she told her date to take her home. Even thoughts of telling Momma the truth had made her cry. But she did it. Lying was not in her DNA.

"Carl, do you have something you're not telling me?"

Carl's response was genuine from all that Melanie could tell. He leaned in with soft eyes. "How can you even ask me that?"

"I don't know. It's your family. I just had a rush of guilt about intruding and pulling you into my suspicions about them. Adam threw me off when he said you might have something to tell me."

Carl shook his head slowly. "Don't fall prey to Adam Barnes. My ties to you are much deeper than they are to Uncle Phil and even to my parents at this point in my life. You know I have a lousy salary deal, so let's just leave it there for now."

Not completely satisfied with the response, Melanie lifted her body straight, stood up, and started to gather up the files that were spread on the table. They were only a decoy and had no bearing on their plan. She was ready to move ahead.

"Wait!" Carl's voice was raised. Melanie responded with a quick shake of her head and faced Carl directly. "Did I tell you about the text message on Phil's phone? And Phil's fake speech problem?"

"Phil's speech, yes. But what text message?"

Carl described the brief view he had of the truncated message from Adam telling Phil, "They're on to me."

"How could you forget that, Carl?!"

He looked up at the ceiling with closed eyes. She heard his exhale and decided it was an honest mistake.

"Okay. Look, we have a little time. Let's think about what that text might have meant." Melanie's tone shifted from frustration to collaboration.

She sat back down as Carl started connecting the dots. "You said Adam let payments process. The text message probably means that Phil directed Adam to make electronic payments to specific customers. Then Adam got scared when you asked to see the subsidiary accounts. Does he know that you found the transfers to our prime accounts?"

"I don't think so. I came to you, no one else."

Carl paused long enough to recall his suspicions when Adam posed a reason for Melanie doing Waverly's work

Melanie put a hand on Carl's shoulder. "Look, we need to get a grip on ourselves."

"Adam did say he talked to people, plural, who were pulling records for you. Maybe someone said more than we know."

"That could be."

Carl explained Adam's possible theory that Melanie was hired because of their relationship. That if something were discovered, she might overlook it.

"We both know I would never do such a thing!" Her tone betrayed her determination to remain calm and empathetic.

"But Phil and my father don't know that, Mel." His eyes locked on hers.

Her cell buzzed. It was Ray. Carl lowered his eyes to break Melanie's gaze. He hated that she was uncovering truths about his family that he could not explain. It was possible that his father was overlooking bribery to protect Carl's bonus. Soon he would have to tell Melanie about his connection with three important customers. He was not bribing anyone, and she needed to know that he was innocent.

CHAPTER 11

Adam finally got a response from Phil who was being discharged later in the day. His new assignment was to do anything necessary to postpone selling company assets. He also needed to be sure Carl did not find out that physical assets were in Locker Eleven. The jewelry was intended to grow cash for Phil.

He sat at his desk putting papers away, tidying pens and desk accessories. He straightened the desk lamp and aligned the desk phone with the corner of the desktop. All habits of leaving a clean office at the end of the day. Before declaring his task complete, he retrieved a check from Phil Walker that was under a paperweight, folded it twice, and tucked it in his pants pocket.

He pulled two aroma sticks from his desk drawer. They were labeled Meadow Breeze and not his favorite. They smelled like air spray used in restrooms. They were the perfect cover for what he needed to do.

A disposable lighter and the two sticks were in his pocket when he started down the hallway and quickly returned to his office. He arranged papers back on the desktop in haphazard placement, strew pens across the surface, and turned the phone on an angle. An emergency had to look like an emergency.

Again, he walked down the hall, this time all the way to the restroom next to the coffee bar. He saw two secretaries at a table near the windows and ducked through the lavatory door before they spotted him.

****

Sharon was walking through the staff snack bar on the fifth floor. She eyed the room to see who was there. No one she needed to worry about. The employees were just grabbing coffee and hustling off to their next task. She stalled at pouring coffee, adding flavored syrup and cream, careful not to splash anything on the paper she held. Finally, her contact arrived.

"Good morning!"

"Oh, hi! Got a minute? I want to tell you all about my shopping spree last weekend. I'll grab a coffee and maybe we can sit near the window."

"Sure! But not too long," Sharon said.

Because Christine was secretary to both Ray and Phil, she had knowledge of legal issues, and Sharon, being nosey, wanted to check on purchases made from a customer. She carried a printed copy of an email written by Carl asking Adam for details of payments made for something purchased from Luxury Home Products.

The conversation was completely fake. It was prearranged in a phone call. Sharon had already talked with the Accounts Payable manager, just as Carl predicted. She then called Christine with a heads-up that something big needed Phil's attention. As they chatted about nonsense, Sharon pushed the paper ever so slightly toward Christine. While Christine was talking away about some dress or shoes or coat, Sharon took a quick look at her watch.

"Oh, I'm so sorry. I've got to get back to my desk. I expect Carl will be in his office soon."

She gave a curt tilt of her head, a wink, and nodded to the sheet of paper on the table.

"Of course! I've got to run too." Christine picked up the paper as if it were hers and the two prepared to return to their respective departments.

****

Melanie's phone buzzed. Before she answered, she checked with Carl. "It's Ray. Are we ready?"

He nodded in reply.

"Hi, Ray." She answered with the tone of confidence she knew how to muster in almost any situation.

"Melanie, I want to move our conversation until tomorrow. I think Phil can be there with us if we wait one more day."

"I thought you wanted to move ahead without him." She shot a puzzled look at Carl and moved the phone so he could hear Ray.

"It's been brought to my attention that I shouldn't do that. Legally. But I still want to see a plan even if Phil isn't here tomorrow."

Carl raised his eyebrows and used roving eyes to communicate. In their code he was saying, "Aha, we've got them on the run."

She ended the call and gave Carl a punch in the arm. Questions ran through her mind as they talked about the brief conversation.

Why would Carl's father have a sudden change of heart? Did Adam get to him? How would Phil get released from the hospital so quickly? And did Phil really pull the legal card on his own brother?

"Melanie, something stinks here."

"Tell me all about the lockers on Floor Three, Carl."

On her first visit to Shore, the elevator stop on Floor Three had caught her off guard, and she had been too shaken to think about the purpose of the lockers. The hair on her arms tickled inside her jacket when she recalled the eeriness of that vacuous space. She remembered lots of metal and chilly air, dim lighting, and lack of cell service. She shivered, thinking that important answers were housed in that stark space.

Carl was on a mission and took Melanie to see the construction. Her legs stretched her tight skirt as she struggled to keep up with him. This time the elevator did not stop automatically. Carl had to circumvent the elevator run. That required a swipe card to open a panel in the back wall of the elevator and for a code to be entered on a keypad.

"How many people can open that panel?"

"Just the four of us who have lockers."

"Four?"

"Dad, Phil, Adam, and me."

Chief officers plus one. Melanie kept that thought to herself. "Why is that floor so secure?"

"Well, they were mostly worried about liability. If somebody got in here during construction and somehow got injured, we'd be in trouble."

"Makes sense. Why is there nothing going on? I mean construction."

"Money. We had to put everything on pause."

Carl answered questions that Melanie fired at him in rapid succession. Everything from how long ago the project started, why the lockers were available for use, why there were so many lockers, what would anybody put in there now if there is no gym, and why the lockers were delivered before the gym was finished.

He could answer them all. His father had walked him through the area and told him everything. Carl relayed the only story he had. People were leaving the office to go to the gym, taking long lunch breaks because of the travel time. The philosophy of keeping people happy to increase productivity was going to be tested. The company could eliminate gym membership fees for employees and offer twenty-four seven access with the right security in place.

"Seems like a stretch, but you have me wondering why Phil gave select people lockers while the place is still being built. Just chief officers and you."

Carl took a few steps, and she watched him flex his fingers as he paced. He turned in a circle and looked at the open rafters, the concrete floors, and three rows of lockers. Then he stopped abruptly.

He called for Melanie to follow him. She walked behind him, her heels creating an echo of measured steps. He stopped in front of Locker Eleven.

"This is mine."

"If only a few people have access, why do you have number eleven?"

"It's temporary until everyone can use them. It was closer to the elevators when this all started."

"What would you use it for if there's no gym?"

Carl put in his combination and opened the door.

"Whoa! Carl, what is this?"

Carl's mouth dropped open, his eyes widened to full moons, and he slowly turned his head toward Melanie. "I have no clue."

Four separate stacks of gold bars wrapped in protective adhesive film were at the bottom of the locker. Each stack included blister packs of one-kilogram bars of gold labeled as pure. They looked untouched. A smaller box held individual gold coins, also in blister packs. Three folders were on a shelf at the top of the locker.

"You didn't put these here?"

"No! What would I be doing with gold?" Carl ran his hand through his wavy blond hair that was damp around the edges. He picked up one stack. "These are heavy. Who did this?"

Melanie felt the weight. "Well, no one would want to carry them around in a pocket. What do you think the value is?"

"Not sure, but right now gold prices are up. I saw something like a thousand dollars a gram last week in the financial news."

"These have to be worth a lot of money, Carl."

"They're not mine!"

"Okay. Regroup. Tell me what you needed me to see in the locker."

Melanie returned the bars, and Carl retrieved the folders. "I have a direct stake in three companies. It was what I bargained for because I had to start in purchasing. My bonus will be based on sales to each one of these companies for as long as I remain in a position outside the C-suite. If they're getting kickbacks to bring their sales levels back up, then I'm the root cause for the corruption. I'd like to think my father and uncle are making sure Luxury keeps ordering from us to save me. But maybe not."

"What is the business relationship with each of the accounts?"

"They'll all third-party entities. They sell our products directly to builders. The credit doesn't get recorded for my bonus until the devices are in homes and we have proof of installation. It's the mission my grandparents had. Provide safe aging at home for people who might not have access to assisted living facilities or want to stay in their own environment where everything is familiar and comfortable."

"Why did you need to keep the files here?"

"I don't trust my secretary. She tells her buddies everything. Office gossip and whistleblower! I bet that by now she has that fake email on its way to my dad's desk since Phil isn't around."

"Well, it looks like there's more than just a secretary you can't trust. Someone's using your locker."

A blaring alarm sounded as lights flashed before Melanie could look at the names on the file folders. They both jumped. He slammed the locker shut, grabbed Melanie's arm, and led her to the nearest stairwell. She cursed her decision to wear a pencil skirt as she hiked it up high to follow Carl. She felt her age as she followed him down the two flights of stairs to the building lobby. They joined a crowd that was rushing out the front doors.

Four fire trucks pulled up along with police and emergency medical vehicles. Within minutes, two people were being carried out of the building on stretchers.

CHAPTER 12

The file folders were stained by sweaty hands. Carl eased his hold but continued to grit his teeth. He told himself this was not what it seemed to be. Intentional fire. Melanie's light grasp of his arm helped his jaw relax. The mist in his eyes was inevitable. He blinked to ward off tears.

"Do you want to talk about anything, Carl?"

"Right now, I need to make sure my people are safe." He turned his back on her.

He walked toward the emergency vehicles. The two injured employees were being treated. He stretched his neck to see who they were.

Pink manicured nails, fashion watch, and small birthstone ring. It was Sharon.

He pushed his way through the throng of bodies, keeping the folders tight to his chest. He needed to wipe his face. When he reached up to clear the sweat, he realized it was starting to rain. Sharon's body shivered on the gurney, and her head was bleeding. The nausea burned his throat as he tucked the folders under his suit jacket.

"Sharon, it's Carl. Are you okay?"

She opened her eyes and gave him a nod and a thumbs-up.

The medic reassured Carl when he explained Sharon only needed stitches and maybe an X-ray. She had hit her head on a door frame when she ran away from flames.

He thanked the medical technicians and walked toward the other ambulance. Adam was already there and spoke loudly enough to be heard. "Christine, just hang in there. You'll be fine." Carl watched Christine slip a paper to Adam. Sharon had taken the bait and handed the draft email off to Christine so it would land on his father's desk. Instead, Adam now had confirmation that someone was indeed suspicious of him.

Carl clutched his folders closer to protect them from the rain and hurried back to find Melanie, stepping in puddles with no regard for his Italian leather shoes.

****

Melanie watched Carl with intent. He was being himself, worrying about people. That was just one of the things Melanie always found attractive about Carl Walker. And there was Adam Barnes, also in the fray, also worrying about people.

When Carl stepped into her sight line, she shifted further away from the building. At that very moment, a window several floors up on the front of the building shattered, sending glass onto the sidewalk where she had been standing. Carl rushed to move her farther into the street. People were screaming and running. Melanie latched on to Carl's arm as he guided her down the block and across the street.

They looked up to see flames through the fifth-floor windows, the C-suite floor. Carl kept his eyes fixed on the building. His head nodded in a rhythm as if he were in a trance.

"Carl? Are you thinking what I'm thinking?"

"Not sure. What's that?"

Neither wanted to say the words aloud. Melanie wiped her palms on the front of her skirt. Sweat mingled with rain was making her hair hang limp around her shoulders. She closed her eyes to take a deep breath, and the puff of release caught Carl's attention.

"Let's not think the worst here. No one would try to destroy the building on purpose," Carl said and headed across the street.

Melanie's shoulders lowered even though the damp weather was chilling. Carl was working his magic on her, calming her nerves regardless of her suspicion of arson.

He led her into a cafe that gave them a street view of what was happening just a half block away. The building was burning, and fire trucks from two different stations were there. Firefighters worked like the gears of a clock, moving among themselves with a sixth sense. Water sprayed out of fire hoses, lights flashed, and the city block was closed to traffic.

Police officers entered the coffee shop. "Everybody out!"

Bullhorns rang out in the street, telling everyone to evacuate as they were closing off the block in all directions. Bodies scrambled everywhere.

"Carl?" Melanie was scared.

"Probably worried about a gas explosion. Let's go."

Melanie's cell rang just as they made it to the next block. It was Dominick Pierce from Waverly.

"Dominick! I can't talk right now."

"What's going on?"

"Shore Industries is exploding!"

"Don't be dramatic with me, Melanie. We know—"

"Literally! The building is on fire."

"A fire? For real?"

"Yeah."

"Keep me posted."

She disconnected the call.

Carl was tending to his personal communications. "I've talked with Holly to let her know what's going on. Now I need to call my father."

Melanie ordered an Uber ride to take them back to her hotel. It arrived within five minutes, and the two of them got away from the scene as directed. Melanie tried to follow Carl's conversation.

She was curious about what Ray was saying on the other end, but she knew it was Holly who was most important to Carl. His call ended, and he ran his fingers through his hair, scrolling the phone with his other hand.

"What did Holly say?"

"Not much." Carl glanced out the window to avoid eye contact. Melanie's heart skipped a beat when she noticed his discomfort at the mention of Holly's name.

"What about Ray?"

"He claimed to be with Uncle Phil since this morning. I thought he was in the office. Otherwise, I wouldn't have chosen this morning to leave the trap on my desk!"

"We thought he'd be there, but I didn't see him around when we evacuated."

"He got a call and was told he couldn't do anything. He'll be notified when he can go to the scene."

"Does that make sense to you?"

"He didn't say who called him, so I'm not sure if it makes sense or not."

They entered the hotel lobby restaurant with moist clothing and scattered belongings. Melanie had only a twisted purse thrown across her body. Everything else was left in the conference room on the same level where smoke rolled out the windows.

"How bad do you think the damage will be? It looked like the fifth floor was burning."

"Those windows were in the restrooms and coffee bar. The fire department arrived early. Maybe they contained the fire."

They ordered hot coffee, and Carl laid the folders on the table. Melanie stared at the fingerprints Carl had impressed on them. His death grip was evidence of how important the information was to him.

"I'm surprised these folders made it out with you."

"Without good earnings from these three accounts, I could lose my house."

What kind of father would pull his son from a prestigious career, pay him so little that his mortgage payments depend on only a few select accounts, and then abandon the ship? Selling Shore's assets would be like telling Carl he was worthless.

The possibilities running through her mind included Shore using Waverly to get to Carl, Carl being tricked into returning to the family business, setting her up as a scapegoat for closing the business, to outright fraud and theft schemes in which she might become an accessory. The heat under her blazer became more than she could tolerate. She peeled the jacket off and started to shiver.

The coffee was delivered as Melanie was pulling her jacket back around her shoulders. She felt Carl watching her with his calm blue eyes, the pools she would drown in if she stayed there too long.

"You're shaking."

"I guess it's damp."

"No, Melanie. I think it's something else."

Tears blurred her view out of the restaurant into the lobby. She tried to focus on the fireplace on the far wall as a distraction but could not.

She closed her eyes and let out a puff of air. "Carl, tell me about these accounts." She had yet to see the names on the tabs.

She listened intently for indicators of exploitation. All three accounts were relatively new customers within the past four to six years. Each was in a different geographic area, with operations in more than one region. There was no real fear of market saturation or intense competition among them. These territories were known as popular retirement states – Florida, Arizona, Texas, and Virginia. Carl divulged that he had taken a salary cut of fifty percent with the balance being made through profits generated by customers who have proven or predicted profitability for Shore.

"You're saying you basically sold yourself to the mercy of Shore since you have no direct hand in sales or marketing."

"Yeah. Dumb move."

"Well, I'm not sure I would have ever counseled someone to accept an arrangement like that." As soon as the words left her mouth, Melanie regretted them. She paused, picked up her coffee with a shaking hand, and put it back on the table before it made it to her mouth.

"This is my family."

"Sorry. You're right. What was it that brought you back to Detroit, Carl?"

"It's a complicated story."

"You know I'm good with complicated."

CHAPTER 13

He had known it would come to this the first time Carl saw Melanie at Shore Industries. If the family did not trust him to do what he does best, then he probably did not belong here. Discoveries from her review could force him to choose between family loyalty and ethics. He needed to consider his mother and his inclination to honor her wishes. He also felt it would be right to mend things with his father. Underneath his father's gentle approach, Carl always considered him to be somewhat selfish, worried about himself over anyone else. There also was the desire to uphold the family name in the Detroit area.

"Well, you know my family history."

Melanie nodded. They were on their second round of hot drinks.

"My grandparents were good people. Shore was founded on their enterprise, their ambition, and the concern they had for aging people. Their own parents had a difficult life in their older years, and that affected them."

Carl noticed that Melanie was still shivering. Her chin was lowered, and she looked upward at him from under her eyebrows as she held her jacket on her shoulders with crossed arms.

"You know, this could be a long story. Better for another time. Maybe you should put warm clothes on. I'll wait here."

"Okay. But that doesn't get you off the hook."

Left alone, he sat bent over his cup with fists against his forehead, enjoying the coffee aroma and hoping for inspiration. What was the gold in his locker and who put it there? He reflected on his mother giving him a bag of heavy gold jewelry when he first came back to Detroit. He rubbed his eyes as he heard her voice. “Keep this for a rainy day, Carl.” He didn’t understand when she said, “This is not for Holly. It’s for you.”

Carl opened his eyes and looked around the hotel restaurant. There were women arriving, probably for a lunch date. They appeared to be in his parents’ generation. He looked at them and searched for gold jewelry. There was none. He rubbed his chin and tightened his lips. He looked more carefully and found a Rolex watch, a pair of diamond earring studs, and one simple bangle. None of the chunky jewelry that his mother had given him.

He envisioned his mother and father going out for dinner when he was a young boy. His mother was saying goodbye.

“Be good for Grandma!” Her charm bracelet rattled on her wrist, and the heavy gold chain around her neck swung in his face. He recalled the face of a fierce lion in the middle of a heavy disk of gold. It scared him, so he turned his head. His mother’s kiss landed on his eyelid before he ducked away.

He shook his head to regain focus. He needed to look at the folders before Melanie returned. He took them in order of their impact on his financial outcomes.

Luxury Home Supply was in Florida and did all their business in the southern part of the state. They sold to builders of elderly apartments but started focusing on housing developers who were designing elegant homes around single-floor living in golf club communities. The folder had one annual earnings report along with their monthly register of orders. Carl scanned their purchases. The numbers had been on a steady decline for the past four months. With just six months left in the fiscal year, this trend would not be good for him. It struck him that the country club environments they catered to would be the vision his uncle Phil and his father held for themselves.

Percy Residential was a company based in Texas with a major operation in Virginia. They sold grab bars to builders of elderly housing complexes. Their largest market was Virginia Beach. Carl kept copies of quarterly earnings reports and the most recent monthly register of their orders. Nothing appeared to be out of order.

The last folder was labeled Stainless Safety. Interestingly, their safety record was far from stainless. Thinking about that fact gave Carl heartburn more often than he cared to admit. The most recent problem was a lawsuit against Shore accusing them of faulty manufacture of joins in longer grab bars. Shore had to pay a healthy sum to keep Stainless Safety from taking the claim to court. There had been no orders since that suit was filed about ten months earlier.

Overall, Carl's prospects were not good. Only Percy would come through with any level of earnings that might augment his income.

His thoughts shifted to the gold bars, their potential value, and where they came from.

He may need to cash in on his mother's jewelry soon, this time without consulting her. The last time he mentioned selling it, she handed him cash. Just as he was succumbing to a sense of dread for what lay ahead of him, Melanie returned to the table.

****

Melanie sat down to her cold coffee and signaled the server for a fresh cup. A change into crisp jeans, cozy turtleneck, and blazer helped her relax and refocus. Her mother would have called these her play clothes, although they looked much nicer than the stained, baggy-kneed pants of her childhood. She hung a shoulder tote on the chair in the hope of retrieving some of her things from the building when the time came. Her crossbody purse was in place for brisk walking.

"Thanks for. . ." She stopped when she caught the look on Carl's face. "What's wrong?"

"That complicated story might be worse than I thought." Carl looked her straight in the eye. "Please don't judge me."

She frowned at him. "Why would I?"

"Because you don't know the whole story. Yet."

Melanie let her eyes peruse the room. There was no one around who looked familiar, no eavesdroppers that she could see. But then again, she did not know all the players at Shore well enough to be certain. "Have you scanned the room for unwanted ears?"

Carl smiled. "You never change. There's no one dangerous in here."

"Then start talking."

Carl gave Melanie a status report on his expected loss of income. He wondered aloud about the value of gold jewelry, particularly when he noted a lack of it on women in the restaurant.

"Okay, now you've lost me. Why do you care about jewelry?"

"That's part of the complication. When I returned to Detroit, my mother handed me a large velvet drawstring bag that was full of gold jewelry."

"Wow!"

"Yeah. Holly doesn't know I have it. It's not for her. It's in a false bottom in my locker."

"If you still have a locker."

"Correct."

"And why do you have this jewelry?"

Carl drew a deep breath. "Here's the bottom line. My mother must have known I would need money."

"So do you know what the gold bars and coins are all about?"

Carl laid out the conclusions he was coming to. His story caused a sensation of prickly wool against her bare spine. This wonderful person sitting in front of her was the victim of conniving men. She held her coffee cup in both palms, taking small sips. Her knee started to bounce when Carl spoke of the lawsuit filed by one of the prominent customers in his bonus calculation. The settlement could have been huge, adding to the drain on company cash. Add that to kickbacks she suspected, and Shore was underwater in many ways.

"The jewelry must have come from my grandmother as a personal gift to my mother. She doesn't wear it anymore, and I don't have a sister. It was handed to me."

"If it belonged to your grandmother, shouldn't some of it go to your cousins, especially Charlene?"

"What had been given to my mother before my grandmother's death wouldn't be part of her estate. Besides, I think it might have been gifts for birthdays and Christmas from my father and my grandparents. I remember my mother wearing a lot of gold. I'm sure it was out of my grandmother's possession before inheritance was in force."

Melanie's knee stilled. Her mouth dropped open, and she leaned in toward Carl. In a low voice, she approached the critical issue. The one that plagued her since she arrived. "Do you trust your father, Carl?"

"Would you?"

She slouched back in her chair and leaned on the arms. She closed her eyes and responded. "No, Carl." She opened her eyes to focus on him. "I'm beginning to think I can't trust your family."

Carl's blue eyes looked gray. She did not know if it was because of a shadow cast across the table by the fake Ficus tree in the corner, or if the color reflected his demeanor.

Her phone buzzed and pulled her away from those thoughts. A text from Adam Barnes.

Where are you? Need to talk.

At my hotel. Is everything ok there?

Under control. You can come back.

Carl gave her a querying look. "Care to share?"

"It's Adam. He said it's okay to return to the building."

Carl asked Melanie to carry his folders in her tote for safekeeping. By the time an Uber arrived, each had expressed their own conspiracy theories.

Carl wondered if his mother's jewelry had been given to him as secret protection from financial ruin and shame because she knew the family business was about to collapse. Melanie imagined that Ray and Adam were scheming against Phil, with Adam playing double agent. Both ideas were too far-fetched to give credence.

Melanie rubbed the back of her neck, already moist with perspiration. She may have overreacted to the chills with her choice of a turtleneck sweater. The hair floating in her face tickled her nose, and she pushed away the annoyance.

When Carl paid the Uber fee, Melanie felt a pang of guilt. Would Shore reimburse him? She could have charged the expense to Waverly.

Flat leather shoes that laced up made it easy for her to slide in and out of the car. Confident that she was prepared to walk into a disaster area, Melanie shifted her crossbody bag into place and followed Carl onto the sidewalk. She was not prepared to have both Phil and Ray Walker greet her.

CHAPTER 14

Carl looked from his father to his uncle and then to Melanie. Ray was holding Phil's elbow as if escorting him into a dining room, taking particular care of his older brother who took short steps. Phil wore a stern face as if he were perturbed by his little brother's doting.

"Uncle Phil! You've made a quick recovery." Carl may have placed a little too much emphasis on the word *quick*, eliciting a sly look from Melanie.

"Hmph."

"It's good to see you, Phil," Melanie said. "I'm surprised you made it here."

"Let's just get inside where we can see the damage." Ray encouraged everyone to walk forward.

Police and fire personnel were still keen on keeping everyone out of the building. Adam Barnes was just inside the door, blocked from moving any farther, and trying to convince the fire chief to allow them to enter. Adam was only able to get them into the lobby. No one was allowed to go into the offices on any level.

Carl relied on Melanie at this point to keep things moving in a positive direction and figure out what had happened. Too many ideas were attacking his brain. Why was there gold in his locker? Why firebombs at the same time he and Melanie went to the locker? Was someone tracking them? Where had Ray been this morning?

He was thankful that the folders were out of sight, diminishing any curiosity. All these thoughts circled into a vortex, sucking all mental ability into his chest where it rallied his heart to a rapid beat. He was grateful when Melanie smoothed the waters with Phil and Ray.

"Phil, are you feeling well enough to be here?" Melanie asked.

"I feel quite strong right now. Of course, by this evening I'll be toast!"

She laughed then addressed Ray. "And Ray, you were lucky not to be in your office when this all happened. Do you know if it started in your suite?"

Ray cleared his throat. "I have no idea. I was getting Phil out of the hospital when the first call came. Need to talk to the professionals here to figure out what happened."

Carl noted that Phil's eyes were darting around the lobby. He was guilty of something. Or was Ray the culprit? Did someone sabotage the timeline for the announcement about shutting down Shore?

The fire chief approached them. Each looked at him with hopeful faces.

"Well, this could have been a complete disaster for the Walker family. Luckily, we kept the fire contained, and there's little damage."

"Does that mean we can go inside?" Ray appeared behind Carl, eager to see the offices for himself.

"Not today, I'm afraid. The origin seems a little odd. It looks like two fires may have started simultaneously in trash bins in fifth-floor restrooms. There was insignificant damage to the surrounding areas. We think the offices are intact. Two people were taken for treatment, minor injuries when they rushed to get out."

"What about the third floor?" Carl asked.

"As far as my firefighters can tell, there was nothing anywhere else. All cement, steel, metal, that kind of thing on the third floor. No problems on the fourth floor either."

"True about Floor Three," Phil replied. "Are you saying we were called back here just to be told to go home?" His eyes searched behind the fire chief.

"I don't know who would have called you back. But at least you all got an update."

Adam added his two cents. "So no other damage, right?"

"We're still checking all floors for any signs of what may have happened, making sure the police have collected any forensics they need."

"You suspect foul play." It was a statement from Carl, not a question.

"Can't say just yet. You'd have to talk to the fire inspector working this scene, but he's busy right now."

Carl nudged Melanie's arm, and she followed him away from the group. "Watch Phil and Adam."

"Why?"

"I know them. Phil can't hide anything if you know his twitches, and Adam is his lackey."

Adam approached, so Carl quickly shifted the topic. "I wonder if we can at least get our cars out of the garage."

"Maybe we should rally at the cafe before we head out," Adam suggested.

Carl ran his fingers through his hair. "Yeah. Maybe."

"That would be fine with me," Melanie offered an upbeat response and gave Carl a look he recognized. Bright eyes and a quick nod meant she was creating a plan.

Adam wandered back to Ray and Phil. When he was out of earshot, Carl turned his back to the center of the lobby and faced

Melanie directly. "He's got something in mind. Didn't he text you to say we could come back?"

She nodded.

"But he didn't have the all-clear from anyone."

"But who called Phil and Ray?"

"Good question. Maybe Adam did, so he could get us all here together."

Melanie lowered her eyes. "But why? If things are still off-limits, why get us here?"

"To talk. He's going to weasel his way out of something."

Carl led Melanie outside onto the sidewalk. Keeping his back turned away from the group and continuing to look directly into Melanie's green eyes, he reminded her of the text message on Phil's phone in the hospital that partially read *They're on to me*.

"Adam wanted to go to the hospital yesterday to see Phil, but I don't know if he did. Our planted email was put in his hands when the secretaries were taken to the hospital. He knows we're suspicious of him."

Melanie breathed out a sigh and put her head back. The rain had stopped, but the humidity made her hair frizzy. Carl smiled slightly at the image. It took him back to a day at the beach outside Boston. The sea air always made her glow, but she complained about bad hair days. This was the Melanie he had once loved romantically. When she did not respond, he touched her arm. "Mel?"

"I was looking at the subsidiary accounts after you left Adam's office yesterday." Melanie kept her voice low.

Carl's face turned pale. He sucked in a breath, waiting for the clutch that would open his chest and allow a full tank of oxygen to the lungs. It did not happen. He tried again. His eyes widened.

"Carl?"

One more effort. A bigger draw and air flowed to the bottom of his diaphragm. He exhaled with pursed lips and was able to talk. "What you found led to our bait for a whistleblower. The account was Luxury. Adam must be in on it."

Carl gave Melanie's arm an elbow bump, and she followed him across the street to the cafe as Adam had suggested. Carl sat at a window table facing up the street so he could see Adam, Ray, and Phil approach if they decided to take Adam's suggestion. Melanie left her tote bag and went to the counter to retrieve drinks. When she returned, Carl saw that she was carrying two black coffees.

"You're coming to the dark side?"

She laughed briefly. "Desperate times, desperate measures."

He did his usual thing. Hung his head over the steaming coffee to inhale inspiration before he spoke. "I think I have it figured out."

Carl asked Melanie to hand him his folders. She pulled them from her tote bag and for the first time saw the names on the folders. Luxury, Percy, Stainless.

"Carl! No!"

"Yes."

Because he was lost in his own thoughts, Carl did not see Adam, who had walked down the sidewalk on the opposite side and crossed the street at the door of the cafe.

"No, yes, what?" Adam's voice was flat.

Carl gave Melanie a quick nod, giving her the lead. "Hi, Adam. Grab a coffee and have a seat."

"Not up for a coffee, actually." He sat down.

Carl looked down at the folders as Melanie slid them back into her tote bag.

"Conducting some kind of business here?" Adam asked.

"I was hoping to pick Carl's brain on an upcoming assignment in Boston."

"Leaving soon?"

Carl let that question sit on the table and watched Melanie ponder her response. Was she thinking of the best way to cover his backside or hers?

"Well. That depends on when I get things wrapped up here. The next one will be there when I return," Melanie said.

Carl shifted in his chair for a better view of Adam's face. "Did you get more information about the status over there?" Carl nodded across the street toward the office building.

Adam stammered. "Uh, no, I guess not."

"What's wrong?" Carl would play this out Adam's way. Pretend everything was completely normal.

"You know what? Let me grab that coffee after all. I'll be right back."

Carl tapped Melanie's foot under the table as he watched Adam go to the counter.

"Watch him. He'll send a text or make a call. Hundred bucks on it."

Melanie laughed openly at the prediction. "You're right. Good thing I didn't take your bet."

Adam returned with a beverage, sat down, and slipped his phone in his pocket.

"What was happening when you contacted me to return to the building?" Melanie was direct in her questioning.

Adam rubbed his hands together and looked in her eyes. "Had a hunch."

Carl crossed his arms on his chest and waited. Adam's pause pointed to foul play.

"Sort of a hunch. I swung by and got the ear of one of the firefighters. He said they were about finished, and the rest would be up to the fire inspector."

"You must have called Ray. I was surprised to see him and Phil there." Melanie was digging.

"I was surprised to see Carl." Adam raised his voice enough for patrons to look their way.

Carl's eyebrows shot up. "Sorry to disappoint you, dude. I do have a stake in all of this. My family, you know."

Adam shifted in his chair. "I guess I just didn't expect you to be with Melanie."

Carl knew he was right. And Adam had contacted Melanie, not him, to return to the office.

It was a little odd that he would be spending time with her. No one had invited him to any part of the review project. Shore Industries contracted with Waverly, his former firm. Melanie had a good reputation, and his family called her, not him, to offer advice. Those facts bothered him still.

"We go way back, as Melanie has told you." Carl's tone was casual, reinforcing that there was no foul play in his meeting with Melanie.

Carl stared directly at Adam, but Adam spoke to Melanie. "Ray and Phil decided to return to Phil's house. Melanie, I expect we need to rethink some of our plans to meet tomorrow morning."

"Our plans? I didn't know you would be meeting with me and Ray and Phil," Melanie said.

"Just like I didn't expect you to invite Carl. And who gave you permission to bring him into the circle?" The veins in Adam's neck bulged as his cheeks reddened.

Carl snapped a look toward Melanie, but her response did not surprise him. "And who said I invited him?" Melanie responded with complete calm and composure.

Adam's phone sounded with a notification, and he reached in his pocket. A disposable lighter landed in the aisle and a folded paper floated under the table. He was fumbling to see the phone screen. "Sorry, need to make a call." When he stood up, he spotted the lighter, picked it up, grabbed his coffee, and walked out on the street.

"I didn't know he smoked," Melanie noted.

"Something's rotten at Shore." Carl's voice was flat.

Melanie watched Adam walk away from the cafe with his phone to his ear and a coffee and lighter in the opposite hand.

"Agreed. I think I'll grab a ride back to the hotel and pick this up tomorrow." She pulled up an app on her phone and ordered a ride.

Carl knew it was best to let things go for the day, and said goodbye as Melanie exited the coffee shop. He reached down to pick up the paper near his foot and slowly unfolded a check for ten thousand dollars, payable to Cash from Phil Walker's personal checking account. He tucked it in his breast pocket with a tap for safekeeping.

He called Holly for a ride since the parking garage was blocked. The boys were in the back seat and shared stories of their visit to the Detroit Institute of Arts. Carl could feel the smile on his face when he heard how happy they were to avoid a terrible school lunch and see lots of big colorful paintings. He laughed when the two started singing the school pep song. "Did you have a school song in elementary school, Holly?"

"No."

He tried again to engage her in a family conversation. "What about school lunches, were they decent?"

"Don't remember."

Holly was staring straight ahead, driving with intent. Carl noticed her tight grip on the steering wheel. He turned to look out the passenger window.

The landscape changed from city blocks to suburban parks. When they turned into their Troy subdivision, Carl had to blink away tears.

CHAPTER 15

Melanie rolled over, hit the snooze button on the alarm one more time, and stared at the ceiling. If half of her night visions were correct, she had the makings of a crime triangle right under her nose.

She saw Ray colluding with Adam in a park. She knew that it had to be Campus Martius because the soldiers' monument was in the distance and businesspeople walked across a paved center. She was enjoying the day on the plaza until she recognized what was happening. Ray was talking with his hands and shaking his head while Adam looked at him with puppy-dog eyes.

Melanie pulled the covers around her neck to avoid the scene. They were standing off to the side when her dream faded away. She rolled over to another vision with Phil on the phone with Adam. They were in their respective offices just before the fire. She could see their faces wrinkled in stressful poses. The heat in the bed pushed her to toss the covers to the side.

Then there was the endless loop of Ray telling her they needed to have their plans in place before Phil could recover and return to work. She shivered, woke up enough to pull a blanket back over her body, and thought about Phil plotting to shut down operations at Shore to postpone a meeting. She rolled over again and thought of the opposing side. Ray had tried to sell out when he thought Phil was incapacitated but had stopped that plan.

The worst dream of all was Carl melting gold jewelry in a cauldron over an open fire. He was dressed in welder's gear and used a long iron rod to stir the pot as he tossed in heavy gold chains, rings, bracelets, pins, and buttons. A laugh resounded with every toss and steamy air surrounded him. The hair on Melanie's arms stood up when she watched the witch-like Carl working in a wooded glen permeated by red and black air.

She sat up, turned the alarm completely off, rubbed the goosebumps on her arms, and headed for the shower. It was time to face her questions head-on. With simplified makeup and practical attire, she made a quick exit from the hotel.

Melanie ordered a ride and wondered if she would be able to get into the Shore offices. She checked local news on her phone and found no alerts for roads being closed. The only sound bites about the fire reported that no real damage was sustained and two people were treated for minor cuts and released from the hospital. She was taking her chances and hoping that her things were still in the conference room.

A pleasant surprise for the morning was the ability to enter the building without a problem, with the door attendant in place and elevators working. The first order of business was to confirm that her rental car was still in the parking garage. No damage was done anywhere in that area, and cars that were parked looked fine. Adam's reserved space was empty.

Melanie returned to the offices and toured the facilities. Yellow tape closed two restrooms, and the coffee bar was partially taped off along the outside wall where the window was boarded over. Signs simply read *Do Not Enter.* The conference room was untouched. Her papers were exactly where they had been left. There was a smoke odor lingering but nothing strong. Cleaning staff had done an incredible job overnight. The missing element was people, and a tour of the C-suite told her she was completely alone.

Because Adam's office was always open, Melanie wandered in. She could smell a hint of pine, one of his afternoon aromas, over the faint fire smoke and wondered if Adam had been in the office overnight. That would explain why his car was gone. Papers were scattered across the desk. Without getting too close, she strained to see if there was anything of interest. She was able to see a document that looked like a lawsuit. An envelope covered the top. The small print included the words "Luxury Home Supply v." but she could not see any more than that. She did not want to jump to conclusions, but it looked like Carl's cash source would not throw him a lifeline this year. She reminded herself not to predict anything too soon.

"What brings you to my office so early?"

Melanie spun around on her toes. "Oh! Hi, Adam. I was noting how little damage was done yesterday. With all the excitement I expected things to be smoky and water stained. Yours was the only open door, so I peeked in. Sorry."

"I'm just surprised to see you here at all." Adam's eyes scanned the room as if he were verifying her story, making sure everything was in place.

"I probably have a meeting today. I haven't heard from anyone about a change. Yes, I'm here early. Needed to be sure I could still get to my documents." Adam's dark eyes and soft jaw drew her attention to his innocent side, the puppy-dog face she saw in her night visions. "Are we not supposed to be here?"

"To my knowledge, the building is open today." Adam looked at his desk before continuing. "I have a few pressing matters, so if you don't mind, I'd like to get to work."

"Of course. Is there anything urgent?" Bad question. "I mean, is it something that might cause Ray and Phil to postpone my meeting with them?"

"Um. Not really. They both chose not to join us yesterday in the coffee shop, so neither of us had that opportunity to know their plan."

"See you later, then." Melanie settled her crossbody bag on her side and pulled her sweater jacket closed before she exited the room. The words "neither of us had that opportunity" echoed loudly in her brain. His statement was true, but Adam probably had another opportunity to communicate with Ray and Phil. He did not lie exactly.

She got set up to continue her work with new information. Luxury Home Supply. She needed to scrutinize those transactions a little more. Especially refunds issued to them. Her fear of who might be involved in kickbacks was adding urgency to the matter.

****

Carl used Uber to get to the office and checked the garage before entering the building. His car was fine, and he saw Melanie's rental right where it had been yesterday. He wondered if she planned to come to the office early. As far as he knew, she would be meeting with his father and uncle in the afternoon. His goal was to track down Adam and ask about the check he dropped on the floor. But first, he would talk with Sharon and Christine.

The two secretaries had a terrible scare in moments of chaos the day before. He felt responsible for their bad fortune since he had left the trap and enticed Sharon to investigate his fake email. They ended up being at ground zero when the disaster hit.

As soon as he was in the lobby, he accessed the company directory and called each of them offering whatever time away from work they needed to recover. Of course, Christine wanted to speak with Ray before deciding. Sharon was pleased to know the offer was made but was feeling well enough to come into the office.

Knowing there were no serious injuries, Carl was prepared to continue solving the puzzles of jewelry, gold, and greed. The Shore staff was dedicated and committed to the company. If they only knew what he suspected, maybe they would be looking for different employment.

He was alone in the elevator and tried the control box for Floor Three. It still opened with the programmed process. Rather than risk getting caught, he closed the panel and exited onto the fourth floor. He took the stairs down one level and pushed the door open carefully, listening before rushing in. He paused at the sound of voices.

"Locker Eleven. Right there."

Something scraped, like metal on metal. His teeth clamped together in response to the rasping sound. The clank of a slide bar that secured the locker door announced that someone was successful in opening it. "Ah. It's there. All of it."

"You sure?"

"Yeah. There were twelve bars. I'll take them now."

"Not so fast, hot shot. My niece doesn't expect to buy that new house yet since Phil won't sell the company."

Carl's heartbeat tripled. My father? And Adam? Carl wondered if the bars were his mother's jewelry melted down. Was that even possible? There could not possibly be that much family jewelry. The door slipped shut when he let his guard down in a moment of enlightenment. Panicked, he ran down the stairs one level, hopped on the elevator down to the garage, and got in his car.

When he pulled out of the parking structure, Adam and Ray were standing on the sidewalk watching him drive away.

"Siri, call Melanie."

The call went to voicemail. Carl hung up without leaving a message.

Without thinking, he drove to Starbucks, his quiet place to regroup.

He set a black coffee in front of him, lifted the lid, and breathed in the energy. Vibrations from his phone interrupted the experience. It was Melanie.

"Hey, thanks for the call."

"Where are you?"

"Starbucks. We need to talk."

It took Melanie nearly thirty minutes to make her way to Carl. He was on his second cup of coffee. The caffeine was working its way through his veins when she walked through the door.

He stood to greet her, almost dancing around the table to invite her to sit down.

"Are you okay?" she asked.

"Fine. I heard my father and Adam in the construction area on Floor Three. They were in my locker. Adam was trying to take the gold bars. He knew there were—"

"Slow down! When did this happen?"

Carl sat down and started tapping the table. "Just now. Well, an hour ago maybe."

"Your father is moving today's meeting again. It will be tomorrow. Interesting that his text came about an hour ago."

"The same time they were at my locker. He must have something important to take care of with Adam."

CHAPTER 16

Melanie learned more than she wanted to know from Carl. He was drinking his mood booster and emitted full-blown anxiety. It was not so much what he said as how he delivered his message.

Carl had unearthed the crux of evil at Shore Industries. He had a theory that his father recruited Adam Barnes to be his scapegoat. Carl was sure Adam took the jewelry from the compartment under the base of the locker, had it melted down, and planted the results back in the locker. The twelve gold bars would be easier to offload without suspicion if traded slowly over time for hard cash, and the coins would make perfect gifts to procurement agents.

Melanie let Carl vent. She jumped when he hit his fist on the chair next to him. She'd never seen this side of him. In the past when they opened Pandora's box, there was no personal connection to the evil that escaped. This time the unleashed greed was close to home, and the revelations tipped Carl into a vindictive mode. She pushed the hair off her heated neck when he raised his voice enough for other customers to look their way.

"How can they possibly think I wouldn't notice?"

She laid her palms on the table and leaned in. "Carl, step back for minute and get your emotions under control."

When he had taken a deep breath and relaxed a little, she gave him a look of askance. "How did they know the jewelry was there?"

"Good question."

"Are you sure it's what and who you think? Your father and not your uncle Phil?"

For the next thirty minutes, the perfect pair of problem solvers brainstormed reasonable scenarios. Their conclusion was that Carl's mother was in on the scheme.

Carl had told no one other than Melanie about his mother's jewelry. He speculated that his uncle Phil must have asked about a specific piece of jewelry that Carl's grandmother had worn. Another possibility was that Joyce had slipped and mentioned the jewelry she had given to Carl.

Given other open questions, they still concluded that Phil knew Carl held the family heirlooms, and Ray was using a non-family member, Adam, to do the dirty work of getting cash out of the precious pieces. Surely, there had to be a monetary benefit for Adam.

After hashing out those possibilities, Carl produced Phil's ten-thousand-dollar check made payable to Cash.

Melanie stared at the check on the table. She wiped the sweat from her palms before dragging it closer. Ten thousand dollars. A personal check. She grabbed her cell phone and snapped a photo.

"What should we do with this?" Carl asked her.

"Sit on it for a while," she replied.

****

It was after ten o'clock, and there was no sign of Ray or Phil in the C-suite. Carl smelled deception when he learned Ray changed the meeting time because of an important luncheon with Joyce at the Detroit Athletic Club. He knew of nothing significant happening at the Club. He texted Melanie.

Ready?

Be there in 5.

Their plan was in place. Melanie headed down the hall carrying an empty folder, Carl greeted her partway, and they detoured to the stairwell.

They made it to the third floor and pushed the door open without a sound. Carl signaled Melanie to hold it ajar while he tiptoed into the open space. Cement dust painted the lockers, the rows of metal frames were rearranged, and locker doors were hanging open in all but one row. Every open locker was empty.

"Surprised, Carl?" Adam's voice carried an evil tone. He wore black and stood behind the row of lockers closest to the stairwell door. He carried a black leather duffle, large enough to carry a change of clothes. And twelve bars of gold.

"Adam! What happened here?"

"I guess you didn't know. Phil wants this area taken back to just the bare structure. Thinks that Shore Industries has a chance to pull out of its financial free fall if we're a little less extravagant with employee perks."

"What does that mean?"

"Ask your girlfriend. I'm sure she planted the idea."

Carl closed the door and stepped farther into the room, hoping Adam had not seen Melanie. He ran his fingers through his hair and squared off to look directly at his opponent. "Another meaningless statement. If you're talking about Melanie, yeah, we do good work together when it comes to corporate turnaround. But what's the deal with this space? Spending more money to take away unfulfilled promises to staff is not how you bring a failing company back on its feet."

Adam gave a smirk and forced a laugh. “Do you think the COs of Shore really thought Miss Sullivan would do anything to help us? Are you that naive?”

Carl was getting deeper into the fog with every piece of information Adam doled out.

“Maybe the Chief Officers are hiding something, and that includes you, not me. And why are you even here? You must be part of a coverup.”

“Figure it out.”

Adam was out of sight when Melanie pushed her way in from the stairwell. Carl blocked her and put his finger to his lips, silencing her until Adam was out of hearing range.

“Oh, and before I forget, it’s not too likely your father and uncle will really want to meet with Melanie any time soon. Just a heads-up. They’ll be busy,” Adam called out.

The sound of the closing elevator door drifted over the rows of lockers. Carl summoned Melanie to join him.

The two of them searched the room looking for Locker Eleven. They found it in a far corner removed from the numerical order of others. The door on his was closed and locked. Carl took a deep breath. “Here we go.”

****

Melanie stood back and watched Carl. His face tightened and his lips clenched into a straight line as his shoulders lifted with his deep inhale before he got to work. It took two attempts to hear the click. Melanie’s body relaxed with Carl’s success. If someone had changed the combination, they would have had another hurdle to overcome.

The door swung open to reveal the gold bars. All the blister packages were in one open box and not bundled in plastic packaging. The coins appeared untouched.

"Don't touch them, Carl!"

He turned to her, his eyes stern.

"You know better. Don't get your prints on them."

"You're right. I don't know what I was thinking."

Melanie handed him the thin scarf that was draped under her sweater jacket. "Use this and make sure your hands stay under it."

Carl wrapped the cloth around his hands with enough slack left between his wrists to be able to maneuver the small blister packs of individual bars. He was careful to lift them just enough to count ten pieces.

"There were twelve. Two are missing."

"What should we do?" Melanie's voice cracked with trepidation.

Carl just looked at her, shaking his head lightly. She saw his skin flush and eyes harden as the seconds passed.

"I could just kill them."

Melanie wondered if Carl could kill anybody. The man she knew could not euthanize a suffering pet. This matter presented a different situation and with it a personality she'd never imagined in him.

"Before we do anything, let's check the rest of the locker. You said there was a false bottom."

"I need to take these bars out. Can they go in your bag?"

Without giving much thought to his request, Melanie opened her tote and let Carl slide the box sideways into the canvas bag. The weight tugged Melanie's hands as she worked to keep the load steady. He covered the box with the scarf and worked on removing the panel at the bottom of the locker.

"Fingerprints?" Melanie warned Carl about leaving evidence.

"It's my locker. The bottom would have my prints."

Melanie let it go. Carl got under the locker base easily, and she noted the surprised look on his face when he returned the metal sheet before she could see the contents. He used his sleeve to wipe the areas he had touched and closed the door. After spinning the combination lock, he wiped the surface and grabbed Melanie's arm.

"We need to go."

"Not with these things in my bag!"

Carl worked fast to get the box back into the locker. He directed Melanie out of the building and into the parking garage.

"Get in your car and hand me the keys."

"Where are we going?"

"Not sure. But Adam didn't see you with me, so taking your car makes the most sense."

Melanie trusted his judgment and did as he asked. Carl pulled out of the parking garage without a trace of Adam in sight.

"I haven't seen Adam since I returned from our planning meeting," Melanie said.

"Well, the plans we made are gone! I didn't expect to see more jewelry sitting in the bottom of the locker."

Melanie tipped her head. "What?"

"Yeah. My mother gave me a bag of jewelry. There was a second bag there. Black velvet. The drawstring was open enough for me to see lots of gold."

"Where would that have come from?"

"Hold the questions. I don't have answers."

Carl drove in silence. Melanie watched him clenching his teeth, which told her he was devising a plan. She waited for the brainchild to be born.

"Where are we going?"

"Home. I mean to my house."

CHAPTER 17

Her hands were clasped tightly in her lap as Carl drove directly to his house in the suburbs. His navigation was automatic, and Melanie thought this place must be his safe zone. It was Melanie's first visit to Carl's private world in Detroit. All the notions she had of Carl Walker's dream home were demolished. The suburbs were not the rolling hills and expansive manicured lawns she pictured. The automotive executives of yesteryear lived in a land removed from the metropolis they rolled through now.

Sidewalks lined streets laid out in quadrants running directly north-south and east-west. House after house looked nearly the same. Gardens defined each residence, trees were sparse, and backyards were fenced for privacy. Most backyards had small swings and jungle gym sets for children who likely all attended the same schools and rode the same school buses. She envisioned the older ones kicking a soccer ball or skateboarding in the street after rush hour traffic had ended in the afternoons.

Surrounding the large subdivision were main roads to any convenience a person needed. And the shopping was not shabby at the nearby Somerset Collection. As they passed by the mall entrances, Melanie noted the high-end retail establishments. Nordstrom, Neiman Marcus, and Saks Fifth Avenue were anchor stores. She could only imagine what lay in between. She made a note to visit before leaving town.

Carl pulled into the driveway of a simple tri-level on a small plot of land in an unassuming subdivision. Melanie followed him to the lowest level into a room that was a pleasant surprise. One wall was a full stone fireplace with a hearth and mantel that were well appointed in mountain cabin decor. Heavy carved wooden candlesticks were supporting large pillar candles with embedded woodland samples while family photos in wood frames flanked the mantle.

She ran a quick inventory of high-end furnishings in leather and handcrafted built-in cabinets lined with impressive first-edition leather books. She wondered if these were Holly's choices, hand-me-downs from the Walker side, or Carl's selections. Given the options, she decided the books were likely given to Carl by his mother. Joyce Walker seemed to be someone who would want her only son to have a very impressive home, even if it was not in keeping with the moneyed Grosse Pointes.

While Melanie was lost in her assessment of the room, Carl had already pulled two glasses and a bottle of wine from a small bar adjacent to the fireplace and opposite bay windows overlooking the backyard patio.

"At this hour? It's not even noon."

"I don't care. This kind of brainstorming requires lubricant. My father would be hitting the bourbon by now. For all I know, he is!"

They raised their classes and clicked loudly. Melanie gave Carl a sly glance and wondered what he was thinking. At that very moment, Holly walked down the stairs from the second level dressed in a brown suede skirt, soft knee-high brown leather boots, and beige cashmere sweater.

It was Melanie who had introduced Carl to Holly within an hour of meeting her at a Christmas gathering. The spark the couple generated had been a surprise. Carl was enamored by the woman Melanie had labeled as a wealth seeker.

Melanie had met the Walker family at Carl's wedding. They were genuinely nice people. She had wondered then if Carl's future would take him back to Grosse Pointe, a perfect fit for Holly.

"Oh! Hi, Holly. It's been a long time."

"Yes. It has."

Carl lifted his head at the sound of the boys shouting their hellos. "What are you doing here now, Daddy?"

"Whoa, my buddy! I could ask you two the same thing."

Holly got close to Carl. Her chin jutted forward. "They're both still coughing. I took them to the pediatrician." She turned to Melanie. "I hope you're enjoying your morning drink with Carl."

"Hold on, Holly. This isn't what you might think." Carl spoke louder than he intended.

"Just an observation." Holly took her youngest son's hand and led him out of the room, the older one following.

Carl flopped into the leather armchair and blew out a lungful of air.

Melanie set her glass down on the edge of the bar before taking a seat on the matching sofa, facing Carl. Her crossbody purse pulled on her shoulder, reminding her that they had jumped into a drink well before planning their next move.

"Carl, I'm sorry."

"It's not your fault. I should have thought ahead. I just came here automatically. This is the place I come when I need space to sort things out. I didn't expect anyone to be home."

"Why don't I leave? We can connect later this afternoon."

"No!"

Melanie sat up with a jolt. "Carl? Are you okay?"

"No. I'm not. Things aren't good here, as you can see. But right now, I need to uncover what I think is rotten business at Shore."

Holly came back into the family room. "Really, Carl? What is rotten business, exactly?"

Carl stood up and stepped toward Holly. She stood taller and looked him in the eyes, defiance beaming at him. Carl's hands clenched and his jaw hardened, but he did nothing to change the response. "None of your business, Holly."

"Oh. But is it Melanie's business?"

"Holly," Melanie butted in, "I'm here because Carl's father and uncle asked Waverly to do some consulting. Through that project, Carl and I have figured out that I may need to speak with the chief officers of Shore to review financial issues with me. I asked Carl to help me find the key accounts for review. That's all."

"And what's rotten about that?"

"Well, you understand that when you confront family members about anything financial, it's rotten. It's a tough topic," Melanie said.

"The Walkers have enough money to buy the city of Detroit if they wanted to," Holly answered before she looked back at Carl. "That better be all it is. Shore is taking way too much of your time from me and the kids. Or is Melanie taking up your time this week? Enjoy your morning brainstorming wine!" She pivoted and left the room, her suede skirt moving the air with a swish.

"I'd better go." Melanie turned to leave but Carl stopped her.

"That's the worst thing you could do right now. After that little speech, we need to be brainstorming."

Melanie smirked at Carl, sat back down, and started developing a list of unanswered questions they believed were key to solving the cash flow issues at Shore. It was not hard to imagine that the chief executives were looking for ways to get cash for bribes and kickbacks to produce bigger orders. These dealings had no place in Melanie or Carl's business practices. The entire scenario was complicated by Carl's need to keep the Luxury Home account in good standing and ultimately support his personal bank account.

The first thing Carl wanted to know was who put the extra jewelry in his locker and where they got it. It was not hard to dream up lots of scenarios. The fact that Adam was running around carrying a duffel bag, showed up in total black clothing, and was in a position that allowed him to cook the books solidified Carl's evil thinking. Melanie did not completely buy into that line of logic.

"There's something about Adam that tells me he's running," Carl said.

"I almost agree. But I think he's being used and is scared."

Carl squinted and shook his head. "No. He might even be the instigator of all of this."

"Do you think your uncle is above crime? We have transactions that point to a coverup he's running."

"I would say we have things pointing to my father. It was my father and Adam at the lockers talking about what to take and how much and when."

"True. Maybe your uncle Phil doesn't have anything to do with it. So why did Adam need to talk to him in the hospital?"

The brainstorming session went on for over an hour. After one glass of wine, the duo put a cork in the bottle and left the house. But not before Carl checked in on his sons and, by default, Holly.

Melanie waited in the car. When he came out looking defeated, Melanie chose to deploy her silence technique and let the conversation happen as Carl was ready. They were halfway back to Detroit before either spoke. It was Melanie first.

"Are we going into tomorrow's meeting with Phil and your dad as if we know nothing about the moved lockers and the bars?"

"If Adam mentions it, we'll have to say something. Otherwise, we can stay away from those topics for now."

Melanie held onto that thought. She tried to sort out the implications of Adam keeping quiet versus his talking about the gold. Would silence mean he was hiding something from the brothers, or would it mean they all were hiding something from her and Carl?

"If Adam's into something with my father and Uncle Phil, he won't say anything. He'll try to cover everything up and pretend I didn't catch him." It amazed Melanie how she and Carl were still tuned into the same airwaves in their thinking. They used to joke and say they finished one another's sentences. It went deeper. They read one another's minds, too.

"But it could also mean Phil doesn't know anything about the gold or the jewelry," she said. "Now we think Adam went back and took two bars."

"Exactly. I think Uncle Phil needs some money, and Adam is getting it for him. Adam must know exactly what goes on but doesn't want my father to know he's part of Phil's bribery."

"Could Adam be stealing for himself?"

"That's what we need to flush out. It's very possible. I think Phil wanted the jewelry and bars out of there before the company was liquidated. That's why he mentioned the lockers when he was first admitted to the hospital."

"Do you know how much each bar is worth?"

"If my calculations are correct, Adam walked out with over two hundred thousand dollars."

CHAPTER 18

Melanie managed to get about six good hours of sleep. Breakfast in her room gave her time to prepare the way she preferred. She was no further ahead in figuring out if both Phil and Ray were in on a jewelry scheme of some kind. She perused and flagged emails for follow-up before taking a leisurely shower. Her selections of clothing were intentional, and she exited the hotel in a navy pants suit, white pleat-front blouse, and small navy beads. Her brown lace-up shoes were comfortable for the long day ahead.

As far as anyone knew, today would be the day to meet with Ray and Phil. No one had canceled yet, even though Adam warned that Phil and Ray would be busy and unable to meet with her. There seemed to be no premise for that declaration.

When Melanie arrived at the office, she and Carl hashed out their plan, agreeing to follow protocol. She reminded Carl that this assignment was hers and technically he was on the client's team. Melanie could see the hurt on Carl's face. She needed to be a strong negotiator so he would not lash out at anyone.

The decision to grab lunch before the afternoon meeting resulted in a fast-food meal eaten in the conference room. More than once, Sharon interrupted. Melanie could feel the tension. Carl was professional, almost short, when answering Sharon's many questions. She knocked lightly on the door, spoke softly, and apologized for interrupting each time. Melanie wondered how anyone could be afraid of Carl, who was caring and concerned about her wellbeing after the fire just two days earlier.

"Is she always that sheepish around you?"

"Who?"

"Sharon. Don't you feel it?"

Carl looked sideways at Melanie. "It's not me. She's afraid of her shadow, even though she plays office gossip and digs up secrets. I think it's the chief officers she's afraid of. I'm family, so even though I'm not one of them, I am in her eyes."

"That's too bad. She needs to get to know you better."

Carl offered his warm smile, closed his eyes, and gave a single nod. "That might help. But I don't trust her. She's an alarmist."

****

A few minutes ahead of the allotted time, Melanie was in the C-suite waiting for the key players to arrive. She was expecting to see Ray, Phil, Adam, and Carl. Stress mounted when she considered what might be uncovered during the dialogue that she anticipated.

For Melanie, the purpose of this meeting was to present a timeline for the closure of Shore Industries. Waverly sent her there to write a plan for the company to move forward in any way that was most beneficial to the founding family. She was already six days into onsite work in addition to the billable hours recorded prior to arriving in Detroit. With a company in a crisis like Shore, time was important. Every day and every dollar were essential to the bottom line.

One question remained. Had bad business created a downfall or had a downfall created bad business? She could only wait to see how her approach to the closure would land. It was likely that chaos would break loose.

Ray and Phil walked into the conference room five minutes early. Phil was moving slowly, but Ray did not offer much assistance. They looked like typical business partners, not brothers.

Carl followed a minute later and was greeted with disdain. "What are *you* doing here?" Phil's brows were pinched together.

"Hi, Uncle Phil. Melanie invited me."

"Yes, I did, Phil. Carl has been helpful in the review of his department's records. There may be a need for his input on what we communicate to employees."

Before either Ray or Phil could respond, Melanie moved on. She distributed a spreadsheet showing the dates and details of her work on the project. "When our firm does onsite work, we always present the client with this breakdown at the start of the action plan meeting. That way, if there's anything omitted, we can address it now. Revisit results from each phase if necessary."

The brothers buried their heads in detail while Carl took his seat and opened a journal. He glanced at Melanie who gave him her corporate smile in return. He answered with a nod and looked at Ray before focusing on his journal and pen, like a child putting on his best behavior for his elders.

At precisely the scheduled meeting time of two o'clock, Melanie closed the door and took a seat next to Carl. She opened her folder and distributed copies of the timeline for closure of Shore Industries.

"Maybe Adam should be here before you continue," Phil said.

"Oh, of course! Would you like me to contact him?" Melanie was glad to see things going her way. Without Adam in the room, there would be no easy segue into the dialogue that needed to be had. The possible reveal of gold transactions.

"I've got it." Ray pulled out his cell, hit the speaker, and dialed Adam.

"Yeah, Ray. I got the bars."

Carl shot a look at Melanie who remained unfazed.

Ray paused too long, and Adam tried again.

"Ray? I picked up the bars, like you said."

"Adam, you're late for a two o'clock meeting with Melanie. We're going over her final recommendations and action plans for Shore. She's here with us now."

"Hi, Adam!" Melanie poured on the charm.

"Oh, yeah. Sorry I'm late. I thought the meeting was being canceled."

"Why?" Ray asked.

"I...I don't know. Just did."

"Get here as soon as you can." Ray disconnected the call.

Carl looked from Ray to Phil to Melanie and back at Phil. When his eyes returned to Ray, Melanie saw a stare that divulged his real feelings. "What *bars*, Dad?"

Ray shifted in his seat. "I can't say I really know. You know Adam! It's probably supplies for the workroom." A single forced laugh escaped. "I *did* tell him to pick up protein snacks, those bars everyone seems to like."

"Right," said Carl. He gave Melanie a side glance and made a shift to appear he was studying the timeline for Shore's closure.

Phil cleared his throat before speaking. "I'll be in my office until Adam gets here." As he stood to leave the room, Ray nodded his agreement with that decision and left the conference room with his brother who shuffled his feet as he walked away.

Carl breathed out a deep sigh. "They're running away from any more questions. I need coffee." He headed to the coffee bar down the hall.

Melanie used the time to rethink her approach. The bars mentioned by Adam had to be gold bars. She needed to get Carl's input on the possibility of gold being transported somewhere. But where? And why? Was Ray trying to save Adam by tricking him into taking the gold to a safe place?

Before Melanie could finish her train of thought, Carl flew back into the room and announced, "I've got it!"

Melanie jumped at the urgency in his voice.

The door closed softly, and Carl's voice dropped to a whisper. "Sorry. I hope I didn't alert my father and Phil, but—"

Phil pushed the door open and entered with Ray and Adam. "Got what?"

Carl's eyebrows shot up. "The best coffee we ever had here," he said, embarrassed that he nearly announced another theory of corruption.

"Well, that can wait. Let's get started. Melanie, do you have another copy of the timeline to share with Adam?"

"Of course." Melanie slid a copy across the table and moved to the end for better nonverbal communication with Carl. She straightened the folder in front of her and opened the meeting.

"Shall we begin with a first read of the timeline?"

Everyone nodded their agreement, and Melanie offered her proposal of how to inform each department of the pending liquidation. Silence surrounded her words. The air was heavy with the scent of males squelching their thirsts for blood.

Ray blushed a deep pink, Phil turned crimson, and Adam was red from collar to cheeks. Carl had regained his composure. All the colors of a red sky at morn when sailors take warn.

The timeline was aggressive. The men in the room were either in a hurry to close Shore or ready to kill the man seated next to him for causing the debacle that brought them to this juncture. Melanie was not sure if her proposal was met with disappointment over the length of the timeline or total resistance.

She had been careful to suggest small group meetings and one-on-one appointments where fragile conversations might be indicated. Many line workers had worked in Shore manufacturing plants for more than twenty years. The shutdown would dismantle this family of employees.

After the first read, Melanie paused and waited for questions or comments. No one offered anything. Perhaps they were reviewing the details, thinking of questions, or simply smoldering over the proposal.

When the pause became painful, Melanie broke the silence.

"What questions do you have about the sequence of events or the overall timeline?"

Phil slammed his hand on the table. "Why are we paying you? We're not here to close the place down. I've made that clear from the beginning. Adam has been working hard to generate more income and being sure that the accounting is correct on all transactions to be sure we're not just making errors somewhere, and—"

"Phil, step back," Ray interrupted. "We've had this conversation, and we don't need to drag non-family members into the mud."

Adam shifted his eyes around the room. "Are you asking me to leave?"

"No!" Phil's voice bounded off the walls.

"Calm down, Phil. You don't need another stroke!" Ray's forehead beaded with moisture.

"Might I offer a suggestion?" Melanie's voice was soft, calm, but firm in her businesslike manner.

When all the men around the table looked her way, she continued. "It's important to keep the right pair of lenses for the work we're doing. Today we're looking at two things in one. Yes, it was a hard decision to move in the direction of liquidating assets. But that recommendation was presented after more research that followed our first meeting. Phil and Ray, we left our last meeting ready for me to develop a timeline, and the request was for me to develop it as quickly as possible. Unfortunately, Phil had a little setback, and the building emergency delayed us until today."

"What has any of *that* got to do with any of *this*?" Phil was still agitated.

"I'm setting the context for this meeting. At our first onsite meeting last week, a decision was made for this course of action. Today is about making sure we understand how we will roll out a major plan with care, empathy, and compassion for everyone who will be affected."

Ray cleared his throat and tugged at his tie.

Adam eyed Phil and twisted his cuffs into alignment.

Phil said, "Let's move on."

"Thank you." She paused to gain control of the room. "I'd like to know what questions you have for me."

It was Phil who jumped into the dialogue first. "What can we do for our employees? They've been loyal through the past couple of years when times have been tough. No Christmas bonuses, no paid days off just for good measure, no overtime in the plant, and I could go on. What do we do for them?"

"All of those extra niceties were beyond their normal employment conditions. We shouldn't need to do anything for them, but we might be able to find a way to fund a good severance payout. We're in trouble and need to shut down if we're going to save our personal assets," Ray replied.

Carl expressed regret for not pressing to review company operations earlier in his tenure and thanked Phil for being concerned about the staff. Adam said nothing.

Phil locked eyes on Adam. "Adam, you've been involved in making sure our sales quotes include good profit margins, right?"

Adam looked like a wrecking ball was heading his way. He tugged on his suit jacket and licked his lips. "Well, yeah. Orders were slowing down on a couple of accounts. So, um, we tried cutting prices, but that was worse for the bottom line. Then we, ah, found a way to use consulting fees without increasing overhead. We can charge to recoup some salary costs that way. Yeah, so that's helping." There was a pause and when no one responded, Adam continued.

"For example, Luxury Home Supply is one customer that wasn't really sending much business to Shore in the last six or seven months."

Melanie and Carl locked eyes in a moment of shared enlightenment while Adam continued.

"I had one of the salespeople talk to their buyer. Turned out, they didn't know about safety bars for some applications. Not so much about buying them, but how to install, or how to train installers. So we charged consulting fees for the sales staff to spend a few days onsite."

The marked lack of confidence in Adam's story made Melanie's fingers tingle. She rubbed her hands together and faced Carl directly.

Adam continued, "We did that in a couple other cases—"

"Adam, do you mean to say that you have trumped up charges to customers?" Carl was direct and authoritative in his approach. "By that I mean, maybe there isn't really any consulting going on, since that's not a service Shore offers. Salespeople had to put a little extra time into explaining a product to sell it. That's not consulting."

Adam shifted his weight in the chair, ran a finger under his collar, and rubbed the side of his nose.

All the telltale signs of lying were laid bare in front of them. Adam was fidgeting, sweating, and giving way too many details about consulting fees. Melanie left this side of the business conversation to Carl. It was his strong suit.

Ray took a deep interest in what Carl had just said. "Adam? Is this the case? We're not a consulting business. Never have been and never will be. Liability would be too great for us."

"I'd say Adam has been creative in finding ways to generate some income," Phil said.

"What kind of risk does that pose for Shore?" Melanie queried.

"For what?" Adam leaned into the conversation.

"If one of our sales staff gives bad advice on installation and someone is injured because of a product installation failure, we could be in deep trouble with lawsuits!" Carl raised his voice.

A snapshot of Adam's desk flashed behind Melanie's eyelids. Luxury was suing Shore. And maybe it was not the first time.

"Are there any outstanding lawsuits that were not part of my focused operations review?" Melanie asked.

Adam looked at Phil with the same puppy-dog eyes he wore in her nightmare.

Carl stood up. He stepped back and positioned himself behind Adam's chair in direct eye contact with Melanie. He gave her a near-imperceivable nod. They were back in the game together, and Carl had just tossed the ball to her court.

CHAPTER 19

Carl watched Melanie run with his cues. His chest expanded with pride to know that he could still work with this talented professional. Melanie, the woman he once loved but who held on to her own dreams with no consideration for his desire to have a family. But look where that got him in life. His growing inability to satisfy Holly's need for career, prestige, and a wealthy lifestyle was a consistent source of anxiety.

"Adam, I'm asking a question. It's especially important for me to know about lawsuits." Melanie's voice pulled Carl out of his self-evaluation.

"Well, there's always something legal to be managed," Adam replied.

"What's currently on the table, Adam?" Ray asked.

"Nothing unusual, I'm guessing," Phil added.

There was silence. Adam looked down at the button on his suit coat and picked at a piece of lint.

"Adam?" Melanie picked up the lead, but Adam still didn't answer Ray's question.

When the air became uncomfortable, she added, "If any kind of legal action is pending, particularly from Luxury and related to consulting, this is the time to fill us in."

Adam took a deep breath that was audible in the room that had gone quiet. All eyes were on him, including Carl's, as he repositioned himself at the table.

The surreal moment caught Carl smiling. His head was nodding slowly when Adam turned to him.

"Knock it off, already. You're the one with jewels in your locker!"

No one at the table flinched. It was a clear sign that everyone knew about the jewelry bag. He had been the last to know that his secret hiding place was anything but secret.

"What an interesting comment, Adam." Carl drew on his practiced stance as a consultant on Melanie's team. "Why do you mention the contents of a locker at this particular time?"

"We're asking about lawsuits here, Adam." Melanie picked up the interrogation method she knew so well. "Has Luxury filed a lawsuit against Shore?"

Adam dropped his chin to his chest and mumbled his reply. "Yes."

Ray looked at Phil. "I'm guessing you knew about this, Phil."

"Of course not! I leave petty things to people I trust. I'm sure this suit is nothing out of the ordinary. Right, Adam?" Phil raised his eyebrows, lowered his chin, and looked over the top of his glasses at Adam.

Adam glared at Phil for a few seconds, then turned to Melanie. "Just how well do you know this family?"

Carl gasped quietly. Was Adam insinuating something about him by mentioning jewelry in the locker? He had to trust Melanie. She would uncover the truth about the lawsuit, the jewelry, and the gold. He had to give her space before stepping into the fray.

"I know one person quite well, as you know. My years of work with Carl tell me there is nothing out of line in his business dealings, ever. That includes his work here at Shore. My investigations over the past week confirm that fact. What exactly are you trying to imply?"

Adam pulled on his lapels and looked back at Phil. "It might not be Carl causing the problem."

Phil's face was puffing up with embarrassment or anger or both. Carl had seen that look more than once in his life. It never ended well. The last time it resulted in a stroke.

"Uncle Phil, can I get you some water?"

"No! I'm fine. This young man thinks he can push his mistakes off on us. Well, that's not going to happen. Believe me."

Ray folded his hands and asked a very pointed question. "Tell me, Phil, what mistakes would those be?"

Carl knew what was coming. Two brothers were about to dig up lots of old private family dirt. The stories of who tried to control the business, which of his grandparents favored which child, who had a larger family to support, and on and on and on.

They started talking about an old accounting error that cost Shore hundreds of dollars in the days when that was a good deal of money.

"Melanie, maybe we can meet with Adam for a few minutes while my father and Uncle Phil take a break."

"Perfect idea. Adam, if we could go to your office? Let's all meet back here in thirty minutes. Does that work for everyone?" Melanie gathered her notebook and pen as she spoke.

Carl thought old business war stories seemed insignificant today when there was a major financial and possible legal crisis facing the family.

****

Melanie was relieved to be with Adam and Carl alone, out of the critical eyes of the Walker brothers. She chose to stand until Adam set the tenor in the room with instructions to sit at the small table in the corner. He was selecting common ground, an equal playing field. Sitting across from his desk would put him in control. The small round table and four chairs created a team. She wondered if Adam knew these signals, that he was relinquishing the upper hand. Or was he just at his wits' end with no clue how to dig himself out of the hole he had just dug?

Carl sat in a chair that backed into the corner. Melanie sat with a view out a window. Adam grabbed bottles of water from his mini fridge before sitting across from Melanie. He faced a bookshelf of artifacts, industry publications, and product models.

"This is the first time I've had an opportunity to look out your office windows. It's really a pleasant view of the street. I can see one of Carl's preferred coffee sources from here." Melanie smiled. She was breaking the ice.

"Yeah. It's nice on a sunny day." Adam's voice was low, humble.

"Adam, I don't want to be your adversary. If anything, I want to collaborate to resolve whatever is going on." Melanie was being kind, offering an olive branch as she often did. It was her way of getting more information and honesty from a client while staying professional.

"I support that," said Carl. "Working at Shore isn't always easy, and I'm more aware of that than anyone. My family can be demanding, and they don't like compromise."

"You can say that again," Adam said. "You fell right in line with them in there. Sometimes I feel like your uncle's pawn."

Carl didn't respond. Melanie thought he had fallen in with the family temperament for a moment but was sure no one knew he was working with her now.

"Is that the case now, with a legal battle?" Melanie walked into the dialogue that could get Adam to talk about the document she had spotted on his desk

"Yes and no. I mean, yeah. There's that. But there's so much more."

Adam looked at Melanie. Those sad eyes caught her off guard. They left the conference room because of Adam's harsh implications, and now she was looking at the man in her nightmare. A victim. A man with whom she could empathize. Did Carl see Adam the same way she did?

"Phil will do anything to get his way. Including having me find ways to postpone meetings with you about shutting down the family business."

Melanie looked from Carl to Adam before continuing.

"So Adam, you don't smoke, do you?"

Carl smiled. Adam rotated his face toward the windows and said, "No. I light aroma sticks. And I get paid well to take care of Phil's wishes."

"Are you thinking about jewelry in a locker? Arson?" Melanie used her questioning techniques to get Adam to expand on his work for Phil. He could choose to stick with her inquiry about a lawsuit, or he could start to unveil illegal gold trading if that was happening. She was not convinced yet that Adam had connections to such business dealings, but maybe he had tried to bribe Luxury to place specialty orders.

"What do you know about me? I mean, aren't you supposed to check employee backgrounds?"

"Yes. And I did. You have a good pedigree. Stanford, Harvard Business School, held jobs at McKinsey and Bain, not to mention your family's business in Boston. You stand to inherit a hefty sum from Barnes Chain when. . ." Melanie realized that what she was saying would open the floodgates. Barnes Chain. Gold chain manufacturer, supplier to jewelry fabricators. A connection just sparked for her. Adam had access to gold processes. She needed Adam to talk about gold bars.

A slight tap of her foot against his shoe was all that was needed to pass the baton to Carl.

"Wait a minute! Gold chain? Adam, it never crossed my mind. What's going on with Phil and you? And maybe my father!" Carl feigned his surprise. Melanie was surprised at how well their plan was working.

Adam let his head drop back. A loud sigh and a drop of his shoulders told Melanie that Adam was ready to surrender.

Melanie's phone rang. Ray reported that Phil was exhausted and requested they resume the meeting on another day.

CHAPTER 20

From here on, she once again would work through the weekend. Melanie was unhappy with her situation. She had hoped to find time to explore some of the Detroit area, maybe shop Somerset, get a healthy meal followed by a good night's sleep, and even board a plane bound for Boston in a day or two.

Her assignment was scheduled to end yesterday. Ten days were agreed upon, and she was scheduled to deliver the action plan before leaving.

She usually traveled with another consultant, but now she understood why Waverly sent her on her own. This assignment was riddled with problems that Dominick, Managing Director, must have uncovered. He was too savvy to miss red flags. Or was it Ray who requested her to come alone because of the cost?

She was frustrated at the number of unanswered questions that stood in the way of setting the path for Shore's action plan. Sure, she had a timeline for communicating with employees and a boilerplate roadmap customized for specific needs to liquidate within six months. Carl had admitted the intertwining events puzzled him also.

A hot shower, breakfast delivered to her room, and thinking time were needed. Not necessarily in that order. She started her day by jotting notes.

Carl has heirloom jewelry: one bag.

Someone planted jewelry in the locker: one bag.

Did the gold bars and coins come from Barnes Chain?

What is Phil's connection with the gold?

What is Ray's connection with the gold?

~~*How is Carl involved?*~~

Is Carl involved?

She sat back and looked at the list and added more inquiries.

Was the building emergency ordered by Phil?

How did Phil recover from a stroke in a week?

Her phone buzzed on the nightstand. She hesitated to answer Carl's call. The last thing she needed was to hear Carl's voice and be thrown into a subjective mindset. On the fourth ring, she sent an automatic message to say she would contact him later.

She continued the list.

Did Adam commit arson?

Is Adam the culprit or a victim? Both?

When she was satisfied, the list was put aside.

Hot shower water eased her shoulders. She let it fall over her hair and face, taking in the potential of renewal, hoping the water would wash away her confusion and clarify her perspective.

It was Saturday, a day to dress down. Her mother used to call Saturday a play clothes day. Melanie wore the same outfits she would put on after school. She loved the memories of selecting clothes for school and church when her mother asked her to dress for an occasion. Even with a tight budget, Momma made sure their clothing was stylish and versatile.

The first thing that made sense today was a comfortable pair of jeans, a cotton pullover sweater in a seasonal rust color, and a print scarf to add a little warmth to the neckline. Her crossbody bag finished the look, and she stepped into soft brown leather loafers. Momma would be proud of the way she carried the lessons of personal appearance into her professional life. But this would not be a play day.

Hair and makeup complete, she took inventory of what she needed—laptop bag, light jacket, car keys, and phone. She was ready for breakfast in the lobby restaurant. She opened the door, and Carl was looking back at her.

He stood in the hallway, eyes dark and tired, hair tousled.

"Carl!" Melanie reached for him and guided him into the room.

The same suit he had worn the day before needed a trip to the dry cleaner. His collar was open, and he was not wearing a tie.

She led him to the sofa in her suite and sat next to him. When he opened his mouth to speak, tears trickled down his face. He squeezed his lips together and shook his head.

Melanie rubbed between his shoulder blades and waited. He wiped his face with his palms and kept his face covered. After a few seconds passed, Melanie removed her hand and waited again. Silence was the best approach, she knew. He needed to feel safe before they talked.

"She's gone, Melanie. Holly left with my boys."

The mix of emotion that swallowed Melanie left her speechless. Carl did not deserve this. But he did deserve a better marriage than Holly was willing to give him. Melanie needed to say something, but words did not come to her.

"Mel, did you hear me? She left! With my kids!" Carl choked on his last two words.

Melanie knew she could not look at Carl because the tears in her own eyes were for the wrong reason. She was sad, but not because Holly left him. He lost the most important thing, the thing that had kept Melanie from marrying him. His kids. Maybe there would be a chance to rewrite their history.

"I don't know what to say, Carl."

"You don't need to say anything, I guess. Just having you here to listen is enough."

Melanie treaded carefully on every word. She did not want to say something that would shut Carl down, stop him from telling her more. "What would you like to do? Have you had a meal?"

"No. Not even my thinking coffee. I was up all night, driving around looking for her."

Driving around looking for her? Why would Holly be somewhere that he could find her? Did he go to Holly's friends' houses? What about the kids?

Too many questions to ask. She took the safe route. Food.

"Carl, you need sustenance, like breakfast. I was about to go down to the lobby restaurant. Come with me. We'll get that coffee and some nourishment."

It was still early for a crowd to be out on a Saturday, and the restaurant was quiet. They chose a booth in a back corner and ordered coffee and Danish pastry to start.

Melanie hid her hands in her lap, embarrassed by a tremor that revealed her remorse. Her mind raced in too many directions. Her ongoing affections for Carl, his possible involvement in corruption at Shore, Adam's role in illegal activity, and the magnetism she felt toward both men.

She was never good at this sort of thing, tending to emotional needs while navigating a business dilemma. That's why she loved working with Carl. He was more inclined to empathize with clients. She was a bottom-line kind of gal. She shoved Adam out of her mind to focus on Carl.

****

When Carl felt a little more clarity in his thoughts, he thanked Melanie for being there for him. She did not really feel what he was going through. How could she? She had never married, never had kids, and never wanted them. Maybe her life aspirations were wiser than he thought. The heartache he felt cut him to the core. His boys were his life. They were the reason he left Boston and his career at Waverly. Before all of that, he left Melanie for kids he did not have. Having been an only child, he longed for laughter, occasional chaos, and years of joy a bigger family could bring.

He had respected Melanie's wishes to live a childless life, but their breakup had not been easy on him. There was a piece of his heart that would always belong to her. He had bucked up for at least a dozen years, all in the hope of living his American-family dream life.

"How's that coffee treating you?"

Melanie's question pulled Carl out of his silence. "It's working its magic. Thanks."

Melanie probed a bit. Carl appreciated her interest, slim as it was. He filled her in on the final straw that pushed Holly to pack her bags and leave.

When Holly found Melanie at the house with Carl, she set a mission to learn everything about Shore's financial situation. She talked to her mother-in-law, Joyce, and learned that Shore was in trouble.

Carl saw the distant look in Melanie's eyes. She was there for him, but only in her presence. When he had laid his sadness on the table, satisfied that his emotional distress was substantiated, he swept the crumbs into a neat little pile and made room for a different topic.

CHAPTER 21

Melanie believed she could guide Carl into the dialogue they needed to have. Carl had finished pouring out his soul, doubting the integrity of every family relationship he had, and eating a decent breakfast. Before shifting topics, she needed to know one thing about Holly's departure.

"Carl, after everything you've told me, I'm wondering something."

"Go ahead. I'll try to answer."

"You said you drove around all night looking for Holly. Where do you think she could have gone?"

"She's left before. I drove by a couple of hotels and houses. Her friends. Sometimes the kids stay with their friends overnight, so I checked with those families."

"Would she go back home?"

"She's not there. I called you from home before coming to your room."

Melanie nodded. This was not the first time Holly ran. She would probably come back, and Carl would take her in. He would stay with her for his kids' sake. And maybe for himself.

"What else were you wondering?"

"Oh nothing, I guess. Maybe I just don't understand your family dynamics."

Carl laughed. "Well, that's two of us. I'll meet you at the office in a while. I know you just want this project to be wrapped up. Yesterday's confession from Adam opened a new gift from Pandora."

"Take your time. I could work here, but I've decided on the office in hope of some divine inspiration striking my laptop."

She had not heard the phrase "a new gift from Pandora" since she and Carl took down two corrupt executives in Providence. It was the first time they had discovered forgery.

As Melanie drove away from the hotel, she caught sight of Adam Barnes walking out of The Coffee House, a little place opposite her hotel where she and Carl had occasional offsite conversations. He was dressed in black and carried a familiar leather duffel bag. A list of possible offenses ran through her mind – fraud, money laundering, bribery, and arson. Theft was a maybe.

A bolt of lightning flashed her memory of a text from Adam on the day the building caught fire. He wanted to talk with her but was deterred when Carl was with her. She never followed up with him, and maybe it was time to do that.

****

Carl found Melanie slumped in a chair in her makeshift office. The conference room had become her space with no meetings booked there during her assignment. Her scent of mingled citrus and vanilla jettisoned him back to better days. The days when the two of them slumped as she was now on long weekends in remote conference rooms that offered far fewer amenities than Shore.

Boxes of documents that Melanie had requested for the initial research were stacked in one corner. She was holding a tattered folder, squinting at a legal document that read "Luxury Home Supply vs. Shore Industries." Carl leaned over Melanie's chair to read the fine print.

"Hi. What do you make of this?" Melanie handed the folder to Carl.

"Four years ago?"

"Yep. About the time Shore started to fall apart."

Carl thought of only two things. Adam had been hired about five years earlier, and Phil had divorced his wife about ten years ago. Had Phil started to pull money from Shore after the divorce and five years later hired Adam as the new Chief Financial Officer to collude with him?

As if Melanie read his mind, she introduced the potential of dirty hands. "If I remember Adam's resume correctly, he came to the company about six years ago? Maybe a little less?"

"He would have been here for a little while when this lawsuit was filed. Are you thinking what I'm thinking?"

"That Adam has been paying companies to avoid lawsuits?" Melanie's voice rose at the end of her question, leading Carl to think he was off base.

"Isn't that within the realm of possibility?" Carl looked directly at Melanie.

"How can that be, given everything he said yesterday?"

Adam had fallen apart in their brief meeting. He willingly had offered his side of the story and accused Phil Walker of fooling him.

When major accusations of price gouging and breach of contracts had led to financial hardship, Phil fired the CFO and encouraged Adam to accept the position in a premier company with a long history of success.

Adam had shifted his eyes around the room without focusing anywhere when he described confidential meetings with Phil. He had described his path to success as muddy, while Phil maintained his pristine reputation as an upstanding businessperson.

Adam had detailed his private story in a moment of weakness. His rocky start had been defined by stealing from his own family's business before he was even of legal age. His parents had kept the incident private and honored their commitment of a good education. They also had added a promise that he would never benefit from Barnes Chain's success directly.

Listening to Melanie now, Carl lost patience. "Do you think Adam told a sob story about not having a family just to entice you? To connect with you on a very personal level?"

"Why would it be for me?"

"Mel, come on. Crocodile tears from a grown man about to be caught in a major crime enterprise. Adam is a fake. He wanted you to believe him by creating some bond over a childless life and retiring all alone."

"And you think I'm all alone." Melanie's voice was small.

"I'm sorry, Mel. No. You're not alone. You're a magnet for friends. Besides, you'll always have me in your corner."

Carl needed Melanie now. His whole life was caving in. But was Melanie softening to Adam, taking sides with him, sympathizing with him? She had never been that gullible.

Melanie flipped through another folder. Across the table, he eyed her between pages of the lawsuit he was scanning, rubbed his forehead, and tried to focus. He was ashamed of having blurted out the potential of a lonely life.

From what he could tell, Melanie had recovered or at least put the unpleasant thoughts into a box for another time. "What do you think, Carl? Is the Luxury thing something you knew about? It's your account for premium bonuses."

"You're right about my compensation, but this is old. I mean, it kind of makes sense that no one mentioned it to me. I've only been here a year, so things probably turned around after this happened."

"Or not."

Carl felt his cell phone buzz in his pocket. It was Holly. He held the screen up to Melanie, and she left the room.

"Holly! Where are you?"

"Hi. You don't need to worry. The boys and I are going to spend a little time Up North. Joyce offered us a few days at the cottage. I have the boys' school assignments."

"You planned this without telling me?"

"It didn't take a lot of planning. I made a call to the school to pick up their assignments. Since they're still both coughing, I had no trouble getting them excused. The kids think it's a special treat. Teachers are apparently glad they won't be spreading germs to everyone else."

"Holly, do you really think this is the right thing for them?"

"No. It's not. It's the right thing for me. I'll be filing papers for separation while I'm here, Carl."

Carl's vision tunneled and the room started to spin. Before he could say anything else, he grabbed the wastebasket and vomited.

****

Melanie heard Carl retching and through the glass wall could see him curled over. Her heart pounded hard when she realized he must have just received devastating news from his wife. She decided to give him space and take a walk outside.

The elevator was slow to arrive. As she waited, she remembered her cell phone and returned to the conference room to retrieve it. Carl had already left. The stench was not pleasant, so she gathered her things, and left the door open for the cleaning crew.

Out on the street, Melanie took in the sunshine and puffy clouds of the fall day in Detroit. Most of what she needed was on her laptop. She opted to return to the hotel where a balcony awaited her and room service would bring anything she needed or wanted.

Settled outside in a webbed chair with puffy white clouds sailing across the sky, Melanie envisioned the islands of white as segments of life moving before her. Days with Carl as her partner, in life and in business, were the biggest of the soft cushions. The two of them held together through winds of change for a long while. They slowly fragmented when the changes related to personal goals, each spreading as small puffs into the vast blue horizon.

Was change coming again? Would they reform their beautiful world, reconnect based on a comfortable history together if Holly left? Melanie doubted it. Too much had happened. And Carl had children. Kids were not in her vision, especially not little ones at her age.

Closing her eyes did not clear her mind. Instead, her stomach did that familiar thing. A ball was slamming her in the gut. She doubled over and inhaled to a count of five, held it for a count of four, exhaled to a count of six. Four repetitions did the job of easing the pain. At least for now.

When the clouds faded away and a gray sky prevailed, Melanie went back into the hotel room. She dialed Adam Barnes to get some answers. He picked up on the first ring.

"Hello, Melanie."

"Hi, Adam. Do you have time for a cup of coffee this afternoon?"

"Well, I could meet you in about twenty minutes or so. Where?"

"You probably know The Coffee House, the cafe across from my hotel. I'll see you there."

She packed up her laptop and freshened her makeup. Melanie was crossing the street when Adam exited through the lobby door onto the sidewalk.

"Wait up!"

Melanie turned to look at him through squinted eyes. "What are you doing in the hotel, Adam?"

"I use their garage. Gotta make it look legit, so I walk through the lobby."

"Always on the sly, huh?"

Adam sighed as his shoulders lowered.

Melanie led the way and ordered a decaf skim vanilla latte. Adam asked for a double shot, cold brew, black. She noted the contrast. Hers was fluff. His, a cold slap in the face. Much the same with Carl and her. Light and sweet versus dark and bitter.

Melanie sipped the sweet creamy coffee and let the steam open her senses before beginning a conversation. She wondered if that's how Carl's black coffee worked for him.

Adam appeared pulled apart, scattered, maybe even fearful when he pushed up the sleeves of his sweater and pulled them back down more than necessary. His face was tight, and she could see his cheekbones creating contours of that chiseled look she admired.

"Relax, Adam. We've already had the hardest conversations. You confessed. Ray knows what you're up to. Phil continues to deny everything, and somehow, I need to wrap all of this up in a pretty package for an ultimate action plan. It just needs a big red bow. They should liquidate before it's too late."

Adam nodded at her but did not speak.

“You know, there are times when little pieces of information aren’t significant at first. And then, when it’s time to finalize a plan, those tidbits surface as clues, indicators of something I’ve missed in my investigation. I’m kind of sensing that might be the case with Shore. I’ve let some comments go by the wayside, and it’s time for answers.”

Adam pulled at his sweater sleeve again, then raised his chin to look Melanie straight in the eye.

“You don’t believe anything I’ve told you, do you?”

“You’re wrong, Adam. My problem right now is that I do believe you. That you have been manipulated by Phil. That you think there is no way out of a corrupt employment arrangement.”

Adam sat up straighter and looked around the shop. “You do?”

“Why wouldn’t I? I give everyone a fair chance. I can see the possibility that Phil has you under his control. In fact, I almost think, even after your confession, that you’re still doing his dirty work. Am I right? Because you’re afraid?”

Melanie watched the man turn into a boy. Adam Barnes, the strong, handsome, charismatic businessman, wore drooping eyes and a faint smile. His cheeks were blushing.

“You are so right.” He paused to scratch the side of his nose. He glanced to the right and continued. “So yeah, I did just take some pieces from the lockers to a gold dealer.”

“Lockers? As in several?”

“Different ones for different jobs.”

“Who else is involved?”

“I don’t know. Phil arranges that. Construction workers, I think.”

Melanie turned an evil look at Adam and waited.

“They just help get stuff in and out.”

"How many people have the combinations to these lockers?"

"Just a couple, maybe a few. Like half a dozen. The combinations came with the locks. No one seems to have changed them for themselves."

"Is that why the elevator doesn't always need a passcode process?"

He nodded. "People need to get in and out at all hours."

"Why are you doing this?"

Adam picked up her hand and said, "I'm trapped. Help me."

His warm touch softened her face, but her mind was still reeling with this discovery. She pulled her hand away and met his eyes directly.

"Who do you steal from, Adam?"

He looked away and closed his eyes momentarily. When he looked at her again, he tipped his head and said, "I do not steal from the Walker family."

****

When the end of the day rolled around, Melanie was happy to pour a glass of wine and hop on a FaceTime call with Liz. It had been too long since they'd had time to talk in anything more than sound bites that kept Liz informed of what was going on in Detroit.

"What's happening over there in Detroit? Sounds like you got more than you bargained for."

Liz was perceptive. It was true that the Shore Industries assignment was not what she expected. Anything but. Old feelings wrestled her psyche, and a new man on the block was carrying her into no-no land.

"So aside from the possible kickback scenario there—"

"You mean definite bribery and maybe money laundering! I have no doubt things are illegal here."

"Okay. Aside from that, though. What's going on with Carl? Can't you two figure this out like two adults? I mean, really, you belong together and you both know it." Liz never minced words.

Melanie could not fool Liz about her lingering feelings for Carl that had never evaporated the way she wished they would. Carl made his choice to marry Holly and pursue a family. She had ended their love relationship long before that.

Melanie closed her eyes and sighed, sipped her chardonnay, and leaned into the camera. "Girlfriend, get off that train. He's married and has kids, just like he wanted."

Liz laughed but Melanie kept her stern eyes focused on her until Liz paused to blot her lips with a cocktail napkin. "Okay, okay. There must be something going on there, though. Spill it."

"I'm pretty sure there's nothing going on with Carl in the way of illegal business dealings. In fact, he's pretty upset with his family and seems to think they are corrupt, or at least not completely truthful. Even about a lot of things in the past."

"Mel, I never thought Carl was involved with anything like that. I'm talking about him and Holly and you. Is it weird to be with him again and know that there's trouble in paradise?"

Melanie had to think about that for a minute. She relaxed on the small sofa. It was not cozy enough to wrap around her and offer comforting warmth like her soft cushioned loveseat at home. "Maybe it is. But. . ." She paused long enough for Liz to be suspicious.

"But what?"

"It's not anything, really. But, Adam, the CFO, he's the one giving me weird vibes."

Liz's brows shot up and her eyes widened.

"Don't look at me like that. He's handsome, suave, eligible, I think about my age, and very much involved in something not good."

"What's his pedigree?"

Melanie listed all of Adam's prestigious affiliations. As she did, it occurred to her that Adam used layman's terms for accounting, had no explanation for his departure from reputable firms, and needed to be saved from a sketchy business deal in Indiana. Maybe he was not really an accountant. How could he bluff his way through his employment history?

"You know how to spot them, don't you? Is he available?"

Melanie laughed lightly. "He is what one would call a happy bachelor who might be worried about aging alone. Besides, his ethics are in question. He gets nervous, antsy, like he's hiding something. And I hardly know him personally."

Liz had an incoming call.

"We need to pick this up later. Gotta run. Hugs!"

Melanie was left wondering if Adam Barnes was a complete con. Was Carl completely clean, though?

She stared into her wine glass that was half full. If she were such a great business consultant, why was it so difficult for her to identify and cut her own losses? But would that mean retiring to avoid Carl or admitting that Adam was a bad character? Or both?

CHAPTER 22

The alarm sounded in unison with her ringing phone. Melanie reached for the buzzer first, then answered the call from Ray.

"Hello?" Melanie was tentative. Ray wouldn't usually call her at this time, and especially not on Sunday morning.

"Good morning."

It was not Ray's voice.

"Who is this?"

"It's Joyce. I need to have a word with you. Might I pick you up after church and take you out for brunch? Just us two."

Melanie did a quick rundown of why Carl's mother might need to have brunch when they had only met a couple of times. When she did not answer right away, Joyce continued. "If that's not possible, then maybe tea later in the day?"

"That might be better."

When the details were agreed upon, she got to work. She needed every piece of information she could possibly gather on Joyce Walker, including any involvement she had in Shore Industries. At least she won the gift of extra time and managed a compromise on where they would meet. She wanted to keep control over the length of their time together.

Today would require business attire with a feminine flair. Lady-to-lady discussion, which Melanie assumed this would be, demanded the airs of sophistication without the sharp edges of a business-as-usual appearance. As her mother would say, "Put on some church clothes, Mel. We're going somewhere fancy."

A green tweed jacket dress had not yet been worn during this trip. This occasion was perfect for the muted fall colors of gold and tan. Without much effort, Melanie would fit into the society crowd, something she and Carl used to laugh about when they worked in Providence and schmoozed clients in Newport or traveled to Philadelphia to dine in five-star restaurants with top executives of Campbell Soup Company. The irony was not lost on the scenario of top chefs preparing exquisite meals for people who marketed condensed soup packaged in a tin can. Those days were history. Many of the former Waverly Consulting clients were out of business, merged with other companies, or in the hands of private equity firms.

Times had changed. Had she changed with them? Was she too stodgy and set in her ways? She'd wondered about her relevance in the current business climate, but every new assignment pumped blood through her veins with fiery resolve to get the best outcome for every project. She loved the success of turning a company into a profitable operation. Maybe her age gave her unique perspectives that could be seen as an asset.

It was never easy to deliver bad news like she had done at Shore, but liquidation was the best answer. Taking down individuals in the process was not something she wanted to do, especially not to Carl. And it scared her to think of the repercussions of ruining Adam's position.

She had to pull herself out of the negative thoughts and bittersweet reminiscence to power through this day with Joyce Walker. Maybe she could learn something that would spare Carl and Adam.

Without finding much information about Joyce Walker, Melanie walked into The Whitney on Woodward Avenue with tension in her limbs and a light throb in her temples. Keeping control of the meeting would not be easy with nothing to toss at Joyce, a winning zinger or innocent inquiries about what to do with out-of-style jewelry. She would need something witty to leave a positive impression, get the information she needed, and walk away with secrets.

Joyce Walker entered The Whitney wearing a pantsuit and toting a large designer bag on her shoulder. Melanie had misread the event. Before succumbing to embarrassment, she reminded herself of some good advice from a personal shopper. She had told Melanie to wear an outfit with confidence because one can never be overdressed, except when showing up at work in a ball gown. Momma would agree. Melanie pushed her shoulders straight and joined Joyce.

"Right this way, Mrs. Walker." The maître de escorted them up a grand staircase. While it was not a typical day for high tea at The Whitney, Joyce's request was met with an abundance of service. The second floor offered a quiet place to talk, and waiters delivered scones with berries and clotted cream shortly after they were settled.

Joyce did not waste time stating her purpose. "Melanie, I am very aware that you and Carl have a strong past together."

Melanie felt her throat constrict and wondered if Carl knew his mother was entertaining her. She made a conscious effort to relax her face muscles and follow with her shoulders, in turn relaxing her throat enough to speak. "We were a good team when Carl worked at Waverly. We have many good memories of projects we tackled together."

"I'm talking about more than that. When I met you at Carl and Holly's wedding, I could see how my son adored you. I wondered if he was marrying the wrong woman."

Melanie felt the pain of the split. Even though she and Carl had agreed to part ways and remain friends, his marriage to Holly was difficult to live through. The wedding day had been marked with sadness for Melanie as she watched them exchange vows in the church. When Carl locked eyes with her during the bride-groom dance, a visceral reaction had pinched her chest. When Holly took time to mingle in the crowd, Carl had invited her to dance. Her solo attendance had allowed the pleasure of getting lost in the music and enjoying Carl's arms around her body without guilt. Until she had returned to her hotel and realized her feelings were not proper. It was her own fault that Carl had married someone else.

"You may not know it, Melanie, but Carl still adores you. I can tell. He's my son, and a mother knows her son."

That was something Melanie would never understand. Besides, no one really knows another person, ever. At least she hoped that was true. There was a certain level of secrecy in everyone's life. Hers involved a love affair with a man outside her mother's approval during the years she worked her way through college. At times, he had offered to pay tuition bills, and she gratefully accepted the help. When she finally was earning her own money, he had been paid back in full, her way of protecting her self-esteem.

"We did have a particularly good relationship, personal relationship, for a long time. But that ended. We stayed close friends and colleagues for many years." It troubled her to think she had missed Carl's signals of continued sentiment for her.

"When you arrived here last week, Carl pretty much came undone. Do you know that? His whole life is in turmoil and—"

"Wait. Did you invite me here to blame me for Holly's leaving Carl? Because if you did—"

"No. I did not invite you here for that. I'm sorry to mislead you. It's true that I'm a little bitter over Carl's situation. It saddens me that you and he didn't see eye-to-eye on family matters."

Carl must have talked to his mother. A pang of remorse hit Melanie, but she slammed the door on guilt about choosing a childless existence. Her own experiences told her children can suffer even in the most loving homes. And she was learning that adult children can be dragged unknowingly into dangerous relationships.

Joyce continued. “Having our only son as part of Shore Industries seemed like a promising idea, but the writing was on the wall long before he arrived.”

Now Melanie was really confused. She played ignorance and did not let on what Adam had shared with her. Did not give in when Joyce prompted her with topics that could lead down a dark path. Joyce paused more than once, each time with a sigh, a rub of her temples, or a straightening of her napkin. Not once did Melanie express empathy. She was playing Joyce like she would play a royal flush. Soon enough, she would be able to lay all the Walker family cards on the table.

Before starting her third cup of tea, Joyce excused herself to use the powder room. Melanie quickly ran downstairs to a separate ladies’ room to relieve herself and made it back to the table before Joyce. Feeling more comfortable, she prepared to open with a question as soon as Joyce was situated.

After stopping at two tables to say hello on her way back to Melanie, Joyce hinted at the poor selection of location. “I’m surprised to see people here today. I was thinking it would be more private.”

“Do we need privacy, Joyce?” This was not exactly the question she had in mind, but she could work around to her main point.

“Yes, we do. There are a couple of things I want to give you, but maybe not here.”

That was unexpected. Melanie tipped her head to the side in askance.

"I won't keep you in suspense. There's some jewelry I want Carl to have. It's in my bag. If people leave before us, I can slip it to you."

Melanie's fingers went cold, and her feet twitched. She needed to stay as far away from jewelry transfers as possible. But how was Joyce involved?

"Why give it to me if it's for Carl?"

"You know you shouldn't ask questions when you already know the answers, and you shouldn't ask questions when you don't want to know the answers. Now which of those two scenarios fits you, Melanie?"

Now she was in a tailspin. Her phone buzzed in her pocket. Etiquette told her not to look. Panic told her to run and take the call.

CHAPTER 23

Carl pulled into his parents' driveway. Typically, his father would be home reading multiple Sunday newspapers and his mother would be at church. When he rounded the end of the driveway toward the side garage, he saw his uncle Phil being escorted in the back door by what appeared to be a medical aide.

He waited and watched as Phil shuffled his feet and allowed the gentleman to hold his elbow. When they reached the two steps leading into the sunroom, Phil stopped. Carl watched the conversation between the two men. Phil was shaking his head, and the young man was demonstrating how Phil should use his cane and the side rail to navigate the steps.

Before they took the first step up, his father appeared in the doorway. He put his forearms under Phil's arms and directed the aide to stand behind Phil. Together, they got Phil into the house.

Carl took his foot off the brake and let the car roll into his old parking spot. The one off the end of the driveway, a patch of lawn that had been filled in with square cement pavers when he got his first car at age sixteen. When the car was parked, he sat for a moment, contemplating how he could possibly tell Ray what he had hoped to convey if Phil was going to be in the room.

The aide exited the house, waved to Carl, and climbed in his own car. Carl signaled for the driver to stop and approached the window.

"I'm Carl, Phil's nephew. How is he doing?"

"Better. It's not been easy for him, but you probably know he's a stubborn man. Won't give in."

"Yeah. Well, thanks for helping him," Carl walked ahead to the sunroom entrance.

He knocked as he opened the door, surprised to see Joyce. "Not at church, Mom?"

The explanation was simple. She had stayed up late, wanted a little time to relax, and was going to a later mass. With a peck on his cheek, she retreated to the kitchen.

"What brings you here this morning, Carl?" Ray asked.

"I was hoping to have a conversation with you. Looks like a bad time." Carl turned toward Phil who was seated in an armchair across the room.

"Good to see you, Carl," Phil said.

Carl nodded in response and breathed in the scent of home. The terra cotta tiles, yellow walls, sunken fern garden, and morning sun filtering through a large window set a warm mood. He could smell the soil of the potted plants, Sunday banana muffins straight from the oven, and fresh coffee. The picture window framed an artistic landscape of grass that stretched out in a border of red, orange, and yellow chrysanthemums. At the far side of the lawn, a stone patio led to the edge of the lake. Everything was perfect in his mother's world.

When a smile stretched across Carl's face, Ray smiled back. They held one another in a visual embrace, and Carl warmed to his father's familial side.

"Your uncle and I were going to talk shop. How would you like to grab a cup of coffee and join us?" His voice held none of the tight tone of the past several days.

Phil gave a harrumph, but Carl ignored his uncle's response and accepted the invitation.

He went to the kitchen for coffee and a muffin, only to overhear Joyce on the phone.

". . . this afternoon. I'll let you know when."

Carl edged closer to the coffee pot to hear Joyce better as she walked into the adjoining dining room.

"Yes, Adam. That's what I said, The Whitney. . ."

His mother was now out of listening distance, but Carl believed something was terribly wrong. He set a muffin on a plate and took it with his cup of black coffee into the sunroom.

Ray was leaning forward in his chair. "We've done what we can to bring in business, Phil."

"And we are bringing orders. Percy is buying, right?"

Carl watched Phil. He was pale and gaunt, but now his cheeks showed signs of a blood pressure surge. The dark circles beneath his eyes appeared black against the pink flush, and Carl chose a positive path to calm the waters. "Phil, that's great if Percy is increasing orders! What caused that change?"

Phil looked at Ray for a response.

"Phil has been working with them. They had a few setbacks and needed some information on products they never thought of using in some of their installations. Phil and Adam gave them more suggestions on custom ceiling-to-floor grab bars." Phil sniffed loudly to accentuate the definitiveness of the explanation.

"Some of those rails require specific materials, sometimes a thicker stainless outer shaft for the mid-bar curves. I haven't seen any requests for my department to order that kind of material."

Phil avoided Carl's eyes when he tried to justify the increased sales.

"Well, we also sweetened the deal a little. Gave them a special discount for some of the typical orders they give us. Maybe the specialty items are on hold."

Carl sipped his coffee to avoid calling a liar a liar.

"What are you saying, Phil? You didn't get orders for the ceiling-to-floor bars we talked about?" Ray's voice was louder.

"They're happy for now," Phil said before adding, "How about some orange juice? I have a pill to take."

Ray slapped the arm of his chair. "Sure, big brother." He left the room with a scowl on his face.

In his father's absence, Carl carried on the questioning. "What are some of the discounts we have to offer? I know about the five-percent offer based on longer lead times for large quantities. What else?"

Phil bit his lip and was saved from responding when Ray returned with a glass of juice.

"I'll hold this while you get your pill. Is it in your pocket?"

Phil looked at his watch. "Oh, it's way too early for that."

Ray put the glass down with enough force for juice to slosh onto the table.

"Okay, Phil. Did you pay a kickback of some kind to Percy?"

Carl was surprised by his father's blunt question.

"Don't accuse me, when—"

"Stop, Uncle Phil. I came here to talk with my father about Adam." Carl paused to let his statement settle with them. "There's something you need to hear."

Phil's chin dropped, and he adjusted his glasses.

Carl said only two words. "Adam confessed."

Phil slumped back in his chair and lost his fight to keep his weak arms and legs situated.

Ray reached across the table that separated their chairs and put a hand on his brother's forearm. "Phil, I can't let your poor business decisions impact me and my family."

His father's candid words gave Carl reason to let out a sigh. He was not surprised when Ray asked him for specific details about a confession.

"Adam set the wastebasket fires with his incense sticks."

Phil flamed red when he reacted. "That's not true."

"Who have you paid to keep that quiet, Uncle Phil? Adam confessed that you directed him to stop business until you were back."

"That boy is not fit for—"

Carl jumped out of his chair and reached in his pocket. "And this check dropped out of his pocket on the day of the fire," he announced before Phil could finish.

"Stop!" Ray sprung out of his chair and left the room. He returned before he walked through the kitchen doorway. "I am reporting you, Phil. Joyce has stopped me from turning you in for years. Now I'm done."

He left Carl and Phil staring at one another.

"That check has nothing to do with the fire. I was in the hospital. It was just a little something to keep Adam motivated."

Carl tore the check into tiny pieces and sprinkled it like snow on Phil's lap.

CHAPTER 24

"Excuse me, Joyce. My phone is buzzing, and it might be urgent. I'll be right back."

Melanie was fishing in her jacket pocket for the cell phone as she slid into the alcove near the ladies' restroom. She huddled in a corner to answer the call from Carl.

"Hello?" She kept her voice low.

"Where are you?"

"I'm with your mother at The Whitney."

There was a long pause.

"Carl?"

"Leave."

"Why?"

"Just leave. Go to your hotel. I'll meet you there."

"Carl, I can't—"

He was gone and she knew he would not pick up the phone if she called him back. Melanie composed herself and returned to the table.

"Is everything okay?" Joyce asked in a tone that sounded like she was suspicious of the call.

"It is, yes. But I probably need to be leaving in a few minutes to get some work done before tomorrow morning. What is this jewelry you mentioned?"

"So you don't fit either scenario? You don't know the answer to your question, and you want to know the answer."

Melanie just stared into Joyce's eyes and waited long enough to make her host uncomfortable. This time Joyce did more than straighten the napkin. She pulled it from her lap and slapped it onto the table. The teacups rattled and people looked their way.

The heat under Melanie's collar rose to her cheeks, and Joyce pushed her chair back far enough to put her bag on her lap. She dug to the bottom of the main compartment and pulled a large black velvet bag tied with a red braided drawstring barely high enough to be visible. Melanie could see the size and imagine the weight of its contents before Joyce lowered it back to the bottom of her purse.

"Why me?"

"I gave Carl pieces of my heirloom jewelry when he returned to the flock. I told him it was for him, not for Holly. This is that jewelry, with more that I added recently. I don't want Holly to have it, and Carl can't have it in his possession right now."

"How is this jewelry with you if you gave it to Carl already? I'm confused."

"I had someone get it out of Carl's possession for me so he wouldn't cash in on it."

Melanie squinted at Joyce when the confusion was only compounded by the answer.

"Let me explain something. Carl needed money once, and I gave him cash. I don't want him to use this jewelry to pay bills, so I had false jewelry planted in its place. That's all you need to know."

"If it belongs to Carl, why can't he have it?"

"The Walker family is careful to keep its investments and profits within the bloodline. Holly is not Walker blood, and Carl gives her anything she wants. Her family is scattered across the states, her parents divorced years ago, and she was never close to her only brother. Bottom line, she's just after Walker money because she has no support system. And her tastes are very expensive, in case you missed that."

Melanie was surprised that she and Joyce had the same impressions of Holly.

"Carl will never let you walk out of his life completely. I'm sure Holly will be divorcing him. When that's over, you can give these things to him."

Melanie shifted in her chair, crumpled the napkin in her lap, and thought about Joyce housing Holly and her grandsons in a cottage in northern Michigan. Carl was keeping financial things from Holly. Melanie's head was spinning.

"Look, I need to leave. Can we postpone this transfer?"

"No, Melanie. I need to get rid of it."

"I can't take it while I'm traveling. I'm sorry."

Melanie stood to leave, but Joyce grabbed her arm and pulled her back down.

"Let me give you a little more information."

Melanie listened to an incredibly devious scheme. Joyce had received a call from Holly asking questions about Carl's financial health. Anticipating the worst of battles over a growing jewelry investment, Joyce coaxed Holly out of town to keep her from prying. She needed time to get ownership transferred.

"It was clear to me that Holly's state of mind was deteriorating and affecting Carl and his boys," Joyce rationalized.

"You have me here to assist in decreasing Carl's personal net worth before a divorce is filed."

"Well stated. Carl cannot have these pieces until much later. I cannot have them because Holly will know they are intended for Carl. That means you need to take legal possession until the time is right to return them to Carl. I have a document that will transfer ownership to you. We'll both sign and date it today."

"This plan does not work, Joyce. How does Holly even know about the jewelry if she's never seen it? And I don't believe Holly can sue Carl for your jewelry."

"She can and she will if I die before the divorce is final," Joyce responded with no emotion.

Melanie sat in awe of how a mother would devise a scheme based on a complete misunderstanding of estate and inheritance laws. If the jewelry had belonged to Joyce's mother-in-law, there had to be documentation in a will that passed the heirlooms to Joyce. Otherwise, they would go to Phil or Ray. Was Joyce dying? She looked healthy enough.

Melanie felt her head jerk in a single involuntary tic, tension pressed on her chest, and thoughts raced in all directions.

"Are you ill? Does Carl know?" Her words rattled in her mouth.

"Calm down, Melanie. No, I'm not dying, at least not that I know of. I just need to protect Carl. If something happens, say the divorce takes years, then those jewels could land in the wrong hands."

"Only if they were not given to you by your mother-in-law before she died. Besides, you said you already gave them to Carl."

"I'm not willing to push the fine line that far," Joyce said. "And I did give jewelry to Carl. And he still has jewelry. He doesn't have the valuable pieces right now."

"Well, you don't expect me to take this bag now, do you? It wouldn't even fit in my purse, and I'm in a hotel. I need to travel back to Boston on a plane. There's no way it will be safe with me. Not now, at least." Anxiety over assisting Joyce for Carl's sake was manifested in warm dewy skin, and her dress clung to her torso.

"Did you use the valet to park?"

"No, I parked across the street."

"Good. Don't walk out without me. I have appearances to uphold. We'll go downstairs together after I sign the bill. Then we'll get in my car when the valet brings it around. I'll drive you back to your car. We will pretend we are saying a long goodbye. Can you agree to that?"

Melanie followed Joyce Walker down the stairs and out the door of The Whitney. She climbed into the passenger seat of the Cadillac not knowing what was waiting for her.

She expected to jump out of the car when they pulled up behind her rental. Instead, Adam Barnes yanked open the passenger door, and Melanie froze. Joyce grabbed her arm and told her to stay calm.

Melanie looked from Adam to Joyce, not knowing who to trust. There was no chance she would escape to her own car. She ran a hand through her hair, wrapping it around her ears, stalling.

"Do you want to get out of the car?" Adam put his hand out to help Melanie.

She looked to her hostess for guidance.

"Why don't you climb in the back seat, Adam? We can talk here for a minute."

Melanie reached to release her seatbelt, looked at the time on the instrument panel, and turned to face Adam. Joyce stopped the car and turned off the engine. An anxious grip tightened in Melanie's stomach when she thought about Carl waiting at the hotel.

"What is going on? Has high tea become a theft drop of some kind?"

Adam knew what Melanie meant, but Joyce did not.

"Theft drop?! What are you insinuating?"

Joyce's loud response and red face signaled Melanie to back out of the topic with caution. "Someone needs to tell me the truth here. I'm very confused as to why you need to offload jewelry."

"It's not what it looks like," Adam began. "You need to separate Shore Industries from what Joyce is trying to do."

Joyce balked at Adam's statement.

"Ray tells me everything about Shore, so I'm aware that Adam has been employed to increase the value of our personal assets."

"But there's more than family jewelry in—"

"Melanie, remember you need to keep Shore separate from what Joyce is doing," Adam interrupted, repeating himself.

"You keep mentioning something going on at Shore. I know everything from Ray, unless you're hiding something, Adam." Joyce raised her voice to get Adam's attention.

"No!" Before continuing with his explanation, Adam gave a short laugh that indicated his story was a lie. "Melanie is referring to other assets that aren't part of the family inventory."

"Gold bars?" Joyce asked.

Adam nodded.

"Why is Adam here now?" Melanie asked.

"Because he will be your bodyguard while you carry this bag on city streets," Joyce explained.

"I've explained that I cannot take this bag now," Melanie repeated.

Adam nodded his agreement with Melanie. He offered to accept temporary ownership.

Melanie climbed into her own car, and Adam followed her back to the hotel in his vehicle. On the drive to the hotel, she saw families walking in the fall air, couples holding hands, and elderly men on a bench. A mother and daughter waited at a crosswalk as she pulled to a stop. An intense sense of loss struck when the little girl hugged her mother's skirt.

She missed Momma deeply and wondered about the meaning of love, thankful that her family had not been lost in riches. Her eyes filled with tears that she brushed away before pulling through the intersection.

Soft music on the radio made her think of her parents dancing to stereo music in the living room of their small house. Melanie's father had been a workaholic who earned a modest income and died of a heart attack when she was in the fourth grade. The night before he died, she had hugged the two of them as they waltzed in a threesome.

Momma had loved staying home, doting on Melanie until she had to work to support herself and her only daughter. With no skills, the minimum wage income barely covered their needs.

Melanie had attended Northeastern University on scholarships and was thankful for the school's cooperative work program. During the five-year program, she had spent six months in the classroom and six months of paid on-the-job learning. Scholarships augmented by student loans, her own income, and her secret cash source had allowed her to earn her degree.

"Momma, love is so complicated," she said aloud.

CHAPTER 25

Carl paced across the lobby. The wait for Melanie to arrive was too long, and every plausible reason for the delay only opened new doubts about his mother. His eyes misted with relief when Melanie walked through the doors, but she was not alone.

Adam was in step with her, their heads together as if to protect their conversation from bystanders.

Carl sniffed back the flow of emotion and stepped into the main thoroughfare to the elevators where Melanie and Adam could see him. It was then he saw the duffle bag. What was Melanie doing? Before he could follow his path of logic to something satisfying, juicy, or maybe evil, Melanie was speaking to him.

"Carl, I'm sorry it took so long. I couldn't get away from the business your—"

"Business? Adam, what are you doing here? What's in the duffel bag?"

"Not here." Melanie pulled Carl's arm and led him to the elevators where they were crowded among other hotel guests. The lift to her suite was a long, silent ride into the unknown. They were the first to exit the car. Adam had to ask people to excuse him as his bag bumped hips and thighs when he worked his way from the back wall of the car.

Melanie took Carl's arm on the walk to her room, signaling her support. He had no idea how she would respond to his intended request now that she was working with Adam. Melanie let go of him and unlocked the door. Stepping back, she motioned for Adam to enter first.

When they were inside, Melanie gave Carl an abbreviated summary of what happened at The Whitney.

Adam opened his duffel bag on the table. Carl was aghast that his mother had given Adam dinner rings, pins, necklaces, gold bangle bracelets, chains, and earrings. Strings of pearls in every length, ornate brooches of rubies, diamonds, emeralds, and other stones he could not name. Beautiful gems were in small green velvet bags left unmounted. If Carl tried to imagine the value of it all, he would be wrong.

He studied the sparkling and gaudy accessories and slowly shook his head. He fell back on the couch and turned to Melanie. Her eyes were open wider than Carl had ever seen before. Their green color was enhanced by her tweed dress, dancing against her fair skin and contrasting the hair that skimmed her shoulders. For a moment, he saw her wearing the emerald brooch and one of the diamond dinner rings.

"Carl, what are you thinking?" Adam pulled him from his fantasy.

"Nothing you would understand, Adam."

Carl caught Melanie studying him.

"I had no idea my family owned this much jewelry."

There were too many questions to think straight. Why did his mother fall for Adam's offer to take Melanie's place in owning this bag of excessive value?

Melanie suggested each item be inventoried and put into a safe.

"What safe? Adam can't take it to his apartment. He's got other *stuff* there, don't you, Adam?"

Adam tugged on his collar. "Not this kind of stuff. It's all in bars. Some gold coins. It won't get mixed up." He rubbed the side of his nose and looked away.

Carl forced himself not to call Adam out on the lie.

Melanie booted up her laptop and created a spreadsheet. They worked together to list each item, take a photo, and create a full inventory log. Melanie offered to sleep with the jewelry and not let it out of her sight. Together, they would take the items to a reputable gemologist for appraisal. Adam fought to use his connections, claiming it would be easy to get a quick appraisal and not involve unknown people. Neither Carl nor Melanie fell for his suggestion that sounded like they would be dealing with corrupt players.

When Adam finally agreed to leave the jewelry with Melanie, he left the hotel.

Carl and Melanie let out a collective breath. They ordered room service and prepared to solve yet another mystery surrounding Adam Barnes.

"How could my mother have signed a document turning possession of these things over to Adam? I just don't understand what she's thinking."

"You must have had a bad vibe today when you told me to leave Joyce this afternoon. What was that about?"

Carl paused long enough to consider the potential meaning of all the pieces of information that were starting to come together for him.

Before he could respond to Melanie's question, they were interrupted by delivery of their meals. He turned his attention to setting out the food and thought about the best way to break the latest news to Melanie.

When they had finished their salads, Carl knew it was time to answer Melanie's question. He took a drink of water, wiped the sweat off the glass, and sat back in his chair.

"I hate to be the one to break the news to you, but I talked with Phil and my dad this morning."

Melanie leaned in with attentive calm.

"The bottom line is that Dad is going to turn Phil in for fraud, bribery, theft, and money laundering. Anything he can prove."

Before walking out of the hotel, Carl called Holly. When she answered her cell, he could hear voices in the background. His sons and a man.

"Hi, Carl. What can I do for you?"

"Nothing. Just wanted to hear your voice." The silence was painful. "Are the boys alright?"

"Of course. They love it here."

"Who's there with them?"

"Oh, just a friend."

"You have friends who live up there?"

"Does it matter who it is, Carl? I do have a life outside of taking care of your household and my kids."

My kids. Your household. "It sort of does, Holly. The boys are mine too, and the household was created to suit your wishes. But it is also *ours*. What are you doing?"

"What am I doing? I'm preparing to leave you, Carl. This isn't the time for a conversation. The boys are in the next room enjoying their evening with a gentleman who enjoys their company and will help me through this process. You'll hear from my attorney about a legal separation this week. We'll see what happens from there."

Holly ended the call.

Instead of driving home, Carl went back up to Melanie's room.

CHAPTER 26

Now Melanie suspected Adam would turn the jewelry to cash so Phil could continue bribing purchasing directors. Maybe Phil would try to put cash back into the trust accounts for Charlene and Al. Either way, it was a losing proposition. The value of the trusts could never be recovered, and sales would never reach a level high enough to bring Shore back into profitability.

The night was long and difficult. Carl's return to her room put a cramp in Melanie's style. She wanted to take a long bath and think. She needed to think. Instead, she called housekeeping to bring extra linens and set up the pull-out sofa.

It was not at all like old times when they used to hold one another late into the night, watching movies and snacking on popcorn.

Carl's presence confused her. He was a married man with kids. She walked around the suite staying busy, tidying the kitchenette. He stared at the television.

She should have said no when he returned, but as his friend, she had to offer him the comfort of knowing she was nearby. Carl had become a needy man, not something she had ever seen in him.

When Melanie considered talking about Adam's role at Shore, a single tic of her head snapped her thinking aright. Her pulse tumbled, reminding her that Holly had left him and maybe he would be single again.

She pushed that line of thinking into her chest, and Adam filled her vision. The two men were so different, but so similar. Both were keen businessmen, although Adam had a shady side. Both were strong personalities, capturing the attention of women. Each had his own flirtatious side, neither inappropriate. Both attracted her in all the right ways, head and heart. She shook her head when Carl looked away from the television.

"You're restless."

"I guess I am. Maybe I need to go to bed. Goodnight, Carl."

She walked into the bedroom carrying her laptop and purse and the velvet bag. Melanie quietly closed the door.

She lay awake. Thoughts of Adam being wrangled into a convoluted scheme, the challenge of finding cash in the slim accounts at Shore and protecting Carl's income left her exhausted but wide awake.

The covers smothered her, drowning her in conflicting emotions. She wanted to shake Adam for being so stupid, and she wanted to hold him and assure him she would help defend his innocence. There was no way he could be so evil unless he was being blackmailed by Phil. But what dirt could be held over Adam by the mastermind of their corruption?

Melanie's dreams were filled with catastrophic events. A bomb in her rental car, with a shower of jewels raining on the pavement in the aftermath. Carl falling off the Ambassador Bridge, possibly pushed by Adam, his sons and Holly watching. Adam behind bars with no one to defend him. She tossed and turned. It was two o'clock when she last noted the time.

When her cell chimed with a text message, she struggled to move the pillows and roll over. It took a few seconds to realize it was a weekday and she had a huge task waiting for her. There was no opportunity to succumb to her grogginess. It was already seven o'clock.

She closed her eyes, and the phone chimed again reminding her that a message was waiting. It was Carl.

She sat straight up, remembering he was in the living area of her small suite. Making sure she was covered, she slipped her feet off the edge of the bed and reached for her clothes. Expecting Carl to be asking about breakfast in the room or in the lobby, she threw her blouse over her pajamas and stepped out of the bedroom.

Carl and Adam sat on the sofa looking at her.

CHAPTER 27

Carl watched Adam looking at the beautiful woman in front them. Large curls were tossed across the top of her head and dark circles accentuated her puffy eyes. This image was a complete divergence from the stylish professional who had arrived just days ago. Adam tried to look away, but her vision was locked on him. He stood to greet her, and Carl gave Melanie a knowing smile.

"Please. Sit, Adam. I'll get dressed."

Adam sat back down, and Melanie returned to the bedroom.

"Nothing went on here, Adam. I crashed on the pull-out bed. I didn't want to go home to my empty house."

"I get it. But you were lucky to have been with her in the past. She's gorgeous and smart."

"This time, you're not lying." Carl chuckled at the thought that he and Adam agreed on something.

Melanie returned in a pair of jeans, a sweatshirt, and athletic shoes. A tote bag carrying jewelry was in one hand, and her crossbody was in place. Carl saw the spark of attraction in Adam when he responded to Melanie's presence with a flirtatious smile and greeting that indicated he noted every detail of her appearance. "You look ready to run if we need to."

Their day started with breakfast in the lobby. Melanie kept the tote bag nestled between her feet. Carl put a cup of coffee to his lips, sniffed and lowered it three times before taking a sip. Adam wobbled his head, drank his coffee steadily, and ordered a refill. Carl gave Adam a stink-eye glare.

****

Carl picked up Adam and Melanie at the lobby entrance. He was attentive to his surroundings on the walk to the garage and on the drive to the front of the hotel. He was anxious about being followed or having the tote bag snatched from Melanie before he got to her. His anticipation was like playing hide-and-seek with his cousins when they were kids. The attic of their grandparents' Grosse Pointe Tudor home had steep sloping ceilings, and Carl liked to hide in the eaves. The dark had spooked him, and he shivered with fear when Albert's eyes appeared from nowhere with a flashlight held under his chin. Eyes were out there now, too, he was sure.

Melanie climbed in the front and buckled her seatbelt. She positioned the bag between her feet. Carrying a tote bag seemed like a reasonable decoy. The top was zipped, making it look like a typical day bag many women carried. Papers sat on the top.

Adam was behind Melanie where his face was not visible in the rearview mirror. Carl turned to look at Adam and said, "Maybe you should turn off your phone."

A scowl of insult flashed on Adam's face, but Carl did not care. He was not taking a chance that Adam was communicating their travels to a clan of thieves. Melanie shot a look at Carl, but he ignored her.

They drove out of the city in silence. Carl thought about the ludicrous predicament of his family. Some lawsuits had been settled, but not without breaking the company in half, splitting the brothers, and making the chasm wider than it ever needed to be.

The Walker family planned to reference rising costs as an excuse to shut down a once-thriving operation. His own father had not invited him to initial discussions focused on a turnaround plan. Instead, Carl had been targeted as the fall guy with a finger pointing at his management of materials procurement.

Now he was getting appraisals on heirloom jewelry that his grandmother wore with pride. These were beautiful works of art. The elder Charlene Walker had transferred ownership to Ray, her younger son, during Phil's pending divorce twenty years ago. When Phil's wife remarried and his mother was no longer living, the jewelry should have been returned to Phil with the younger Charlene taking possession as part of her inheritance. Carl had concluded that his mother laid claim to the forgotten fortune.

History was repeating itself. Holly was not to have these precious pieces that needed to stay in the family bloodline. Could he not choose just a couple of items that Holly would love to wear? She was his wife, after all, and he had no daughters to inherit them.

He wondered if temporary possession had been given to someone else in the past. Are women really that greedy? He knew Holly would be. But he doubted Melanie would care about material things. His cousin Charlene wanted money for a house. She was greedy too. What about Charlene's brother Albert? He seemed like a guy who would just want things to be in order with no disputes or wasted emotional energy when Phil died.

Maybe Carl was more like his cousin Albert than he knew. Thinking about Al's scary eyes in the big house still made him see evil, yet he could recognize that under a tantalizing spirit, Al did not create a fuss over personal assets. He probably wanted Shore to be his stable revenue source, but heirlooms were of no interest to him. It was Charlene who liked all the drama. She wanted a bigger home, more money, and a guaranteed flamboyant lifestyle. No room for marriage or kids for either of his cousins.

The streets stretched on, city boundaries blended into other cities and townships, all in one big metropolis. They traveled out of Wayne into Oakland County, once one of the top five richest counties in the United States. The mansion-like homes and stretches of manicured lawn reminded Carl of why he returned to Michigan. He had dreamed of giving Holly a beautiful house and large yard that looked like these. The days of automotive executives living the suburban lifestyle he dreamed about looked quite different now. Especially from his newest vantage point.

The research he and Melanie had done the night before led them to an independent jewelry appraiser in northern Oakland County. They were taking a chance that the business would be open on a Monday morning, hoping they could not only get a ballpark appraisal, but also procure a lock box for storage. They would be sure that two of their names were on the box for entry. The unannounced arrival was intended to avoid any leak in their plans.

Carl pulled into the parking lot of the small brick building on a side street in the township of Lake Orion. An unmarked police car pulled in behind him.

"Where did he come from?"

"Detroit." Adam was the first person out of the car.

"He had us followed by a cop," Carl said.

"Are you sure? Do you have a taillight out or—"

"He followed us. Buckle up!" Carl yelled at Melanie.

He put the car in reverse, got turned around, and sped out of the parking lot.

"Carl, stop! We can't run away."

"We can't stay either. Adam is going to turn on us."

Melanie tracked the guardrail and kept an eye on her side mirror. She avoided Carl's angry face and watched for the police. The cruiser took time to get turned around to trail them and had been caught behind a tractor trailer truck that was unable to pull over. Carl lost them when he turned onto a service road.

"Where are you going?"

"Grosse Pointe. My mother got us into this mess, and she'll have to get us out of it."

Carl's cell phone rang in the cupholder. It was Adam.

"Should I answer it?"

Before he could reply, Melanie had pressed the speaker button.

"Carl, pull over and wait for us. I'm with the cops."

"What's going on, Adam?" Melanie asked.

"You're running from the police! That's what's going on!"

"We need to know what you're doing." Melanie pressed for an explanation.

"That's not important. Carl! Pull over. You're only looking for more trouble if you keep running."

Carl ended the call with remote control on the steering wheel.

Melanie put her hands on the dashboard. "You can't run from the police!"

"They can't chase me without suspicion of a felony or that we're dangerous."

"But you're driving way too fast."

"So I can expect a speeding ticket in the mail."

CHAPTER 28

Melanie squeezed the door armrest when Carl made a hands-free call to his father's cell and Ray answered. She had to focus hard to follow Carl's conversation.

"Dad, are you home?"

"Yes. Why?"

"Melanie and I are on the way. The cops are after us, and Adam is with them. Make room for us!"

Ray's voice cracked when he asked Carl for details. Carl navigated the highway at nearly one hundred miles an hour. He managed to shout, "Make room in the garage in about forty-five minutes!" before disconnecting.

Melanie turned in her seat. "I don't even see the flashing lights anymore."

Carl continued driving well above the speed limit. They were less than thirty minutes from the exit to Grosse Pointe. From there, a series of turns and another ten minutes would put them in the safety of his parents' garage.

Melanie saw sweat trickle down the sides of Carl's face and struggled to adjust the air conditioning and fan, her hand slipping around with the speed of the lane changes he made. The air chilled her more than the fear had heated her. The tote bag on the mat in front of her tipped when Carl swerved to another lane, and she pushed it around with her feet. When it was comfortably secure, she put her head back on the headrest and took a deep breath. Just as she released the tension, a siren alerted her.

The police car was beside them.

"Where did they come from?!" Carl hit the gas and sped around the car in front of him using the left lane. The police car sped up in the outside lane, turning into the center lane just as Carl pulled farther ahead.

Melanie squeezed her eyes shut and prayed aloud. "Oh, dear God, keep this car safe!"

Carl swerved when the police pulled ahead of him. The fender of his car grazed a barrier on the driver's side, pushing them into the rear of the police car that spun around and landed in the middle lane facing in the opposite direction.

Carl sped up again. The screaming engine forced Melanie deeper in the seat, and she squeezed the door armrest again.

"We're so close. Hang on, Mel."

Another siren blared past them, going in the opposite direction on the highway. Melanie saw the rooftop and flashing lights. She forced herself to turn. The lights whipped through an emergency turnaround and sped in their direction.

"Another cop is coming behind us!"

Carl looked in the rearview mirror and slowed down to avoid slamming into the car in front of him. Melanie grabbed the handle above the passenger door, now holding on with both hands in expectation of speeding up and swerving into another lane. The sirens and lights sped by. It was an ambulance headed for the next exit.

Melanie let go of the handle, but too soon. Now, Carl did hit the gas. The car fishtailed and she screamed.

"Hang on, Mel!" Carl was white-knuckled and focused on his getaway drive.

Something made Melanie reach for the cell phone. Without thinking, she hit redial and Carl's father was on the car speaker.

"Carl? We're ready for you, but what's going on? The police are here."

Immediately, Carl hung up the call with the control at his fingertips. Melanie needed to think about the endgame, but she was too focused on her safety to think that far ahead. Putting the pieces together, she surmised that the police car that they managed to lose called for backup to show up at the Walker house in Grosse Pointe. It must have been Adam who tipped them off about a possible destination.

"I'm not sure where to go." Carl had slowed the car down to the speed limit. He made his way to the right lane and took the first exit off the highway. They pulled into the parking lot of a strip mall.

"What do we do now, Carl?"

"I think we need to call the police."

****

They sat in the car staring through the windshield. It took the state police less than five minutes to arrive. Two officers exited the cruiser. When a female officer walked to the driver's door, Carl lowered the window and handed over his license and registration.

Carl waited while she checked his credentials.

He carefully looked straight ahead and took his time with what he had to say. "I'm going to hand over the jewelry to be returned to Adam. Make sure the signed document is on top of your tote bag. Melanie, I'm sorry. I panicked. I was afraid Adam had his accomplices in a police car."

Melanie nodded and leaned over to reach for the tote bag. A male cop walked to the passenger window with a gun drawn, yelling to be heard through the glass. "Leave the bag alone. Out of the car, ma'am, with your hands up."

Carl's eyes were closed when the female tapped on his side of the car. She ordered him to get out with his hands in the air. By now, a crowd had gathered. Two more police cars sped into the lot with sirens and lights. Officers jumped out to hold back the onlookers.

Carl's ears rang, then crackled. He saw a black tunnel. The sound of Melanie's calling out in pain cleared his head. "Leave her alone!"

"You just need to be quiet, Mr. Walker. Don't cause a bigger scene than we already have here."

Melanie was escorted to one of the police cars in handcuffs. Before Carl could move, cuffs were snapping on his wrists. The pain was sharp, and a burst of noise involuntarily escaped him.

"Get in the car." There was no choice. His head was lowered by a firm hand as he was guided into the back of a police cruiser. He lost sight of Melanie.

Carl watched as the officers searched his car. They retrieved Melanie's tote bag, her crossbody, and both of their cell phones. He watched them pull things out of interior compartments and the trunk. The cuffs rubbed hard on his wrists. His face burned with embarrassment, creating more pain than the cuffs that chafed behind his back.

He had made an unwise decision in a moment of panic, and it did not look like the police would believe him.

****

Melanie cooperated with the officer. She tried to explain why she had the tote full of valuable jewelry and where they were going. She knew better than to say too much, but in her attempt to prove that she and Carl were innocent, she talked about the document.

"Why is your name here, crossed off, and signed by someone named Adam Barnes?"

She wondered what to reveal about Joyce Walker's scheme that was vague at best.

"Adam took possession of the jewelry when I refused to take it from Mrs. Walker."

"Will your buddy there, Mr. Carl Walker, say the same thing?"

She answered out of instinct. "Of course he would! It's the truth."

The officer left her. Melanie was afraid to move. Her wrists throbbed, her neck was stiff, and her upper back was tight. The tortuous position she kept to prevent the handcuffs from scratching her wrists reminded her that she was not as nimble as she used to be. It was time to play safer games in business. No more assignments that required chasing the bad guys. Who are the bad guys at Shore? The answers were getting cloudy again.

Ray Walker went to the Oak Park State Police Station to collect Carl and Melanie when the police found no reason to hold them. Fines would be issued for reckless driving and refusing to stop for the police, hitting a moving police vehicle, and possibly more. This was one time that Carl was thankful for his clean record and the Walker name that erased potential consequences of bad decisions. Ray drove Carl and Melanie to Madison Heights to pick up Carl's car. Joyce and Adam were at the Walker home in Grosse Pointe being questioned by police officers.

Melanie thought about Ray leaving his wife and Adam at home talking with the police. A shiver ran up her arms. She clutched her tote bag and crossbody in her lap and folded her arms on top. The back of the headrest where Carl sat in front of her became her focal point, and she listened to father and son banter over the occurrences of the morning. She could see veins bulging on Ray's forehead and wondered if his health was at risk. Carl apologized for running, and Ray gave no hint of understanding.

The ordeal took a lot out of Melanie. The muscles in her arms started to weaken, her elbows slipping to her sides. Her knees slightly relaxed to the side, and her head fell back. The signs of low blood sugar were creeping up on her, and she guessed that Carl needed his therapeutic coffee. They had not eaten since breakfast, and now the sun was low in the sky.

An hour later they were on their way back to Detroit in Carl's car. Ray had the jewelry, and Adam would have to find his own way home from Grosse Pointe. Neither Melanie nor Carl wanted to see him tonight.

She thought of her home in Boston and wondered what the sunset might look like tonight. She and Momma might have found enough extra cash to go to the top of The Pru on a day like today. It always helped them relax.

****

Melanie was alone in her hotel room. After a satisfying meal, Carl had decided to face the discomfort of his own house. She undressed, climbed into bed, and fell into a deep sleep. She was awakened by a notification on her cell phone. Frustrated that her phone was not silenced, she looked at the screen. It was close to eleven o'clock, and Carl was awake and texting her.

> My father is shocked. The jewelry was NOT my grandmother's.

She was a fool. She believed Joyce and Adam's story about protecting Carl by keeping the jewelry ownership away from him. Instead, she was nearly pulled into the distribution of dirty goods without knowing where they came from.

A deep breath calmed her hands enough to respond.

She paced, looked out the window, and paced some more. By midnight she talked herself into letting the worry go and pulled the drapes closed. There was nothing to do tonight. She succumbed to exhaustion and fell back on the pillow. Carl was right. She had managed to avoid a personal disaster.

****

When the early morning sun peeked through the drawn drapes, Melanie awoke wet with sweat. Her first thoughts were of the police chase.

Of all her years spent uncovering corrupt business practices, she had never been dragged into the depths of crime that could muddy her own shoes. She'd done nothing wrong, but her role in liquidating Shore Industries was beginning to feel like a trap.

Throwing off the covers and heading to the shower, she focused on her last communication with Carl. He was pleased that she had not fallen for his mother's plan. And so was she. But something still felt wrong.

Her muscles were gnarled. Eating seemed like a bad idea.

It would make sense to connect with Ray and Phil today and tell them no more delays would be tolerated. Yesterday's events took her too close to bad business that she could not accept, even for Carl Walker.

She would confirm her initial timeline for liquidation of assets and emphasize her plan as the best strategy. The Walker brothers needed to be told in plain language that she would contribute nothing more. There was no fountain of cash to bail them out of the Luxury lawsuit. Step one: Get Carl to agree with her.

She would then call the Waverly office and let Dominick know she was finishing up the project. The sooner, the better. Ray and Phil would have to handle Adam and Joyce in whatever way they chose. Count her out.

CHAPTER 29

Carl walked into his favorite Starbucks for the first time in more than a week. It felt good to see familiar faces and follow his routine. The people here were smiling, passing pleasantries, and generally a little more relaxed than the crowds at coffee shops closer to Shore.

Pastries were just coming out of the oven, sending aromas of bliss through his senses. Coffee and a raspberry scone would give him the energy he needed to keep positive vibes running. He liked knowing he had Adam in an awkward position. He learned more by collaborating with him than Adam would have ever wanted to divulge.

Carl had pieced together enough information to imagine Adam and Phil directing an enterprise of thieves with layers of mules who hauled stolen goods.

Melanie stepped in the waiting line behind him and jolted him out of his brain space when she said, “I’ll be out of here soon!”

He spun around to have his face nearly touching hers. “Melanie.” His own soft whisper surprised him, but he did not let on. Her breath was close and warm, and he remembered the taste of her melon lip balm.

“Yes! It’s me.” Melanie stepped back, a smile on her face. “And I’m feeling like this will be a great day.”

“Because you plan to leave?”

“Because we can tell Phil and Ray there is no money in a legitimate pipeline. If they want to pursue whatever Adam is up to, that’s not my project. I’m not holding the jewelry, so I don’t need to drag this process out any longer.”

"What about the ethical side of things? Where is the Melanie Sullivan that would never let corruption go unreported?"

"Next, sir?" The barista pulled their conversation apart, and Carl ordered a coffee. He skipped the raspberry scone.

****

Melanie's jaw clenched at Carl's question. She put a hand on her stomach and ordered herbal tea instead of her usual latte.

In typical scenarios, she and Carl would report any illegal business practices directly to the authorities, especially when the company's principals were involved. Their training and experience told them that working through a company's officers never ended well. In one case, Waverly suffered a lawsuit for defamation of character when they cited a chief officer's side business in their final reports. The claim against them had been a stretch, and Waverly was able to find a loophole. The client, in the end, had been charged with money laundering. The Shore case had multiple components of potential wrongdoing, and Carl needed to be the person revealing their discoveries. Otherwise, they could be in a similar situation again.

By the time she added sugar and cream to her tea, Carl had found a corner table where he sat with his coffee. She joined him and waited for him to say something. He inhaled and sipped several times before acknowledging her presence.

"Melanie, please consider staying here. Dominick will understand. I need you to be here when the liquidation begins."

"What you really want is to report the jewelry scheme to the authorities."

She looked at Carl's pleading eyes. The warm blue pools begged for her compassion. She should not have stated the obvious. His desperation was clear, and she could not turn him down. Either they agreed on how to proceed with their findings as a team, or she would leave. There could be no partial truths revealed.

When Melanie pulled a small notepad and pen out of her crossbody, Carl thanked her, and they started strategizing their approach.

It was mid-morning by the time they arrived at Shore. Melanie was surprised to see Joyce. Adam was in his office packing boxes while Joyce and Ray watched him. She let Carl take the lead.

"Adam, what's going on?"

Adam shot a look at Melanie before responding to Carl. "That depends on your girlfriend."

"That was way out of line," Carl said.

Melanie's face flushed. How could Adam think she and Carl had a relationship? Carl was married with children and not hers for the taking, unless Adam had no rules about such things.

Ray saved the conversation from going down the wrong track. "Adam, just pack up. Carl, why don't you and Melanie leave the room?"

Carl blew air out of puffed cheeks and turned away. "Maybe that's a smart suggestion," he muttered as he left the office, leaving Melanie on her own. Before Ray could tell her again to leave, she tried to get the information she needed.

"Ray, could I have a minute with Joyce?"

"I prefer that she stay here with me. Go ahead and get on with your day. We'll talk later."

Her face hardened, but she nodded and headed to the conference room. Ray's rejection stung. Melanie was a consultant, not family, and she should be treated with much more respect than that.

A missed call and voicemail from Dominick popped up on her cell. It had come in about five minutes earlier, just before she and Carl entered Adam's office. She was too preoccupied to feel the buzz through her bag.

Her return call went straight to Dominick's voicemail. Her heart beat a little faster when she thought about the implications of the missed call. Was he pulling her out of Shore? She dialed Carl. No answer. She hung up and sent a text to locate Carl.

The reply arrived after ten minutes, and she did not like the response that he was unavailable.

No Dominick, no Carl. Adam was escorted out of the building by security, and Ray would not let her talk to Joyce. Sweaty palms and tingling fingers caught her attention: fight or flight. She chose flight.

On the way down to the garage level, the elevator stopped at the lockers on Floor Three. When the door slid open, Dominick was staring at her.

CHAPTER 30

When he came around the corner toward the elevator carrying a briefcase, Carl stopped abruptly before bumping into Dominick. It took a moment to register what was happening.

Melanie held the elevator open and invited them into the car. Dominick stood still while Carl took a step forward and spoke.

"Melanie, let me explain."

She turned to Carl with a look on her face that posed the question, *What the hell is going on?*

Carl felt her eyes burning into his while he tried to explain. "I contacted him last night, and he caught the last flight out of Boston," he said, "but I didn't know he would get here by this morning."

Dominick came out of his silence. "Hi, Melanie. I left you a voice mail."

"It's good to see you, Dominick. I tried to call both of you. There's no cell service in this cave."

Carl pulled Melanie out of the elevator before the long pause caused delays for people waiting on other levels. He set the briefcase at his feet, placed a hand on her shoulder, and turned her to face him. "Dominick is here to help."

"What about the strategy we put together just this morning?"

"It still works."

"Why didn't you say anything about Dominick being here?"

"I told you he would understand."

"And that was enough?" She turned to Dominick. "Are you okay with the next steps for Shore?"

"I am. I had no idea what Phil Walker was up to when he called Waverly in for a review. I accepted without question."

"Phil called you?" Carl's voice was louder than he anticipated, and he looked to Melanie to confirm his confusion.

"Who do you think would have contracted with Waverly?"

"Given my father wants to sell and Uncle Phil is against that, I thought it would have been my father." Carl shook his head as he continued to put the pieces together.

"Phil is the Chief Executive," Dominick said.

"But why? Phil thinks everything is perfectly fine here."

"Nothing in this family has been transparent," Melanie added. "What's in the briefcase?"

"Take a guess," Carl replied.

"How many?"

"The ten that were left. And the box of coins."

****

Melanie stood shoulder to shoulder with Carl, and Dominick followed when they entered the Detroit Police precinct. Carl's bravery bolstered her own confidence that they were doing the right thing. By turning in the gold, Carl was implicating his family in a possible illegal business enterprise.

She could not predict if that enterprise was lucrative. If the gold produced greater sales to Luxury, Carl's bonus might have been secure. Adam had to find ways to pay for the bars, and money laundering wasn't something she wanted to discover. She shivered in the chill of the police station and tapped her fingertips against her thigh to alleviate the numbness.

Dominick introduced himself and stepped in as Waverly's representative. In the past, Melanie and Carl had handled these situations. She reminded herself that this case was not typical.

None of them imagined a web of lies, deceit, and fraud in a company associated with Carl Walker.

Her mouth went dry as she listened to the conversation. Occasional questions were asked that only she could answer. Some were directed at Carl. No one mentioned Joyce Walker. Recognizing that omission sent up a red flag. Melanie's legs quivered under the rectangular table in the cold, barren room. She pressed her palms into her thighs to steady the shaking.

After two hours of completing reports, answering questions from detectives, and watching the gold get registered into evidence, the police dismissed them. Melanie's head throbbed, and the bottles of water she had consumed were screaming in her bladder. When she excused herself for the restroom, Dominick touched her arm. "Good work, Melanie. This was a tough assignment."

She nodded and walked away to seek relief.

Her thoughts continued to spin in circles as she focused on a sudsy mix that formed a funnel and ran down the drain. She looked at herself in the mirror and imagined Carl's life being washed into a dark and murky stream. During their last assignment together, their relationship spiraled like the water falling through her hands into the drain in front of her.

In that instance, she had not wanted to uncover a fraudulent lawsuit that saved a company's profitability a year before Waverly was contracted. There was solid evidence, and Carl's steady moral compass led them down that path. She had ruined her pristine record with him by arguing the parties involved had taken one wrong step, and since then had righted their practices. But Carl had remained resolute, and they did the right thing. But she had tainted the trust Carl had in her. The fine line could be easy to cross, and Melanie believed Adam Barnes knew that very well.

Carl and Dominick met Melanie in the lobby. Seeing them reminded her of the days at Waverly before Carl left to save his family's company. Dominick slapped Carl's shoulder, and the two laughed briefly. Their open shirt collars and smiles contrasted with her level of distress.

They left the precinct to meet with the Walker brothers at their office. Every time she thought of Adam or Joyce, she had a physical signal that something was off balance. It was the familiar gut punch. Questions remained, and she was sure Dominick was in Detroit to help them find answers in the story. How was Carl feeling about that? This was private business, his family's legacy. No one could deny the positive impact the Walker family had on the city of Detroit.

****

Carl watched Phil and Ray stand up when Dominick Pierce walked into the C-suite conference room. Melanie introduced them out of habit and courtesy. Carl admired her ability to turn on the charm when she swept the room with her smile.

His temples throbbed just enough to tell him something would crash soon. He should have told her that he would be taking the gold to the police. That was something Dominick encouraged.

This meeting belonged to Melanie, but Carl anticipated Dominick's input. Their prior conversation had paved the groundwork for today. He would sit back and watch Melanie and Dominick peel away layers of schemes that had been exposed. The heat in Carl's suit jacket elevated when he thought about his mother, and the tension in his chest made him doubt his decision to protect her.

Melanie distributed copies of an action plan to liquidate Shore's assets. She explained changes that had occurred since her first presentation of a timeline and detailed the review she performed with Carl. They were not successful in identifying cash sources that would be sufficient to settle the Luxury lawsuit.

Melanie outlined a course of action that would generate enough cash to pay off debts and defend the lawsuit. She suggested exploring options for lower retainer fees for outside counsel to work with the Luxury legal team.

Dominick nodded in support of Melanie's plan. The timeline was aggressive, but Shore could stay on track with minimal interruption if everyone agreed and implemented the steps assigned to each department.

"This plan makes no sense," Phil said. "This company is not going under. We can turn it around. I know we can." Phil's pallor and tight lips gave Carl reason to interrupt.

"Uncle Phil, maybe we can listen to the rest of what Dominick and Melanie have to say. Then we can all talk about other ideas if you still feel the same way."

Dominick gave Carl a nod of agreement, and Phil puffed as he sat back in his chair. Melanie smiled at him and turned the meeting over to Dominick, who posed questions.

"Phil, what do you see as ways to increase cash flow and save Shore Industries?"

"I said I'd keep quiet and listen."

"You did say that, but this is a good time to help me understand an option that maybe hasn't been presented for review."

Phil looked at Ray and waited. Ray looked at Carl and asked, "Do you have a sense of what your mother's jewelry is worth?"

Melanie's mouth dropped open. Carl shot a look of panic at her.

"Come on, Carl. Phil was the one trying to trade in the family heirlooms. He had Adam on board to work that angle. It was all to keep Shore afloat," Ray added.

"You condone that?" The pounding in Carl's temples screamed for coffee.

"There's nothing wrong with the principals adding their own assets!" Phil's voice was shaky beneath his authoritative demeanor. "It wouldn't be the first time in the company's history that we had to dig into our own pockets."

The Walker brothers started their own sidebar conversation, recalling multiple times over the years when they had each sold personal assets to invest in Shore.

When Carl noticed the scowl on Melanie's brow, he suggested they take a break as they had not had time for lunch. He needed to get Melanie and Dominick alone.

****

They stayed within walking distance and grabbed food-truck fare to eat in Dominick's hotel room. The familiar routine served them well for days on the road working with difficult clients. Sometimes stepping away from the client's office was needed.

Melanie felt vibes from Carl and Dominick that they were enjoying being a team as much as she was. She also knew that the circumstances were far out of their normal sphere of performance, but maybe that fueled their energy.

Melanie used the time to focus on possible avenues that were not on the table. There was a theft ring that was yet to be revealed. And the person at the heart of the crimes had not been identified.

She pressed through the small talk with Dominick long enough to open the bag of greasy French fries and chicken. With one dip into the ketchup, she was ready to talk.

"Dominick, Carl might not have been completely open with you."

"About what?" Carl feigned ignorance.

"Don't do that, Carl. Either you're on board, or I need to be with Dominick alone."

She watched Carl deflate and felt a pang of guilt for what she was about to say. When Carl sat back and did not fight, she continued.

"Do you know about the police chase?"

Dominick nodded and took a newspaper off the dresser.

Melanie read the headline "Prominent Detroit Family Member Pursued in Police Chase."

She pulled the paper from Dominick's hand and scanned the article. The reporter outlined the pertinent facts, and to her credit, did include that Carl had pulled over and called the police when the chase ended. Details hinted at possible possession of stolen jewelry and gold. But, also to the reporter's credit, the signed document of ownership was mentioned as evidence of no stolen property.

The article concluded that misunderstandings were resolved after interviews had been taken with all parties involved, including Joyce Walker and Adam Barnes. Melanie did not like seeing her name connected to suspicion of theft, but the damage was done.

"Do you know that Joyce tried to have me sign to receive ownership of jewelry?" she asked Dominick.

He nodded.

"What about the fact that Adam ended up taking ownership and then tried to set us up like we were stealing the jewelry?"

"I didn't quite understand that. Explain."

Carl gave the details of Adam leading them into a trap by having the police at their destination when they arrived.

"Why would he do that?" Dominick asked.

"We think he was attempting to accuse us of stealing his jewelry, since Joyce transferred possession to him," Melanie said.

"Turns out there were pieces in there that were not part of any Walker heirlooms," Carl added.

Dominick shook his head and piled on more questions. "Why would Adam involve the law, and didn't Joyce know she was handing off more jewelry than she owned? And when did she figure it out?"

"Adam was covering his own crimes, and my mother just didn't look at what she was carrying until Melanie refused to take it," Carl said.

Melanie's heart sank. Carl was making excuses for his mother.

"Wait a minute! This makes no sense. The police determined there was no stolen property." Dominick looked at Melanie. "What's your interpretation?"

"Not quite the same," Melanie said. "The police looked at the inventory we took and the signed document, so it looked as if Joyce had owned everything we had. I thought so, too. Until now. I'm beginning to think Joyce took stolen jewelry from Adam and hid it in her own stash. She confronted Phil when she learned the truth about finances, and I think Phil pressured Adam to produce cash. Adam needed to protect himself from something Phil knows about him and ended up stealing to keep up with Phil's demands."

"What negative information did Phil have on Adam?" Dominick asked.

"Maybe his past record," Carl answered.

Melanie's food slipped on the table when she jerked around to face Carl. "What?"

"Hear me out."

Even with what Melanie knew, she hoped Adam acted under duress. She saw an innocent man somewhere under the tough skin. She was convinced Phil was the culprit and Joyce was part of a cover up. She would go so far as to say that Adam might have been trying to expose the theft without implicating himself.

If Adam had a criminal record, she would really wonder about her ability to pick out a good man from a crowd of scumbags.

CHAPTER 31

Christine was setting out a pitcher of ice water and glasses when they returned to the conference room.

"Thanks, Christine. We'll need that after a salty lunch from a food truck," Carl joked. He looked at her wrist. "Nice watch." Another Rolex in the C-suite.

She blushed and left the room.

Dominick carried a file of documents, but during the meeting it would be Carl's role to surface details and force Phil to admit his crooked business dealings.

Carl knew he should have given all the information to Melanie, but something tugged at his heartstrings. It would be impossible to report his mother to the police. Protecting her assets from Holly emphasized Joyce's opinion of Carl's wife, but she did nothing illegal when she followed family practice. Uncle Phil should pay the price, not his parents.

Dominick greeted Phil and Ray with jovial banter, comparing food in Detroit and Boston. Carl also thought that, like Melanie, Dominick was good at getting criminals to trust the environment enough to make a mistake, give the truth, and land the plane after a rocky flight.

"The food truck was pretty good, but you can't beat Boston lobsta'!" Dominick stressed the New England accent. The brothers appreciated the humor and relaxed in swivel chairs around the table. With everyone in the right mindset, Carl loosened his tie and addressed his family.

"Dad, Uncle Phil, this meeting isn't easy for me, and I know it won't be easy for you either." He paused to see if there was a reaction.

The silence lingered almost too long when Ray said, “Go on, son. We need to hear anything you and Melanie have to say.”

That was Dominick’s cue to put documents in front of them. He laid out credit reports for Adam Barnes. Ray picked them up and scanned the information before sliding them to Phil, who did a quick review and shrugged. “What’s your point here?”

“It looks like Adam Barnes, using variations of his name, got himself into a deep hole about ten years ago. There was a total of about a quarter of a million dollars owed to credit card companies and maxed out lines of credit at three banks. All of that happened within six months of his leaving a job in New York City.”

“What does that have to do with us?” Ray asked.

“It might not. But it’s curious that Adam built up huge debt, left a good position, and moved to the suburbs of Indiana. Stayed there for about four years working in real estate development and left within months of meeting Phil.”

“Are we on trial or something?” Phil’s question was clipped. He coughed to clear his throat. “How is this part of your review of Shore?”

“Interestingly, there are some unusual payments made to a company that collects gold scrap. We know that Adam owns that company.” Dominick presented the information objectively.

Carl saw Melanie’s wide eyes focused on him and knew she was looking for an explanation that he had not provided. Yet.

Carl watched Phil’s eyes scan the room. The mannerism produced a flash of Phil’s tall tale about ownership of a yacht in Florida to impress a woman at the Detroit Athletic Club. Phil’s habit of lying clouded Carl’s path for a moment. He gave a quick shake of his head to clear the way. “Isn’t that kind of odd, Uncle Phil?”

"So Adam and I struck a deal," Phil started to explain, but his voice was softer than usual.

"That deal may have killed Shore's bottom line," Carl said.

"Is this the arrangement you set up for his relocation expenses? I recall something about that." Ray tossed his brother a lifeline, and his cheeks glistened with sweat.

"Yes. Yes, that's exactly what it was," Phil said. He hesitated before adding too many details. "He had things stored in New York and Allen County, Indiana." He paused to cough. When he collected himself, he continued. "That's where I searched for a manufacturing site in Indiana. You know, we thought at the time it made sense to do some of our work out there where new industry was being encouraged. I believe the tax incentives were good, too."

He tugged at his jacket and tie, wiped his cuff across his forehead, and sniffed loudly. His eyes roamed the room seeking an alibi as he tried to concoct a story. It did not work.

Carl looked at his father, who leaned back in his chair, his head tipped back.

"Did anyone research the gold scrap business before making that agreement, Phil?" Dominick asked.

"No. It wasn't necessary. I figured the kid did something crazy and was trying to pay off his mistakes."

Phil choked and Melanie poured a glass of water for him. He sipped but said nothing more until Dominick prompted him. "So you hired a CFO with poor personal financial management? You must have seen some major benefit in taking that risk."

"I saw potential and wanted to save him from himself. Besides, not all the payments were from Shore. We have a personal arrangement."

Melanie took over the questioning. “Ray, can you tell us why you had Adam escorted out of the building today?” she asked.

Ray sat up and looked at her, his eyes squinting. “Because Joyce figured out that Adam had done something horrible that involved her.” He paused and looked directly at Carl. “Adam tried to move stolen jewelry through your mother’s name. We don’t stand for that kind of activity.”

“Phil, did you know that Adam was fired this morning?” Melanie asked.

“Yes. Ray talked to me, and I agreed,” Phil admitted.

“But you didn’t say anything about helping him with debt of that magnitude. Why not?” Ray leaned forward with his long arms stretched across the table as if he wanted to grab his brother.

Everyone sat very still to hear what Phil had to say.

“The kid needed a clean slate, that’s why. He got into some trouble in Indiana at a real estate outfit he worked for. It wasn’t anything big. He did a few things that he should have been licensed for. Then he had to pay off some folks so they wouldn’t report him. He never took the test to be a real estate broker. When I hired him, I promised to protect him.” Phil’s voice dropped off at the end. He hung his head and stared at his hands.

Ray clenched his fists on the table, purple lines on his neck pulsed.

The conference room phone rang, and Carl jumped to pick it up. The timing was perfect. “Send them up,” he said before hanging up the receiver. “Law enforcement officers are here. They have questions.”

****

Melanie wanted to vanish. She stood to clear space around the table. Maybe Carl was not protecting his mother. Maybe Joyce really was innocent. She eyed Dominick, hoping to catch a clue from him, but he stayed focused on Phil.

The room was quiet enough to hear approaching footsteps. She heard Christine making small talk with what sounded like three other people. A tap announced two police detectives who shared their badges and stated their names.

What she saw was so far left of typical procedure, Melanie let out an audible gasp. A uniformed officer escorted Adam Barnes into the room. Visions of Adam with innocent eyes flashed in front of her, making her throat ache as if she were about to sob.

Adam responded to Melanie with bedroom eyes. He looked her over like a jockey would evaluate a thoroughbred horse, making her suck her elbows into her sides when a sensation of spiders crawling up her spine cause her to wince.

She turned her focus to folders on the table and took a seat next to Carl. She leaned in and whispered. “Maybe we should duck out now?”

“Not happening.” Carl made clear his intention to see this work through to the end.

She sat back with a deep breath and succumbed to Carl’s need to revel in this moment. All indications were that he needed his father to know the truth. Adam was the cause of Shore’s problems. Carl’s diligence in procurement of raw materials was not to blame for financial losses.

Phil was the first to address the oddity that played out in front of them. “What are you doing bringing Adam in here in cuffs?” Emotion brought volume back to his voice.

"We've been talking with Mr. Barnes downstairs since he was taken out of the office earlier today," a female detective answered. "He just confessed to being in possession of personal goods that do not belong to the Walker family. Jewelry and gold coins."

"Phil, you should know that I won't go down without you joining me," Adam said.

Before an argument could break out, Dominick stood up and took command of the room. "It's true that the situation is out of normal procedure, Phil."

"Did you set this up, Carl?" Phil asked.

Dominick did not leave room for Carl to engage. "Carl was not looking to uncover family dirt. There were legitimate reasons that led Melanie to a deeper audit of specific cash transactions."

Melanie's forehead creased when she felt Dominick's words implicated her for uncovering illegal transactions. He did not lie, but the statement was not entirely true. Carl had put things together. He called Dominick in without telling Melanie everything. The enormity of the situation made her pause and think about all the possible implications. Her mind raced.

Less than two weeks ago, she left the final coaching meeting with the C-suite team knowing the demise of Shore Industries would be seen as her fault. But she never thought she would be the whistleblower or turn Carl against his parents.

CHAPTER 32

Melanie awoke to a new day, a new plan, and a headache. She had accompanied Carl and Dominick to the Detroit Athletic Club for cocktails that led to dinner and the finalization of the Shore Industries project. The evening extended beyond a decent hour. The Walker family associations at the DAC were long-standing, and Melanie saw Carl in his element, fully present, delighting in the camaraderie of his old team. Melanie also could see that Dominick wanted Carl back at Waverly.

The Shore Industries turnaround analysis was one of the hardest Melanie could remember in all her working career. It was not a turnaround at all. It was the slaughter of a colleague, and she had to admit Carl was still the only love of her life. He would pay dearly for taking a moral path against his own family.

The first step in the action plan would be more than difficult. The Walker brothers were no longer family. Melanie and Carl tore apart any bonds that may have existed all the years they operated Shore. Begun by their parents before them, with every intent on being an organization that served the greater good of the community, Phil Walker had turned his back on the mission their father worked hard to promote.

Ray Walker would have to tell Shore employees and the surrounding community that the Walker family was running a sham. Phil Walker, a supposed philanthropist and Detroit supporter, had betrayed everyone, and could face charges of fraud, bribery, theft, and money laundering.

Ray would be asked to deliver all the shutdown and liquidation plans alone. Carl wanted to support his father in any way he could, but his own reputation was at stake. Waverly

Consultants were not part of the implementation, and Melanie would be leaving Carl on his own. The thought of walking away at a critical time in Carl's life compounded the effects of too many cocktails the night before.

She looked out at the city view while waiting for room service to deliver her coffee. A hot shower and pain relievers lessened her headache, but nothing could touch the hurt in her soul.

Logic told her to look closer. There had to be a missing piece of this puzzle. Yes, they were moving forward with a solid plan. But what was it about Adam Barnes that kept hitting her so hard?

Those beautiful eyes changed from flirtatious to evil. He was innocent one moment, taking part in uncovering possible illegal dealings by Phil, then covered his own tracks the next. Melanie wanted nothing more than to know this man. To sit with him in an intimate restaurant, smell the rapture of gourmet plates, listen to the seduction of soft jazz, and inhale the woodland scent of Adam's afternoon aromatherapy. The one that lingered on his suit when he left the office.

Her eyes shifted to the ceiling and instead of this titillating scene, she envisioned the other Adam who devoured her with his eyes in front of the Walker men, making her feel cheap. Maybe she liked the way he undressed her with his eyes. There was so much more to learn about Adam Barnes.

A knock from room service interrupted her thoughts.

She opened the door for her breakfast tray and was surprised by the rush of a woman behind the server. The cart was pushed down the hallway away from the door, and the tray was grabbed out of the room attendant's hands by a tall attractive woman who commanded him to leave as she pushed a fifty-dollar bill into his hands. “And keep quiet.”

“Yes, Ms. Walker.”

“Walker? Charlene?” Melanie asked as she stepped backward.

“Good memory. Haven’t seen you since Carl and Holly’s wedding.”

The thought of Phil having a demon daughter raised urgency and panic. “What do you need with me?”

“Get your stuff. We’re getting out of this place.”

Melanie would normally have objected but now felt the need to placate this woman who could be as evil as Phil, but possibly in a physical way. She grabbed her crossbody, cell phone and its charger before saying anything more. Her thoughts twisted and gnarled into the growing ball of confusion about the Walker family and Adam Barnes.

The walk to the elevator was tense, Charlene’s proximity reeking of imminent harm. Melanie knew the physicality of the movement was intended to threaten her, and it did. Afraid to step out of line, she pretended to be friends with Charlene when they joined hotel guests in the elevator.

A car waited for them in front of the lobby doors, and Melanie was not given an inch of lenience when they approached the open door.

The back doors locked, and Charlene climbed into the driver’s seat. A large man sat in the front passenger’s side. A text message from Dominick distracted her, and Melanie did not get a look at the man.

> Boarding plane. Can’t reach Carl.
> Will call from Boston.

A familiar voice asked, “Is everything okay, Melanie?”

Phil sat in the front passenger seat and turned to look at Melanie in the back.

“I thought I was fine until you two just kidnapped me. Where are we going?”

“Hardly a kidnapping. You’ll like the party. Breakfast will be served,” Charlene said.

CHAPTER 33

Carl pulled into Shore Industries parking structure, turned the corner to the reserved section, and was blocked by a police barricade. He hopped out of the car to tell the uniforms who he was and that he needed to get to his office. The hand that shoved his shoulder pushed him against the hood of his car, and he reached back to stop the fall. A tall man in dark sunglasses, brimmed hat shading his face, walked out from behind a cement pillar and dismissed the cop.

"We need to have a chat."

Carl had no chance to get his bearings before the looming figure had him in a tight grip. The strong-arm shoved him into the backseat of a black car and climbed into the driver's seat. He peered through black windows to see the barricade being pulled down as they sped onto the street.

"Who are you?"

They hit the highway in record time.

"Have you really forgotten me?"

Carl knew his cousin Albert's voice. "What the hell, Al?"

"Shut up. Daddy called in a chip."

"Money for a house for Charlene? Is that what this is about? There'll be plenty of money if—"

"Just shut it, Carl."

His cousins always had a way of making Carl fall in line. Since they were kids, he took their orders like his life depended on their approval. Al's spooky hide-and-seek eyes haunted Carl in nightmares. Maybe they had much more power over him than he realized. He had not seen Al in at least five years. The time had not been forgiving and his age showed on his skin, if not in his strength.

The car headed out of the city, going east on Jefferson Avenue. Carl buckled his seat belt for what felt like a treacherous trip and used the movement to pull out his cell.

"Don't even think about contacting your father."

That was not who he had in mind. "No worries there."

Al twisted around to look at Carl directly. This threat was real. What else was going on in the Walker family?

"Where are we headed?"

"Just getting out of town for some clean air." Al turned back to focus on the road. Carl watched the scenery speeding by and wondered if his kids were okay.

He slid the phone under his leg and ignored it.

"Out to the lake, huh?"

When Al did not answer, Carl saw his fate. They would pretend to be a family on a casual weekend or holiday, sitting on the shore of Lake St. Clair swapping stories. Cousins mourning the loss of a family business that had become an icon in Detroit. They would grieve for the brothers who tried to follow in the footsteps of their parents and failed, creating havoc for their own kids. He and Al would fall back into the childhood roles they played, pretending the family was tight, intact in the pending demise of Shore Industries.

Carl's cell phone buzzed under his leg, and he managed to read it. It was Melanie.

Where are you?

As badly as Carl wanted to reply, he knew better. Al would take him to the shed if he did, a reference to family stories and the Walker brothers being disciplined with the rod of correction.

Carl and Al used to wonder if the stories were just legends intended to scare them into good behavior.

"Don't answer if it's Ray or my dad," Al said.

"I do need to reply here. It's personal," Carl answered.

"Must be the divorce I heard about."

A snapshot of his little boys burned in Carl's brain. They were huddled together on a gliding loveseat on the lawn at his parents' house. The sun caused them to squint, but their smiles and rosy cheeks spoke to the day of fun they had spent on the lake. The red, white, and blue bathing suits and towels were bought specially for the Fourth of July outing.

Friendly abduction by Cousin Al. Taking me 2 my parents.

Friendly? I'm in a car w/ Phil & Charlene.

"Hey, Al. When did you last see Charlene? I saw her at the hospital when your father had that episode." He kept his voice familiar, casual.

"Been a little while."

"Is she part of this little abduction?"

Al whirled around. "Is that Charlene texting you?"

Carl laughed. "Are you paranoid?"

"Why would I be?"

Carl shook his head and did not reply.

Might see you soon.

Dom left town. Will call from Boston.

Carl had intended to check in with Dominick when he got to the office this morning. He saw three missed call notifications from him.

Last night, Melanie and Dominick lauded their praises for Carl's steadfast commitment to moral dealings when he took the gold to the state police. He thought about joining forces with them again in Boston. His family business was a fraud, and his uncle needed to be taken down. His parents would be destroyed in the press unless someone stood by their side.

He could see headlines flaming with his name if he supported them. Their darkest secrets would be brought into the light, potentially destroying his ability to remain financially stable and support his family. He had not held his sons close or even talked to them in four days. Holly had made sure of that, or maybe it was the gentleman with Holly who was getting in Carl's way.

They pulled into the circular drive of his parents' home. Ray and Joyce greeted their son and nephew as if nothing out of the ordinary was happening. They did not even flinch at the fact that Al was in town. They walked four abreast to the front porch and strolled through the entry into the living room.

CHAPTER 34

Charlene poured Melanie a cup of coffee at the kitchen breakfast bar. "Since you were pulled away from breakfast, maybe this will help your attitude."

Melanie bit her lip as she had for the entire drive to this place. Charlene was considerate enough to offer cream and sugar, and the first few sips did give her the boost she needed to think clearly.

"How exactly does this family party involve me?"

Charlene gave her a sly smile. "Your boyfriend just came in the front door with my brother, so let's go see."

Melanie stood without spilling a drop of the precious liquid. Ray and Joyce retreated toward the kitchen to join Phil. Melanie focused on Carl's face. Dark circles under his eyes from lack of sleep added to his collapsed posture. She had never seen him look as fragile and defeated. When he realized her eyes were glued on him, he straightened his shoulders and flashed a smile. So typical of him to mask up and march on.

"I could use some of that coffee." Carl nodded at her cup.

Charlene obliged her cousin's wish and headed out of the room. "Black," Carl called out.

"It's not Starbucks, but it works," Melanie said. She hoped Carl would pick up on her attempt to get the cousins to relax and talk.

Albert leaned in and acknowledged Melanie's presence. "So you've had a chance to visit with Charlene."

Melanie tried to read the sentiment, but his dark sunglasses did not help. "Yes. It's been years since we met."

"Yeah. Carl and Holly's big day. Too bad that's not going so hot."

Melanie watched Carl deflate again.

Charlene came back with a steaming cup of black coffee and handed it off to Carl. He breathed in the fumes with his eyes closed. Melanie studied Charlene.

The Walkers were a handsome family, each with specific characteristics that identified them as blood relatives. Their hair was wavy, regardless of the shades that ran from dirty blonde to light brown, and they all had light eyes and defined jawlines. Standing together, they were an attractive party. Melanie wondered if the similarities ended there.

She read Carl's body language and cracked open the conversation. "So why are we here?"

As if on cue, Phil, Ray, and Joyce Walker appeared from the direction of the sunroom.

"Let's get a little nourishment while we chat about how we'll settle this mess with Shore," Ray said as Joyce set down a box of pastries.

****

Carl did not expect the closing phase of Shore Industries to become a family affair. Now all the Walker clan stood shoulder to shoulder. The plans they detailed with Dominick and Melanie called for Ray to finish writing his script and begin rolling out the news to employees by this afternoon. Carl committed to stand by his father through what promised to be a humiliating and unfortunate circumstance. Now the Walker brothers were derailing that course of action.

Phil spoke first. "Let's just say we don't need to abandon our empire just yet."

Eyes darted around the room as silence settled loudly at their feet.

Carl's parents stared at him as they held hands, breathing in unison. Cousins Charlene and Al wore smug smiles, waiting for their father Phil to continue. No one opened the dialogue.

Carl turned to see Melanie staring into the cup of coffee she clutched with both hands. He gazed through the wall of windows, across the lush lawn, and settled on the wooden glider. He imagined his boys giggling as the glider rocked slowly. There was no way he could ever give up his boys.

Ray cleared his throat and broke the impasse. "Carl, we brought you and Melanie here because there is something you both need to know." Phil raised his hand to halt his brother from saying any more. Carl remained silent, uncrossing and crossing his legs, and looking at his cousins for a hint.

"As I started to say, we might not need to abandon the ship just yet," said Phil. "We've had a setback, it's true. I made a huge mistake bringing Adam Barnes on board. I felt bad for the kid. But he's gone now. Out of the picture. We can right this thing."

Phil nodded to Charlene and Al. They looked at one another as if to decide who should talk first. Charlene, of course, took the show. "It's easy. We keep Shore going. Pull in all the favors our fathers are owed and just keep the business running. Nothing is going to come out about kickbacks. No one needs to know."

"What favors can be pulled in to save the company from huge lawsuits that are perfectly legitimate?" Carl asked.

Ray's mouth dropped open. "Carl, that's not correct. There is just one lawsuit out there, and that one can be beat. They have no supporting arguments. Those installations were third party.

Stainless Safety is grabbing at straws. We didn't install rails in that group home. We've never done installations."

"What about Luxury?"

One by one, gazes locked on Carl. Melanie set her cup on the side table and offered her perspective. "If I may, I'd like to give a little input here." Nods around the room let Carl know her words would be taken seriously.

"We know there are financial challenges that appear to be insurmountable on paper. We also know there have been less-than-appropriate, shall we say, exchanges of gifts, funds, thank-you tokens to large accounts. Bribes to get more orders.

"In at least five cases, the charges against customer accounts were not legitimate. You fraudulently billed for consulting services, and Shore is not a consulting firm. You sell tangible products. That set Shore up for the liability claims, not all of which have been settled. And that's not to mention the lack of compliance with the Articles of Incorporation on record that very specifically detail what products Shore can sell."

The tenor in the room shifted. The Walkers squirmed in their chairs, shuffled their feet, looked down, and showed every sign of guilt.

"And I haven't begun to touch on the transactions with Luxury Home Supply. The ones where twenty percent of the sales were refunded, a little at a time, through cash transfers into accounts that don't appear to be Luxury Home business accounts. A little kickback into the pockets of the principals there, maybe? They failed to pay their bills. That's always a risk in business, but writing off bad debt is a standard business practice."

When Melanie finished, she leaned back into her chair. Carl knew her body language. When she put her hand on her throat, her own reminder to breathe, Carl saw that she hated being hard on the Walkers. But she was right. Unfortunately, their purpose for doing business could have easily included consulting work. No one had the foresight at Shore Industries' inception to state a purpose to conduct any legal business. Nor had anyone considered filing for a change in the purpose of the business.

Carl gave her a look of pride and waited for the facts to settle around the room. Charlene and Al both eyed their father, and Carl was sure they knew about the uncouth business he promoted. He also could tell they had no understanding of basic accounting practices when Melanie talked about delinquent accounts receivable.

Melanie leaned in and continued. "So we did uncover potential illegal dealings, no matter how you couch the transactions. I understand you may have been trying to make the sales look better than they are for morale or to satisfy compensation arrangements among C-suite staff." She looked at Carl, who chose not to offer his own employment terms in front of his cousins.

"Police have an active investigation going, and Adam Barnes is in custody. The result could lead to legal charges against Shore.

"Based on all this information, Waverly advises that all accounts be reconciled, cleared with reparation to all affected parties through out-of-court settlement prior to and during the liquidation process. That simply means selling all Shore's assets, making payouts to vendors to clear your debt, and settling outstanding lawsuits. You may need to write off bad debts instead of finding ways to fund the amounts customers owe you.

"If managed correctly, the family's personal assets will not be heavily affected. And, I think, you will avoid company bankruptcy, which I sense is important to your family name."

"None of this is what we want to do." Phil's voice was laced with rancor.

"And what is your proposal, Uncle Phil?" Carl was impatient. His thoughts drifted to Holly, the boys, his mother's intrusion into his marriage. He did not have time for all these crises. His soul deconstructed as he realized his family was not what he thought they were.

"I'm dying," Phil said.

Carl paused and took the pulse in the room. There were no shocked looks, no gasps, no questions asked. Instead, everyone was watching for his reaction, including Melanie. Her eyes were round and wide, awake with caffeine, and questioning him.

"Am I the last to know?" Carl asked.

"Why does that matter? I won't be around much longer, and you're worried about the pecking order of information flow?"

"It's not that, Uncle Phil. We could have approached things very differently if we'd known how sick you are."

Charlene joined Al in laughing at Carl's response.

Ray shot a look at his niece and nephew before speaking. "You two might find this funny, but it is probably as hard on Carl as it is for anyone else." Carl met Ray's eyes and together they sucked in the hurt.

"And you think he would have done something different if he knew his uncle was knocking on death's door?" Charlene offered a snide and demeaning look to both Carl and her uncle Ray.

"Don't say it like I'm not here! I'm still functioning!" Phil found his passion and laid it bare. "We might think differently now since we all know the truth. Let's not liquidate. Please."

Melanie nodded at Carl for him to continue. He had no words. He had just reported his family to the police for possible theft to produce gold coins for bribes, Adam had been arrested, and now he was supposed to rethink the future of Shore. How?

Phil laid out his own ideas, none of which had been considered. Melanie and Carl listened while Ray and Joyce nodded their agreement.

Carl needed Melanie to extend her stay in Detroit and be a partner in the pivot he needed to make.

CHAPTER 35

Melanie crawled into bed, her body aching from the strain of the day. She and Carl had spent time rehashing their path, asking bigger questions, and generally doubting their original decisions. They had a virtual call scheduled with Dominick for ten o'clock in the morning, and she was prepared to support Carl. He felt obligated to stand by his family's wishes.

As much as Melanie knew there could be damage to Carl's professional reputation, she again recognized what she loved about him. She would have done the same for Momma. In her world, standing by family meant helping to put food on the table. The love and care dangling on the apron strings all through her college and early career years were indispensable. She believed she could never ask a child to support her, even though her own mother never expected that kind of devotion in return for the protection and love that enveloped Melanie. Carl had the same level of commitment to his family.

A bigger problem lingered for Shore. They needed a communication strategy to address forthcoming news after a police investigation would lay out all of Phil Walker's connections to Adam Barnes and his evil dealings. Stolen jewelry may or may not be in the mix for Phil, but gifting gold, creating income flow with dirty money, and offering payouts for larger sales orders would all land Phil in a bad place. As if facing his own mortality was not enough.

Melanie shortened her morning routine so she could get to Shore ahead of Ray and Carl. She chose comfortable attire in the form of a loose-fitting dress and warm cardigan she had bought specifically for this trip, tights and flat shoes accompanied by a generous scarf and her faithful crossbody bag. Still, she smiled when she thought of Momma's words when they left home together. "Put on some school clothes, Melanie. You don't want to be in play clothes if we bump into somebody we know!" How trivial it seemed to worry about such things. She would be happy to see her mother in a ragged apron, even if they were going to church.

Learning more about the Walker family gave her a new appreciation for family ties and warmed her to a domestic yearning. Today she would view the Walker family in a new light. When all was carved away to what is most important, they were bonded by blood. And she was bonded to Carl through friendship and, yes, love.

On a pass through the lobby coffee bar, Melanie caught a glimpse of the restaurant patrons. Still early, the clatter of flatware and dishes signaled the start of a busy day.

She focused on adding sugar and cream to her self-serve coffee and looked up to find Adam Barnes watching her from the restaurant entrance. A quick movement caused hot coffee to splash on the back of her hand, the heat stinging her skin. Attempting to move quickly to shift her crossbody bag and grab a napkin only made things worse. Before she could secure a plastic lid on the cup, Adam stood by her side.

"Need some help there?" The sadness in his face reflected a deep loss that she could not connect to his buttery smooth voice. He reached across her to secure the lid on her cup. His hand brushed the back of her wrist where the coffee burned, adding fuel to the sting.

Melanie looked at Adam, speechless.

Their eyes locked, and she detected the woodsy soap scent of a freshly showered man. His eyes shifted to her lips, and hers lowered to his chest.

When a few people crowded around Melanie to reach the coffee carafes, she shook off his male aura and stepped to the side, Adam following with her covered cup.

"Can we go over by the fireplace for a minute?" Adam asked, his voice warm and intimate.

Still lost for words, she nodded and followed him. They sat in barrel chairs separated by a round coffee table where Adam laid her coffee and extra napkins.

"Are you going to at least say hello, or thank you?"

She nodded. "Yes, of course. Thank you." The simple exchange brought her back to her senses.

"You must be wondering why I'm here in your hotel. Am I right?"

She nodded again and scanned the lobby and busy restaurant to identify anyone who might know Adam. She wondered about the charges against him but kept her questions to herself. He should not be walking the streets.

The trap closed in on her, and she fell for it. Adam would try to get her to his side and change the course of his legal problems. Flashes of him in dark clothes, a duffel bag, and sinister eyes alternated with the handsome man who walked confidently through Shore offices in tailored suits. The contrasts jumbled her logic.

"What do you want, Adam?"

"Just a conversation, that's all."

He tugged the sleeve of his pullover sweater, and Melanie took the upper hand.

"There's not much to talk about, is there? Or do you have more confessions to spill?" Her voice was flat, but her emotions were soaring everywhere. This man confused her.

Adam let out a sigh, stretched his neck, and faced her squarely. "None of this is what it looks like."

Melanie was surprised by the laugh that came out of her mouth. It was not genuine, and it was not her. "Sorry, Adam. That is such a cliche. It says 'Guilty' loud and clear."

"Let me explain. You might change your mind."

She looked at her phone. It was still early enough to spare some time if it would help her unravel what was becoming a loosely knit story. "You have fifteen minutes of my time, and no more."

Adam detailed for Melanie how he earned side money from Shore Industries. He explained that pieces of damaged gold chain links considered spoilage at Barnes Chain were sold for scrap, but he was the buyer. No one at his family's business knew they were selling to him. A truck picked up the material and took it to a processing facility where it was melted into gold bars and coins that he offloaded to Phil. Phil paid him at a premium over his cost. He admitted that sometimes extra jewelry from other sources got added into the mix.

"How does Phil pay you? Company money or his own?"

"A little of both, but mostly Shore Industry buys the bars and coins. My company is paid as a vendor. He also puts a commission through payroll, so it's all legit. I pay the income taxes on it."

"How does the Walker heirloom jewelry come into play?"

"It doesn't. It has nothing to do with the gold." Adam shifted his eyes and stopped talking.

"I need a little more than that. You just said sometimes there is jewelry added to the Barnes Chain scrap."

"That's Phil's work. I just help him out sometimes. And it's not all family heirloom stuff."

"Where do the other pieces come from?"

"Can't tell you that."

"Would Christine's or Katie's Rolex watch be one of those non-family heirloom pieces?"

"Maybe."

"What happens to the precious gems that are taken out of the jewelry?"

"Some of the jewelers buy them from us."

The coffee had cooled enough for Melanie to take a sip. The clamor of the restaurant died down, and the street traffic noise picked up. She waited for Adam to continue. When he smoothed his sleeves and touched the side of his nose, she wondered if he was lying. The story details were too vague to be a sure sign of a lie, but his body language aligned with fear and insecurity. When he slouched into the chair, Melanie wondered about his vulnerability and moved on with her interview.

"Why do you allow Phil Walker to make off-book payments to you through a company that sounds illegal?"

"He's paying the cost to produce the coins and bars!"

Melanie finally saw a true emotion when his story changed, and the vigor in his voice reflected a defensive attitude.

"I got caught conducting real estate sales when I was working as an assistant to an agent. I used the income to set up an investment account. I intended to use the income from the commission and the added earnings from investments to buy more of my family's scrap metal. Maybe even buy Barnes Chain without my parents knowing it. I was wrong, okay?"

"Does the investment account exist?"

"Yes, but I took a huge hit, dipped into lines of credit, used credit cards. Got in too deep. Phil hired me and has been helping me pay off everything." He looked left, avoiding eye contact. "I trusted a father figure to do the right thing and guide me in the right direction." He used air quotes to emphasize his lapse in judgment.

"That's lame for your pedigree, Adam."

"Agreed. But it's true. He said he could get my credit restored and maybe help me buy Barnes Chain anonymously."

The thought that Phil Walker would buy Barnes Chain for Adam seemed like a stretch, a dream that Adam was reaching for.

His strong cheekbones, gray eyes, and salt and pepper hair greatly diverged from the image of a young boy seeking guidance from a father. Adam was a lost soul in more ways than Melanie had realized. Creases deepened around his eyes when he pushed back tears.

Without thinking, she reached for his hand and squeezed lightly before she stood to leave.

CHAPTER 36

Carl and Ray were in the fishbowl conference room waiting for Melanie. Ray had a box of freshly baked pastries and napkins on the table. Each had a cup of coffee, and a pot was brewing down the hall. Even though she arrived after them, she had her own treats to share. News from Adam.

Father and son were talking quietly, enjoying breakfast, even smiling and laughing. She hated to disrupt the moment they were having. She was greeted cordially and welcomed the invitation to join them.

"The raised chocolate-covered ones are the best," Ray said.

She reached for the suggested donut and gave Carl a coy smile.

"You hit one of her weak spots, Dad," Carl said.

They were all getting comfortable around the table. Someone would say more than they should if given enough freedom and space. She waited and nibbled. Time passed too slowly for Melanie. The small talk was starting to chafe her brain when the reason for the delay walked into the room.

Carl stood up when Adam Barnes crossed the threshold carrying his black duffle bag. Melanie thought he looked different than he did less than an hour earlier in her hotel lobby. Confidence braced him, and his smile flashed of celebrity. Melanie shifted chairs to make room for him. He laid his duffel bag on the table and unzipped it.

A black towel lay folded across the top of loosely tied velvet bags. They nestled together in a way that nothing could spill out, but their contents shone spectacularly. Melanie tried to imagine the worth of the diamonds and emeralds that caught her eye.

Watermelon tourmaline stones in a tennis bracelet resided alongside pearls, sapphires, and opals. Each piece had to hold a value of tens of thousands of dollars. At least the sapphires and emeralds. Momma would swoon at the sight. All were worthy of adorning church clothes.

"Where did all of this come from?" Carl asked.

"It's a long story, Carl," Ray offered before Adam could respond. "Adam isn't responsible for all of it."

"Actually, none of it. Technically speaking," Carl added.

Melanie waited to see if there would be more information shared without interrogation. She sipped her coffee and nibbled the chocolate donut. Her thoughts drifted to Adam's earlier words about trusting Phil as a father figure for guidance. And now Ray was defending Adam.

The comfort food kicked her brain with an overdose of empathy. How could he have been raised in a wealthy family, sent to the best schools, had respectable business experience, and still be wandering into trouble? When a piece of chocolate dropped on her napkin, she dabbed it with an index finger and sucked it away before catching Carl's nonverbal cue for her to lead the conversation.

Another sip of coffee washed down the last bit of blissful indulgence before she spoke. "Adam, if you are not responsible for any of this loot, why do you have it?"

"You know why. Phil is my puppeteer."

"Cute. So you're saying you dance when the master tells you to? You don't think a big boy should make his own moves? And how does jewelry make you dance?"

"Enough with the rhetoric," Ray interrupted.

"Are you saying Uncle Phil has something on you, Adam?"

Adam looked at Carl with tight lips and gave a single nod.

"Look, Phil has his faults," Ray interrupted, "but none of this stuff is outside his legal right of ownership. As far as I know, this collection is all from the Walker family. Some from our grandmother, who was wealthy in her own right, which is why our father was able to pursue work for the greater good. He couldn't have manufactured grab bars and aid devices that were affordable without financial backing." Ray covered for his brother, and his flip-flop capabilities continued to surprise Melanie.

Ray wanted to sell Shore, then he wanted to put personal funding behind the company, then he wanted to sell again, now he supported his brother's unlikely possession of ridiculous amounts of precious gems. The imminent death of his older brother was creating allegiance.

"So where did it all come from?" Carl asked.

"I just told you," Ray answered.

"No. You said it was in the family. Where was this stuff hiding?"

"In my safe at home. It has never been part of the jewelry trading intended to grow the family heirloom investment."

Melanie rolled her eyes. This fiasco had gone far enough. "You're saying this collection has nothing to do with the bag Joyce was transferring to Adam."

"That's right," Ray said.

Without introduction, Adam pulled out a photograph and laid it on the table.

Carl and Melanie studied it in silence. The Walker brothers and their families, minus Carl, stood on the shore at the lake. Phil with his kids, Albert and Charlene, stood to the right of Ray and Joyce. A beautiful sunset painted the sky in red and yellow behind the Phil Walker family while faded clouds washed away behind the loving Ray and Joyce.

"I took that photo on the day the Walker family hired me to be the guard of their jewelry assets. I have traded some, sold some, and yes, swindled a little out of the hands of a few old ladies. All because Phil threatened to expose my mistakes in Indiana if I didn't turn the family jewelry investment into a multi-million-dollar collection. And I'm close to the goal of five million."

"How can you possibly claim that you are not responsible for your actions? You have swindled your family's gold scrap and used some unethical practices to increase the value of the Walker jewelry collection." Melanie's own words caused her arms to chill when she realized Adam really had been too weak to stand on his own.

"None of my actions are illegal. The scrap thing is my side business. My family just thinks they're dealing with someone else. Some of the jewelry acquisitions were made with a little pressure, but no one was hurt. There was no lying, no theft. Phil buys the bars from me. What's the harm there?" Adam's confidence had elevated to arrogance.

"What's with the photo?" Carl asked.

"I have the same question," Ray said.

Adam addressed Ray. "You were all heading out to dinner. Phil and I shook hands to seal my employment deal, and he asked me to take a family photo. I did. Then you all left for one of your favorite fancy restaurants on the lake. As far as I know, that was the last time Al and Charlene were in town together."

"I don't understand why you would want that picture," Ray said.

"With the deal I made, it felt like I'd sold my soul to the Walker family, so I kept a copy of the photo to remember the devil is not just Phil. The whole private family business is my nemesis."

There was a collective exhale of disgust from everyone except Adam. He smiled at Melanie. "You know I'm innocent. Why do you think the cops let me go?"

"Because Phil posted your bond, maybe?" Carl asked.

"Well, there will be no court hearing, so the bond was voided," Adam answered. "The police admitted they have nothing on me."

"Adam, you are basically saying that you are being coerced for two reasons. One is to keep your personal business quiet, and the other is to keep Shore business dealings private," Melanie said.

Adam was losing his calm demeanor. "I'm a victim of Walker family threats. Phil is paying my debts."

"What about the arson you committed to halt our liquidation plan?"

"There were no charges, Melanie. The foam and water used to extinguish the fire destroyed any possible evidence," Ray said.

"Are you saying you knew Adam set the fire?" asked Carl.

"Only after it happened," Ray replied.

Adam shifted in his seat. Melanie saw him as an innocent child who had been played for a fool when he did not know how to stand up for himself. His chest sunk against his spine and deflated his strength. She watched him closely, the tug on his sleeve, the touch of a finger against his face, the glance across the room. He was not only uncomfortable. She saw defeat, despair, and even regret.

"Look, Adam, this thing can all go away pretty easily," Ray offered.

Three sets of expectant eyes landed on Ray.

"All you have to do is offer to pay the settlement on the Luxury lawsuit, and we can wait out the disposition of Shore until we see where that takes us."

Adam's jaw dropped. Melanie squeezed her fingers into the napkin on the table, and Carl shook his head, but none of them spoke. The offer made no sense. Adam could not possibly pay that settlement cost.

"Look, you probably have enough cash value in the gold you've collected to bankroll Shore. Offer us reasonable terms, we'll take a loan from your gold bar business and move on."

Carl leaned into the table. He tipped his head in thought and said, "That might be a possibility. Adam, have you ever floated a legitimate loan to someone? Shore could work out repayment terms." Carl's voice indicated to Melanie that he was willing to exit the boxing ring without a knockout.

Melanie's phone buzzed. A text from Dominick asked her to call him ASAP.

She excused herself and stepped out of the room.

CHAPTER 37

Melanie gave Dominick an update in preparation for the upcoming ten o'clock call. He was less patient with the Shore project and recommended that Melanie wrap up her work in the next forty-eight hours. He needed her for another assignment in Boston.

"I would be extremely happy to make that happen, Dominick. The problem is that the end of this story is dark. I'm not sure you want to end any project on a negative note. Bad PR."

There was silence on the other end of the phone. She waited, sure Dominick was staring at the Boston skyline, rubbing his chin, and waiting for her to give more details. She could imagine the headlines. *Waverly Consultant Implicated in Bribery Charges.*

"Look, it's not as easy to wrap this up and put a pretty bow on it as I thought it would be. It's Carl, our trusted, once-lauded colleague!"

"He hasn't done anything wrong, Melanie. When families get into these borderline compromises, Waverly has to back away and let the chips fall where they may. Besides, I think I've got Carl interested in returning to Waverly."

The tension left her shoulders as she found a wall to lean against. A video of memories replayed project completion celebrations with Carl and Dominick, late nights over Chinese containers with chopsticks that served as pointers against a slide presentation on the wall, Sunday morning work sessions laced with black coffee and latte. A smile tugged at her cheeks when she closed her mouth.

"That's encouraging, Dominick. How do we get him out of here unscathed?"

"Leave that to me. Just get this thing wrapped up and come back to Boston. I'm here to support anything you need. Including muscle with the law to move a little faster, if necessary."

The laugh that escaped her surprised them both.

"Why is that so funny?"

She could see Dominick's laugh behind the question. "You? Muscle with the law? Never going to happen." Pride filled the empty ache she had for Carl's redemption. He needed to be restored to his former self. With or without Holly.

"Call me with Carl on the line at ten o'clock."

Melanie returned to the conference room to find two men laughing. Ray and Adam had bonded in the brief time she stood in the hallway. Carl was the odd one out. He did not look dejected, beaten, or disappointed.

She wrapped her cardigan close as she returned to her seat. The joviality and conversation lagged as if to cover up a conversation they were having about her. Since when did she ever feel this out of place in a client meeting where she had the lead role? Or did she lose that role here?

"Everything okay?" Carl asked.

"All good. Thanks for asking. Where are we here?"

Adam reached for the photo that was still in the center of the table. "We were just rehashing my employment arrangement and talking about new terms for a contract."

Melanie looked to Carl for details. When he avoided eye contact, she turned to Ray. "That's a shift from where we were when I stepped away from the table."

"Not really. Adam seems to like the idea of loaning money to Shore. That way Shore can settle the outstanding lawsuits, put a lawyer on retainer, and pull us out of the hole. But we need to keep him on the payroll for everyone's security."

"Then what? That's an immediate rescue. You'll still need to scale back, find ways to improve quality, and convince your current customers to continue buying from you."

"There will be plenty of cash flow after Phil dies," added Adam. "If we just keep a lid on all of this stuff until he's gone, Shore will be fine."

"Phil is paying your debts," Melanie replied.

"That's a separate personal arrangement."

Melanie slumped back in her chair, pulling herself into the comfort of her sweater and looking at Carl with a heart full of empathy. He caught her vibe and leaned into the moment.

"Dad, you had a family business. But blood relations aren't important to you. Maybe I should take the hint."

Adam stammered on about saving the business for the sake of the family. He struggled to paint a picture of love and support in the family circle, of Ray honoring his older brother's last wishes, of continuing the bloodline involvement in Shore.

"And who will that bloodline be, Adam? Carl and his boys?" Melanie asked.

"Al wants to join the Shore staff immediately," Ray said.

Carl's palms hit the table. "I think we have a meeting at ten o'clock, don't we, Melanie?" He stood and left the room.

"Carl's right. We have a call with Dominick. Do I understand that it is time for Waverly to move out of your way, Ray?"

Ray nodded in response. Melanie collected her papers, settled her bag across her shoulder and stood to shake hands. Ray stood as conventional etiquette would order, shook hands, and gave Melanie a warm smile. “Thank you for your input.”

When she approached Adam, her body froze, and heat filled her gut. He stood slowly, smoothed his sweater around his waist, and reached forward with both hands. Her palm warmed as he clasped onto her soft skin. She looked down at his firm, tender grip and let her eyes roam up his body to his chin, lips, and eyes. As if in slow motion, she tipped her head and offered a coy smile.

“It’s been a pleasure working with you, Melanie.”

“Good luck with your new scheme,” she whispered.

The words tumbled out before she had full control of herself. She dropped her hand from his clutch and stepped away from the table. Carl was in the hallway waiting.

****

Lunch on the hotel balcony was a pleasant change of pace. The chill of late October was welcome and refreshing. Defeat was never a pleasant marker along her professional path, but Melanie knew it was counterproductive to wallow in what could have been.

Wrapping up this assignment brought a mix of emotions. She would be leaving Carl and was unsure if she could put her feelings for him in a box and keep the lid on it. She was able to separate her feelings of agape love from the passion they once shared.

Mental photos continued to infiltrate her heart. These two weeks of intense emotional weaknesses made her yearn for familiar and comfortable future days in Boston. Working with Carl on his family’s turf was a reminder of her inability to commit to a family of her own, her need to control all aspects of her life, and the heartache she carried for her mother. Grief sucked her deeper into the chair, her body slouching with exhaustion.

She reflected on Shore as a loss in the tally of wins. If Carl walked out on his family's business, it would be the right decision. He was never meant to sit at the kids' table, and if he remained in the shadow of his father and older cousin, there would be no opportunities to eat with them. Carl had called the situation as he saw it. The Walker family functioned like a business. After witnessing his relationships, Melanie understood his parents had lured him back to keep family jewels close, to have a pawn for the empire, and to find a way to keep Holly out of their pockets.

The bigger question now was whether Holly would join him back in Boston. Melanie did not want to lean into that possibility. It was still Carl's face she saw when the topic of love invaded her thoughts. She had wondered if they could have been a happy, childless couple until recent days when she watched Carl's devotion to his sons.

The coffee in her cup had chilled, so she returned to the suite. When she dragged the sliding door closed, she wondered if that would be the last time she enjoyed the Detroit skyline. Nearly two weeks had passed, and while it was not home, the hotel suite had functioned as her respite during the hard days at Shore. She reflected on the night Carl slept on the couch, the next morning resulting in a bonding with Carl, Adam, and her. A bond that came unglued as soon as she trusted it.

Her cell phone buzzed and interrupted her thoughts. It was Carl.

She returned to preparation for her departure. Checking emails about her next assignment, packing, booking a flight for the next morning. Before any of that, she needed her own conversation with an old friend.

"What is up with you, girlfriend?"

That was exactly what Melanie needed to hear. A genuine laugh was enough of a response. She wanted Liz to know she would be back in Boston by noon the next day. With minimal details, Melanie admitted that she had not done her best work at Shore and allowed the "I told you to be careful" comment to float across the room on her cell phone speaker. They made a dinner date for the coming weekend and promised one another that it would be the best dinner ever.

CHAPTER 38

The sun moved lower in the afternoon sky before Melanie left the hotel. A lightweight quilted jacket was enough protection against the light breeze that funneled down the street. In repacking her suitcases, she pulled out a pair of boot-cut jeans that had gone unworn. They paired well with her brown leather ankle boots, matching hobo purse, and cream-colored cashmere turtleneck sweater. A tan and navy scarf cheered the open collar of her jacket, projecting a sense of security and optimism in what might be an awkward evening with Carl.

The idea that she had packed so many work and church clothes for a ten-day assignment was just one sign that she had hoped to impress the Walker family. Why was that important when she knew Carl was clearly off limits? Maybe she had a thread of hope that kept her tied to old dreams of a life with him. Liz had reminded her to be careful, and Melanie knew that was good advice.

She stopped at a crosswalk and looked at the flashing hand telling her to stop thinking about the past. Tomorrow the Walker family and Shore Industries would be in the rearview mirror. But where would Carl be? The signal changed, and she walked across the intersection. A small jewelry storefront with dark windows and gated doors made her think about the side business the Walkers kept—buying and selling jewelry. She gave in to the urge to step inside and see what that world looked like.

An older couple huddled over a glass showcase pointing to specific items for the big man behind the counter to show them. Melanie brushed past the arm of the woman and detected the scent of Ivory soap mixed with mothballs. Her wool coat had tattered sleeves and a torn side pocket.

Melanie made her way around the couple and focused on a display case of pendant necklaces. A marquise-shaped emerald surrounded with small cut diamonds set in white gold or platinum drew her closer. Melanie compared the pendant to others in the case. It was by far the largest and most brilliant. It was also eerily familiar. She wondered if she had entered one of Adam's trading posts. Remaining casual, she shifted along the length of the glass case until she was close enough to hear the couple asking for the price of rings.

"That piece just came in. Isn't it beautiful?" The man helping them slipped the ring into a small plastic bag and set it on the counter.

"We want a diamond to celebrate a big anniversary. But what is that stone?" the husband asked.

"That's a blue diamond in a square cut, about three carats, and the baguettes equal about half a carat of white diamonds. It's set in platinum."

"It's beautiful. I've never seen a blue diamond."

"The price is only thirty-five thousand dollars."

"Oh, my!" the lady exclaimed.

"It's really not that bad, honey," the man said. "With the insurance money we collect, we'll only need to pay about five thousand."

The couple looked like they could be in their eighties. She wondered why the cost was so low for such a precious stone and why they were buying such an impressive ring. And why was there insurance money to cover the cost? None of the details made sense.

Beginning to feel a little obvious, Melanie walked to a case labeled *Heirloom Jewelry*. There were pieces that looked more like estate sale costume jewelry than true heirloom items. She recognized thick gold bangle bracelets that were in vogue in the 1970s alongside chunky gold chains from the same era. Her mind wandered to Adam and the source of his cash flow. This store just might be the kind of place where he sold the Walkers' jewelry.

She unbuttoned her jacket and untwisted the scarf, allowing it to drape open and relieve the heat under her turtleneck. The owner took note of her sudden need to loosen her clothing and asked if there was anything he could show Melanie.

"Yes, there is. May I see that emerald pendant in the case over there?" She pointed to the counter next to the couple where they were still looking at the diamond ring.

When he turned to unlock the sliding door that secured the pendant, the old man grabbed the ring, and the couple ran out the door. Melanie followed them with her cell phone in hand.

She was dialing 9-1-1 when Adam Barnes bumped into the thief who now ran toward the corner, his wife lagging him.

"Adam, stop that man!"

He grabbed her arm and held the cell phone. "Drop the call."

In an instant, Melanie had met the real Adam Barnes.

The cell phone was confiscated and dropped in Adam's pocket, but he did not let go of her.

Their faces were within inches of one another. Adam's warm breath and woodsy scent lessened the threat of his grip on her wrist. When their eyes had locked a second too long, Adam dropped her hand and swiped his other hand across her open handbag.

"I'm dropping you a little hint. You need to understand me better. Now leave."

She had an immediate reaction to tell Carl what happened and pushed past Adam. Her thigh muscles were aching by the time she made it to her car at the hotel. If he had wanted to, Adam could have stopped her.

A fall festival downtown made the traffic slow, and she had to wipe the sweat off her hands more than once. If she did not get to the Greek Isles diner within a reasonable time, she knew she would miss Carl. He would try to contact her and go searching when she did not answer. Something felt terribly wrong, and anxiety grew with every delay.

CHAPTER 39

Carl pulled into the Shore garage just ahead of his father. Al's car was in Uncle Phil's parking space. He pulled into his own assigned slot and thought about how quickly they would find another innocent soul to take his job. Al would not be stacked so low on the team roster to be assigned to the Procurement Director position.

The elevator from the parking level to the office suite was blocked and a sign hung on the doors that read *Under Maintenance*. He walked out of the parking garage and turned the corner to enter the building from the street. A black car was at the curb, and the driver was helping Phil climb out of the back seat. Ray came out of the lobby as Carl approached the car to help. Charlene exited the opposite side of the car.

"Uncle Phil! Good to see you out today," Carl said.

Charlene glared at Carl. Ray greeted his niece with a hug and headed to his brother's side.

"Hear you've abandoned the company, Carl," Phil replied. His voice was soft but steady.

Abandoned the company. Carl wondered if he had abandoned his family. He waited for his father to stand up for him, but it was clear Ray shared Phil's sentiment.

"Well, I'm not sure that's how I would define things, Uncle Phil. Maybe I'm just making room for my older cousins to step in and help keep things afloat."

Phil responded with a hearty harrumph and dismissed his driver. Ray took his brother's arm and led him into the building. Carl watched with sadness as his once vibrant uncle labored with every step. The diagnosis of a stage four glioblastoma brain tumor had affected each family member differently. It was not Carl's place to pass judgment, but reactions ranged from Charlene's near jubilation at the potential of inheriting Shore industries to Al's sudden interest in a C-suite position at Shore to Ray's indifference. Carl really was the outsider. He chose compassion and focused on memories of his youth when Uncle Phil was jovial and fun-loving. It was Phil who teased and tickled Carl when he was little, threw him in a pool or the lake, and taught him how to fish.

Charlene looked at Carl with hard eyes and a set jaw. "What exactly do you think your older cousins will do, Carl?"

"Continue the family *traditions*, I suppose." With a curt nod, Carl walked ahead of everyone and took the stairs up to his office, intending to gather his personal belongings and exit as quickly as possible.

****

It was six-thirty and Carl sat in a corner booth at the diner with a cup of black coffee and watched for Melanie to come through the door. Anticipation of what he had to tell her made him anxious, and he wondered how she would react to his plans.

With the decision to return to Boston, he hoped Melanie would support him in seeking full custody of his sons. His work at Waverly would require travel. Holly complained about his absence for work more than any other aspect of their relationship. If they finalized their divorce, he would manage to be a good father with live-in childcare. He believed his kids would be better off in Boston, where they had spent all but one year of their short lives. The schools were familiar, and they had stayed in touch with regular virtual show-and-tell dates with Boston playmates.

If necessary, he would ask Melanie to testify to his ability to raise the boys, care for them independently, and provide a better home than Holly could. He did not want his boys witnessing inappropriate relationships that Holly may have already exposed them to. Besides, Holly could move back to Boston.

When Melanie was fifteen minutes late, he sent a text but did not get a response. Five more minutes passed, and his pulse picked up a beat. It was not like her to be late without notice. Sometimes her responses to his texts took a little longer, but the length of her silence this time flagged a potential problem.

Carl paid for his coffee and walked out. He headed toward his car that still held two boxes of his office contents. The best option he could think of was to drive to Melanie's hotel and wait for her there. The soundtrack from his stomach was not enough to shift his thinking away from Melanie's no-show. Did she have a car wreck? Was she sick?

He backed his car out of the parking spot and turned to exit the lot. Two people stood in the exit drive, blocking his car. One was Adam Barnes. The other was Charlene Walker.

Melanie was pulling into the lot. She slammed on the brakes to avoid hitting Adam and Charlene. Carl waved her away.

Adam spun around to face Melanie's car and ran to her door. Carl heard him yelling at Melanie.

"Get out of here," Adam screamed at her.

"Give me my phone!"

He saw Adam reach into his pocket and hand her cell phone through the open window.

Charlene yelled at Carl, "You just need to get on the next flight to Boston and leave us to run Shore."

Carl called out, "Mel, go! Don't worry about me."

Carl watched Melanie drive away before he responded to Charlene.

"What is this about? You know I left Shore," Carl said.

"I had a little run-in with your girlfriend earlier today," Adam said.

"Melanie? We're not—"

"Yeah, sure."

"What kind of run-in? She's finished with the project and on her way out of Detroit tomorrow!"

"Let's just say we may have both wanted to buy the same souvenir. I scored it."

"What are you talking about?"

Adam put his face within inches of Carl's. "Just listen carefully. Melanie is a good person, but she might have inaccurate impressions of me." He backed away and slapped Carl on the back.

"And you came here with Charlene to tell me this? How did you even know I was here?"

"Melanie left her phone behind, and I saw your texts. You should just go back to Boston and keep her warm this winter."

Adam gestured for Charlene to follow him. She turned to Carl instead.

"Look, we always knew the demise of Shore would be a disaster if we didn't take control ahead of time. So let's just leave it that the business is still in family hands, but the talented business cousin is off doing his own thing. It'll all work out."

Carl squinted in reply. "*Family hands*, as in you and Al? Funny how different the two of you are from our grandparents, the original Charlene and Albert Walker. Founders of Shore. Pillars of the community. As their namesakes, you two are a disgrace, not to mention your pitiful treatment of your father when he's staring at his demise."

"See you around the family table at Christmas?" Charlene asked.

"Maybe not."

Carl climbed into his car while Charlene and Adam walked across the lot. Thoughts of driving into them crossed his mind, but so did the urgency to talk to Melanie. He needed to know what had happened and why Adam had her phone. Melanie knew something about Adam. The possible scenarios were endless. His mind flashed to thoughts of his boys ending up as collateral in a crime family. Kidnapped, alone in an abandoned warehouse.

The exit was clear, and he left the parking lot. He called Melanie, but her cell went straight to voicemail. He sped up, hoping to find her blue Chevy rental on the road, but it was too dark. Instinct took him directly to her hotel.

****

Melanie walked into the lobby restaurant, still trying to reconcile the shock of Adam and Charlene's behavior. She took the first open booth and pulled out her phone. It was dead. She ordered the daily soup and sandwich and asked the waitress to hold the table. When she reached to push the button for the elevator to go to her room, Carl grabbed her arm. She hugged him and let out a heavy breath of relief.

While Melanie retrieved a phone charger from her room, Carl occupied her booth. She returned to find him breathing black coffee. Neither of them spoke. She was waiting for him to speak first. A cup of soup appeared with a turkey sandwich. Carl sipped his coffee.

"Aren't you going to say anything?"

He looked around the restaurant before focusing on her. "Yeah. I need your advice."

Melanie let out a little laugh. "Tell me you don't want to talk about Adam and Charlene. Because there are some real questions there."

"I need to talk about that, too."

Melanie signaled the server and ordered another soup and sandwich special. "It's on me. You need to eat."

Carl first asked why Melanie missed their planned dinner. When she told him about the jewelry theft and Adam's threat when she tried to call the police, Carl did not respond.

"Carl, did you hear what I said?"

He nodded. "I did. There's still something way off base with Adam and Charlene. Adam said you knew something about him that wasn't true. I bet that's why they tracked me down. But let them all rot in their crooked dealings. I'm out of there."

This man was not the same Carl she had admired for so long. He had been beaten down, and she had not seen that coming. She played with the napkin on her lap and watched Carl position himself to eat soup.

"What did you want to talk to me about?"

"My kids."

She saw the stress in his eyes. The bright light that had always been there when Carl talked about the boys was gone. His face looked longer, thinner. The smile he attempted failed to reach his eyes as it usually did.

Melanie reached across the table to clasp his hand. He looked into her eyes as his lips turned downward when he fought off the tears.

“I’m sorry. But it’s all coming at me fast. I leave for Boston a week or two. I can’t leave my kids here.”

Melanie gaped across the table. “You’re coming to Boston for real?”

“You didn’t know?”

Melanie laughed. “No one confirmed anything.”

Tears and laughter spewed from Carl’s joy, sorrow, fear, and confusion. “Melanie, what about my kids?”

The conversation was finally on the table, and Melanie jumped on the chance to be Carl’s strongest supporter.

CHAPTER 40

Melanie awoke early to the prospect of a clean start with a new assignment for Waverly. She would be in Boston soon. Within a couple of weeks, she would have her old teammate at her side. It would be a great return to business the way it used to be. She had to credit Dominick for getting Carl back to town, a development that would stop her from retiring. Maybe the Shore project did not have the best business outcome, but the results helped her settle the uncertainty she had about her career. This was not time to step away from the work she loved.

Today's travel would be easy after the rental car was returned and her bags were checked at the curb in Detroit. This routine was old hat, as they say. She would call a car as soon as she landed at Logan and be home by mid-afternoon.

Pulling out of the dark hotel parking garage, the sun caught her face and blinded her. A man stepped off the curb in front of the car. She slammed on the brakes, sending her small purse tumbling off the seat. The man screamed an obscenity and kept on walking. A horn blared behind her, and she turned the corner in a daze. At the first safe place, she pulled off the road to collect the spilled contents of the purse that would later fit into her tote bag.

Without paying attention, she scooped up all the items, replaced them haphazardly, and put the smallest items into a compartment she could zip. She felt a small plastic baggie lying at the bottom of the purse, the spare button she clipped off the new sweater she wore two days ago. It was odd that it landed here and not in her suitcase.

An alarm on her phone buzzed to warn her that it was time to get to the airport. She pushed everything together in her purse, closed it securely, and drove to Detroit Metro Airport.

The final boarding call for her flight was the most welcome news she'd heard in two weeks. Her time in Detroit needed to be left behind, and an in-flight movie might help her do that. She looked forward to a great return to Waverly after purging her brain of the Shore Industries project.

She sat in the wide first-class seat and got situated. She put her tote bag with her purse and valuables tucked inside under the seat in front of her, laid her cell phone on her lap, and adjusted the seat belt. Just as she was ready to decompress, her phone buzzed. Melanie closed her eyes, thought of all the possibilities. It was impossible to ignore the pull. Carl was sending a link to a breaking news story.

Jewelry Heist across. . .

The rest of the link was truncated.

"Please turn all devices to airplane mode as we prepare for takeoff." The announcement was crushingly loud.

Melanie's thoughts ran in too many directions at once. Call Carl? Tap the link? Turn off the phone? She got a text out in a hurry to say she was taking off and would call later.

She hit Send and tapped the news link. A local newscast opened just as the flight attendant passed. "I'm sorry, ma'am. Please put the phone in airplane mode. You can get complimentary Wi-Fi soon."

Melanie turned the phone off and stuffed it into the bag under the seat. She twisted the complimentary earphones into her ears, plugged the other end into the screen, and scrolled through her options. The real drama was put on pause.

The series *Suits* came up on the screen. The wannabe lawyer caught her attention. He had the nerve to fake his way into an interview at a prestigious law firm and managed to land a job without being an attorney. All to make his grandmother proud and take care of her.

Is that what Adam Barnes did? Did Phil Walker see a possible scapegoat, or did he sincerely feel a need to mentor Adam? The difference here was that Adam was not trying to make his family proud, and he had a solid background until he landed in Indiana. She had not figured out why he was there and needed to be rescued. Or was his entire resume false?

Carl's text occupied her thoughts more than the drama on the screen.

The jet engines lulled her into twilight sleep. Her hands were holding a needle as she wove fibers together. The long weft threads carried historical backstory while the warp bled around the dark fibers in shocking red tales of corruption. Adam's voice was faint in the background. She heard his words "dropping you a little hint" as a pattern came together in the shape of a diamond.

The announcement to land interrupted the series she was watching, and the change in sound woke her. She disconnected her earphones. It was time to face the real-life plotline that lay in front of her.

As soon as she got into an Uber, she dialed Carl. His phone went straight to voicemail, and the news link he sent was not connecting. She put her head back and thought about the mess she was in. She remembered the baggie in her purse. Maybe it was not a button.

****

Carl paced the carpet in his home den. The news had been running nonstop since he got out of bed. A jewelry heist that started the day before had been discovered when four different jewelers reported missing gems. Their locations were within proximity, and about fifteen people took part in the scheme.

"We are standing in front of ReImagine, a local dealer who sells heirloom jewelry. This shop has been in business for nearly ten years with no thefts, and the owner tells us the neighborhood is safe. Yesterday, a couple ran out of the store with a ring priced at over thirty thousand dollars."

Carl flipped the television off. He had heard the same description too many times. Melanie's story about Adam threatening her if she called the police matched every detail of the theft being reported. When he put the pieces together, he knew Melanie was in trouble.

He looked at the clock. She would land at Logan airport within two hours, maybe less with a tailwind. There was no one he could trust to dig into the events surrounding the theft, and he had to see his boys. There were four hours left in the school day. He distracted himself by emptying his desk in the den, preparing for his move back to Boston.

The workspace reminded him of the life he and Holly had tried to build together. Her expensive taste in furniture and bookshelves lined with impressive first edition books that she acquired through a long search. He tried to thwart the purchases, tried to tell Holly to save the money for private schools for the boys, but instead she insisted on living in luxury. Even though the house was nothing impressive.

Pushing the sorrow away, he focused on getting his favorite office accessories together. The tape dispenser and letter opener were part of a set that he kept in a drawer. They were carved wood with his initials monogrammed on the handle of the opener. Melanie had given him that set at Christmas when they were together. He felt a tug on his lips when he thought about taking these back to Boston.

In the back of a side drawer, he felt a large envelope and gently removed it. Photographs he intended to frame for his office spilled onto the carpet. His sons fishing, dressed for Halloween, opening Christmas presents, and hugging him on Father's Day. He stretched down to gather each photo and looked at the dates and locations inscribed on the back. They were still so young.

Carl fell back into the leather desk chair and stared at the memories in front of him. His family was growing too fast. Holly's smile in the pictures was beautiful. Her face echoed the joy in her heart. Where had that joy gone? He traced her face on the glossy photo with his finger and wondered what else he could do to stop a divorce.

CHAPTER 41

It was a sleepless night filled with new fears about a ring she discovered in her purse. When she had finally talked to Carl, he suggested contacting the police. He believed Adam set her up to be implicated in thefts that were orchestrated around the city. Melanie disagreed. Her instincts told her there was a reason the ring was in her possession. She just had to figure out why. Carl gave her until noon to be in touch. The warnings he cited included jail time for obstructing a police investigation.

She had lain in bed thinking of her mother's jewelry. The best she owned was her small engagement diamond, now tucked away for safekeeping. Her pearls, broaches, earrings, and bracelets were all inexpensive costume jewelry that was tastefully created, timeless, and hard to identify as imitation. Solid-colored clothing in the latest fits adorned with simple jewelry resulted in timeless style. Momma worked magic with their meager budget. When the Walker family drama was behind her, Melanie would have her mother's diamond crafted into something she could wear daily. She wanted a reminder of her humble upbringing and her mother's love.

Before she could do anything, she needed food delivered and a cup of coffee. She placed an online grocery order and considered running to the corner coffee shop before it could be delivered. Even though she was in familiar territory, a heightened sense of vulnerability caused her to pause. Rather than rush into the corridor, she unbolted the condominium door and put an ear to the surface. Footsteps passed by. Another set of footsteps slowed down, then stopped.

She was not sure exactly where the person was standing, but the fine hair on the back of her neck was itchy. A person stood outside her door, but no one had buzzed her apartment. It was too soon for the grocery delivery to arrive. The flight instinct rattled her. She had nowhere to run.

Leaving her hands flat against the door and not moving her feet, Melanie shifted her body to look through the peephole. A man was looking down at his feet and raising a hand to knock. Her breath quickened. She shifted her face away from the peephole and left her palms flat on the surface. A knock rapped against her left palm. She desperately wanted to set the deadbolt again but knew she would signal her presence to the stranger on the other side of the door.

A bang hit her hand again. Her shirt shook over her heart. There was no escape.

She prayed in silence, *Dear Lord, help me stay calm.*

She counted to ten with her eyes squeezed shut, air pumped in short spurts through her nostrils. Every breath a threat of being heard, exposed.

There was silence on the other side.

Melanie pushed her body back from the door without moving her feet or hands. With enough distance from the door's surface, she managed to drop her head and relax the muscles in the back of her neck. When she looked down, a large manila envelope was being pushed under the door. It hit her foot and stopped.

The person pulled the envelope back and tried again, this time wiggling it side to side. It made enough noise against the rubber safety strip on the bottom of the door that she could slide her foot out of the way without being heard. The envelope floated across the hardwood. Footsteps indicated the man was walking down the hallway toward the elevator.

Frozen in fear and not trusting what she heard, Melanie removed her hands from the door as if in a slow-motion film. She backed away and quietly reset the bolt without taking her eyes off the doorknob. She retrieved the envelope and tiptoed into the kitchen where she could sit on a counter stool and still see the entrance. Across the open dining and living areas, she stared at the city through the large windows that flooded the space with morning sun. Her city. Who followed her here and why?

She sat in silence, afraid to open the envelope that had her first name scrawled across it. No address. When her fingers stopped shaking enough so that she could handle her phone, she reached out to Carl.

Someone followed me here???

Melanie put her finger under the sealed flap and the intercom buzzed, causing her to yank on the thick paper and catch a nasty paper cut. With a few extra heartbeats, she grabbed a napkin off the counter and answered the buzzer.

The trickle of blood stopped. She got the envelope open and scanned the first page of a document. Afraid of bleeding on the pages, she shoved the document back in the envelope when the delivery woman knocked. Opening the door, she looked up and down the hallway.

"Is anyone else out here?"

"I only saw one guy getting on the elevator when I stepped off."

The bags were loaded onto the kitchen island, and Melanie watched the woman until she stepped into the elevator again. There was no one else in sight. One man getting on the elevator could have been any one of her neighbors leaving for work.

This was ridiculous. She bolted the door and got to work unloading groceries and making the coffee she so badly needed.

Thirty minutes had passed before she realized Carl had not responded. She did the next logical thing. She prepared for a productive day, loaded her laptop and files into her briefcase, and headed to her office. Not wanting to repeat a mishap like yesterday's, she was more careful with her crossbody purse that she could keep close. A cozy turtleneck sweater and wool blazer were enough to fight the Boston chill.

She kept a hand on her possessions on her way to Waverly. The soft leather briefcase she hugged reminded her of a handbag her mother bought for her at a discount store when she was still in high school. Her only Christmas gift that year, it carried the brand of a television actress. That purse stayed in service for all her high school and college years.

Melanie recalled how she and Momma had walked bravely into a Coach store to look at the luxurious leather goods. The sales associate had complimented the bag that matched Melanie's outfit and referred to it as one of their most popular styles. The mother-daughter duo had continued browsing, said they were only shopping for ideas, and left in laughter. Her chest ached with memories of the outings spent with her mother, her best friend.

Within an hour, Melanie was stepping into the offices of Waverly Consulting. The staff were happy to see her. Special pastries were laid out in the break room. She had not been away much longer than for other projects, but Dominick must have told the staff that she had a rough assignment. There was nothing more welcoming than the Boston cream pie and cannoli from the bakery in The Pru lobby. She bypassed her office to catch up with everyone.

Fall was in the air, and people were sporting heavier sweaters, sipping pumpkin lattes and spiced teas. It was not until she could stop and look around her that Melanie understood how important her home had become. She felt her body relaxing, her arms naturally by her side with even shoulders. These people and this place grounded her in all ways. Soon, her circle would be complete with Carl in the office. Maybe her days of business trips would come to a slow end, but she would not leave her team, her career, or Carl.

Dominick walked into the chatter and caught Melanie unprepared for a meeting. “Welcome home! We’ve been sitting on projects until you were back in the fray. See you in twenty.”

Melanie laughed. “Ya gotta love that guy!”

Her briefcase needed to be unpacked, and her crossbody bag was still in place. She begged off with promises to catch up later and got herself ready to meet with Dominick. A scan of new emails and notes left on her desk let Melanie know this would be a late-night kind of week. Still shaken by the morning events, she wondered how she felt about going home in the dark. That had never been a problem. Until now.

When she retrieved files from her briefcase, the morning’s delivery made her shiver. The contents were very incriminating.

She looked at her phone, but Carl still had not replied to her text. With Dominick waiting for her, she decided to call Carl at noon.

CHAPTER 42

Melanie walked into Dominick's office with her laptop and a cup of coffee. He greeted her with a side hug and an invitation to the conference table. The view of Boston Harbor and skyline distracted most people, but the best brainstorming and planning were generated through this department in front of these windows.

Dominick started with a debrief on the outcomes at Shore Industries. They agreed that the family's final decision was not in the best interest of the company. He added that he was considering a substantial percentage discount on the billing. Melanie added her two cents.

"A discount might look like a favor of some kind for Carl's sake."

"I've thought about that. But the police have all the information, and he had nothing to do with the gold. We did what we needed to do. In the meantime, you noted that their accounting practices do not help their bottom line, and they have an opportunity to change the way they record transactions. They can also take steps toward offering consulting services in a legitimate way if that's what they decide to do."

They concurred that the best outcome was Carl's recognition of the corruption in his family and his decision to return to Waverly. Dominick expressed sincere interest in Melanie's wellbeing. He asked what she thought about Carl's return to Waverly, having reconnected and collaborated with him for nearly two weeks.

She knew the language, the approach, the heart behind the question.

"My head is in a good place. Carl has a lot to work through, and I'm ready to be there for him. I'm happy that he'll be on our team again."

"You have a deep friendship. I hope you can keep that strong in the hardest transition of his life."

"Coming back here?"

"No. Leaving Holly and his kids in Detroit."

Melanie looked at the bay. A layer of morning fog hung above the water like the haze of confusion settling around her heart. Carl was more than a typical friend, and they were more than typical business partners. The term *work spouse* had a deeper meaning for her.

But then there was no doubt that when Adam was near her, she felt sparks.

Dominick needed none of this information.

She made eye contact, paused briefly, and then replied. "He deserves all the support I can give him."

They spent the morning making sure there were no pending details on the Shore project. Billable hours were reviewed, and the signed agreements were prepared for the staff to log and file.

By noon, they finished reviewing upcoming contracts, expected outcomes for each, project timelines, team assignments, and the company calendar.

"Before we head into the work of the day, I'd like to talk with you about something that might be really important," Melanie said.

Dominick closed his laptop and focused on her. "You have my full attention."

"It has to do with a big news item out of Detroit yesterday."

"The jewelry heist?"

"So you know."

"I don't want to assume anything since I only saw headlines."

Her turtleneck clung to her neck as moisture glued the fabric to her skin. She reached up to tug it away under her hairline before starting her story.

"All I can say is that before leaving Detroit, I witnessed two people trying to steal a ring. When I tried to stop them, Adam Barnes appeared outside the door of the store. He grabbed my wrist, took my phone. He told me not to call the police and left."

Dominick pinched his brows together and curled his lips inward before speaking. An exhale preceded his words. "Is that it?"

"Yes." She had the pleading eyes of a child but could not stay in that space. "Maybe not."

He gave his look of "tell me everything," and she explained the ring in her purse, the envelope that had been pushed under her door, and Carl's warning that she was being set up.

She laid the envelope on the table and let Dominick examine the contents. An insurance appraisal for the ring was written in Phil Walker's name. The value was more than four times greater than the thirty-five thousand dollars she heard the jeweler give as a retail price.

"This appraisal is twenty years old. A hundred fifty thousand was a whole lot of money for a piece of jewelry back then. It's still too much to pay."

"I agree, but who put the copy under my door this morning?"

With a call to his secretary, Dominick cleared his calendar for the day.

****

It was not Carl's plan to travel so soon, but with no choice he booked a twenty-four-hour visit to help Melanie get rid of the ring. He hoped also to begin the employment process with Waverly.

He landed at Logan Airport at one o'clock and saw Melanie's early text and a missed call. Traveling with just a backpack, he walked quickly through the airport, got into an Uber, and then checked his messages.

Why did she think someone had followed her to Boston?

Have more info- don't call police.

I haven't.

Good. I'm in Boston.
Where are you?

Wow! At Waverly. Didn't
expect to see you.

On my way.

His first goal was to take care of the ring. He was focused on keeping Melanie's name out of the news around the Detroit heist. With any suspicion of involvement, their reputation for being straight-up business partners would vanish in one bad headline.

He hopped on the elevator with lifted spirits as he ascended to Waverly Consulting offices. He was in his comfort zone, a place of challenging work and good outcomes. A full contrast to Shore Industries where he never knew who to trust.

When the car stopped, the door slid open to a crowd of reporters.

****

Melanie sat at her desk researching jewelry appraisers that could take an appointment right away. Dominick had offered to go with her so two people were present for the appraisal. The Detroit crime was now hitting national news like fire. Smash-and-grab thefts had occurred simultaneously in and around the city. There might be inquiries into her possession of the ring if she were alone.

It was after three o'clock, and she called the last possible local resource. Luck was with her when they gave her an appointment at four o'clock. The jewelry store was located about twenty minutes away, so she packed up and walked to Dominick's office.

"Where are they?" Dominick was talking to the receptionist and waving Melanie into his office.

"Call security."

He hung up the phone and grabbed Melanie by the arm. "Let's go. Back exit."

"Why?"

"I'll explain later. Just move fast."

They hurried to a stairway that led them down four flights before picking up a limited-access elevator to the parking garage.

Melanie held her crossbody close. She had put the blue diamond ring in a small sleeve sewn inside a zipper pocket designed to carry a backup battery for a phone. The value of the ring worried her. With an insurance appraisal of one-hundred-fifty thousand dollars and the jeweler quoting thirty-five thousand to the thieves, she suspected the ring had been stolen.

Dominick had his hand on her back, urging her to move fast and get to his car. They needed to get out of the garage unnoticed. Before they pulled through the exit gate, her phone buzzed.

Reporters blocked me.
I'm standing at the back
of the garage.

"Do you see Carl? He texted. He's here somewhere."

Dominick took a turn through the row of cars.

"Right there!" Melanie spotted Carl.

The car slowed down enough for Carl to hop in the back seat, and they sped out of the parking structure.

"Sit low," Dominick said. Carl and Melanie slid down and lowered their heads. They drove past the front of the complex within view of a mob of reporters.

"What is going on?" Melanie finally asked.

"That mob that was outside our offices. I couldn't get off the elevator. Story hunters."

The most up-to-date news out of Detroit had connected the Walker family to the robberies, Carl Walker to Melanie Sullivan, and both to Waverly Consulting. Carl leaned forward when they were a block away. "My fears are becoming reality. We can't have a false news story ruin Waverly's good name," he said.

Melanie put the address of the appraiser in her phone's GPS, and Carl brought them up to date and what he knew.

"I broke down and called my father. I learned that Charlene was asking Phil for a blue diamond ring she remembered our grandmother used to wear. It was Uncle Phil's, but my father had possession at one time."

"Because Phil was getting a divorce?" Melanie asked.

"You got it. It went back to Phil after any threat of losing it to a non-Walker."

"That sounds devious," Dominick noted.

"It's a secret family weapon," Carl said. He chuckled and shook his head.

"Did Phil give it to Adam to sell?" Melanie asked.

"Not sure that was intentional. But Adam sold many pieces in bundles, without regard for the value of individual items."

"So Phil asked Adam to get it back." Melanie stated. "Was it really for Charlene?" She did not think Phil would hand over something worth that much to his daughter. He needed cash for other things.

"Not sure if he would give it to Charlene or not. But Adam contacted all his outlets to find the specific piece. He never kept a detailed inventory of what went to which buyer."

"That says a lot about his skills as Chief Financial Officer!" Dominick added.

"For sure. Maybe he's avoiding evidence so he can plead innocent to illegal transactions."

"Maybe I really am carrying a stolen ring!" Melanie's fingers tingled, and she spun around to see Carl's face.

"I don't think so. The owner of ReImagine alerted Adam when that couple wanted to buy the ring, but they ran out with it. You know the rest of the story. In the end, Adam paid the jeweler the thirty-five thousand dollars he quoted the couple, hoping to keep the police out of it," Carl explained.

"He couldn't tell us that when he showed up at the restaurant?"

"Charlene was there. She still doesn't know Adam's job includes managing family collections."

"I don't see the logic in any of this story," Melanie said.

"It's the Walker family. There is no logic."

Dominick smiled at Melanie but did not add anything to Carl's conclusion.

CHAPTER 43

Before they got out of the car for the appointment, Melanie pulled out the insurance appraisal. Carl's eyes opened wide when he saw Melanie's name scrawled across the envelope.

"How did you get this?"

"It showed up under my door this morning. Do you recognize it?"

"The handwriting is my mother's."

Melanie said nothing. Her initial reaction had been that the ring was in her possession for a reason. Now she needed to rethink her position regarding Joyce's involvement in dishonest transactions.

She rubbed the back of her neck and wondered why Joyce wanted her to know the value of a ring that belonged to Phil Walker.

She looked at Carl with mist forming in her eyes. Melanie was realizing that Joyce liked her more than she appreciated the mother of her grandchildren.

"Let's do what we came here to do," Dominick said.

She was thankful Dominick pulled her back to her purpose.

The appraiser scanned the documents. "The good news is I have no need to weigh stones or check quality. This document comes from a well-known certified gemologist, so this won't take long. Feel free to browse while I update the values of the stones and setting. We have a lounge with coffee and snacks if you'd like to wait there."

"Sounds good," Carl said and followed the aroma of his vice.

"Carl, what do you think is going on?" Dominick asked.

"If I had to guess, I would say maybe my mother doesn't think this ring really belonged to Phil."

"Do you think Phil plans to sell it and put the money into Shore, or does he really want to give the ring to his daughter?" Dominick's curiosity sounded sincere.

"With Uncle Phil, anything is possible. Maybe his scare with mortality gave him a little religion." He held a cup of coffee close and breathed in. "Let's hope the appraisal is stronger than this coffee."

"Based on Charlene's performance lately, I would guess that if Phil gets the ring back for her, she'll convert it to green as soon as possible," Melanie said.

"You're probably right," Carl agreed.

"But who slipped the envelope under my door? That was scary."

Melanie watched Carl, hoping that he had solved the mystery. She detected something different. He was more relaxed than when she worked with him in Detroit. His jaw softened and stayed that way. His shoulders were low but not slumped in defeat.

"Carl?"

"Sorry, Mel. I don't have any answers. My family. . . well, my birth family is a little messed up."

She tipped her head in question but was interrupted by the salesperson.

"Ms. Sullivan, the appraiser is ready for you. You can follow me to the office."

"I think I'd like all of us to go."

"You and Carl can go. I've heard a couple of emails come in on my phone."

As they followed the lady, Carl leaned in toward Melanie. "Thanks for including me."

"Well, it's not mine!"

The salesperson turned around. "Did you say this ring does not belong to you?"

"Oh, it is going to be hers," Carl said.

Melanie smiled. They were a team, and they played the game very well.

"Well, congratulations! When is the big day?"

"We haven't decided." Melanie poured on a bright face and walked into the appraiser's office. She saw Carl pulling at his finger and slipping his wedding band into his pants pocket. She could not help but wonder about an omen for what lay ahead for him.

When they arrived back at The Pru, the offices were empty and there were no signs of the story hunters. Each locked up their offices for the day. Dinner would be Dominick's treat, the first business evening with the reunited team. They spoke sparsely on the way to the waterfront.

The sun, nearly gone, opened the way for crisp fall air. Carl pulled a sweater out of his backpack and draped it over Melanie's shoulders as they walked down the docks to the restaurant. The quiet of the bay mixed with salt air. Melanie heard Carl take deep breaths. It felt good to be home with him at her side.

"Good evening, Mr. Pierce," the maître de greeted Dominick. "Ah! And Ms. Sullivan. Mr. Walker! It's been a long time. Welcome back to The Pier." The sincere greeting reflected many dinners served to this trio in the past.

"Thanks, Marco. Good to be here." Melanie noted the softened tone in Carl's reply.

They were led to a premier table overlooking the water where conversation started with suggestions involving the ring. Carl wanted to get it back to Phil and back out of the situation gracefully. Dominick agreed that returning it quickly made good sense and noted Carl's desire to keep his and Melanie's names out of the news headlines.

Melanie, though, had hesitations. She wondered why Adam dropped the ring in her bag, who gave her the old appraisal, and whether the thieves were part of the bigger heist. She pointed out the decreased value of the rare diamond.

"Hundred thousand, a drop of thirty percent. That's about right with all the buzz around lab diamonds," Carl added.

"There has to be a reason Adam wanted me to have the ring and for Joyce to make sure I knew the value," Melanie said. "It's curious to me that Phil was looking for that one item at the same time the theft ring was in action."

"Can we agree on a couple of things?" Carl asked.

"Depends on what those things are," Melanie answered.

"You two haven't lost your cadence!" Dominick raised his wine glass and took a sip.

Carl nodded toward Dominick but did not shift topics.

"This is just speculation, but I think Adam told Phil he located the ring and slipped it to you. Then Phil, not remembering the value himself, contacted my mother to see if she still had the appraisal. She would have given it to him if he asked."

"I think I can buy those points. But why did Adam want me to have it?"

"I think he was setting you up. Maybe he wants you to know he can be powerful, and you should not dig into his business."

"That might be the answer," she agreed.

"Whether Uncle Phil sells the ring for himself, his kids, or the business, we don't need to care. He may even have asked my mother to pass the appraisal to you so you would know what you were carrying around. Phil knows you don't trust him."

"Okay, I can understand that, even if Phil is not quite that transparent." Melanie nodded in agreement.

Carl paused before adding his last thoughts. He sipped his Manhattan slowly. When the silence extended, Dominick asked, "What else, Carl?"

"Melanie, don't take this the wrong way. I know you and Adam kind of clicked on some level. Your logical side understands he might be bad news, but your heartbeat tells you something a little offsides with your sensibility when he's around. Am I right?"

Melanie's hackles rose and put her on the defensive.

"Oh, so you think we were attracted to one another, huh?"

"Maybe. He did say you're gorgeous."

Dominick cleared his throat and encouraged Carl to stay on track and get to the point of what to do with the ring. Melanie smiled as she thought of business protocols. She understood work environments of earlier times and never worried about the MeToo Movement of nearly a decade earlier.

"My point is that we can't let a little fantasy version of Adam Barnes take us down a rabbit hole based on Melanie's thinking she was supposed to have the ring, that some sign from the universe needed to be unraveled."

Melanie sat back in her chair with an exhale. "Just what are you getting at?" Her tone was sharp, clipped.

Carl responded gently. "You wondered if you were meant to have the ring. Do you remember that?"

Before admitting his good memory, Melanie drank her wine.

She looked out at the water and savored the best part of the evening. Honesty was on the table.

****

Adam Barnes stepped off the plane and into a waiting car at Detroit Metro airport. On the ride to Shore offices, he reflected on a renewed purpose. Al Walker and his sister Charlene were forces to be dealt with. Charlene was getting impatient to receive the extravagant piece of jewelry, and with Phil's help he had put the essential information in the right hands.

He had done the right thing by hand delivering the appraisal papers. Now that Melanie knew the value of the stone, she would get the diamond to its rightful owner, Mrs. Joyce Walker.

Maybe Boston's Irish luck graced him when he found an innocent, hungry bystander. The hundred-dollar bill he paid to have the man run an envelope up to Melanie's condominium door was worth it. With that dirty work out of the way, Adam thought about the fire in his bones.

Melanie was a special lady.

CHAPTER 44

A jewel carrier and an armed guard stood in Melanie's office at six o'clock in the morning. The carrier presented proof that he was insured and personally bonded for values up to four million dollars for the work he would do. Melanie placed the ring in a box and photos were taken of the transaction. She signed the required paperwork confirming the ring had been transferred to the carrier after the package was tagged and tucked into a locked box. Carl witnessed all the signatures, and he walked with the carrier and the guard downstairs to the courier entrance at street level. There, another guard sat in a locked and idling armored van. This pickup was the only one along their route in the early hours of the day.

Delivery of the ring to Ray Walker in Detroit was guaranteed by ten o'clock in the evening Eastern Standard time. Ray would hold the ring until he could personally see his brother Phil, whose physical state was deteriorating quickly.

Melanie was thankful that Carl had labeled her poor judgment last night. It was true that Adam Barnes puzzled her. There was chemistry there. But he was not always a good guy. Or was he? She still wondered if he had good intentions and repeatedly ended up following bad advice. Maybe he was a professional fraud, and she might never know the man behind the mysteries.

She did know that Carl knew her better than she knew herself.

During her momentary preponderance, Carl returned to her office with coffee and pastry.

"Have a coffee with me before I head to the airport?"

"That was a quick stay!"

"It was. But I'll be back for the long haul in a couple of weeks. Until then, we'll be working together remotely."

Melanie accepted the hot cup, and they sat in leather chairs near the window of her office. The sky was orange and red. Neither spoke. They just took in the view. Sipping and nibbling, a favorite pastime, especially with your dearest companion at your side.

When enough space had opened, Melanie asked Carl how he felt about his transition.

"Great! I'm doing the right thing."

"What about the boys?"

"I'm working on that."

She employed her best listening skills, nodded, and waited.

"I'm hoping Holly will want to come back to Boston. She's not that happy in Detroit."

"What does that mean for you?"

"That I'll have my boys nearby, we can try for shared custody, and who knows? Maybe we can save this marriage. I'm not convinced she hates me."

Melanie smiled but turned to avoid Carl seeing puddles growing in her eyes. "I hope things work out best for you."

"How can it not? Even if we do get divorced, I'll have you to work with. We're an impressive pair of consultants, Melanie."

Carl stood to leave. He gave Melanie a hug, swung his backpack into place, and tossed an empty cup into the trash.

"What's that saying? Red sky at morning—"

"Sailors take warning," Melanie finished for him. "But I'd say yellowy orange might not count. You'll have a smooth flight home."

"It's the storm I'll have to endure with Holly when I get there."

"Before you go, let me apologize."

Carl gave her a questioning look and waited.

"The last project we did together here, at Waverly, wasn't my finest moment. You, as usual, were right about walking the straight and narrow path of business ethics. I hope you see me as completely on the right side of the law."

He smiled. "Of course I do. We all have our dalliance, at least when we walk through what-if scenarios in a project. I've never thought for a minute that you would compromise yourself or your colleagues with bad decisions." He kissed her cheek and turned toward the door.

"Good luck with Holly, Carl."

"Bye, Mel."

He left the office, and she ran to the door. "Keep me posted!"

"Will do." He waved over his shoulder and exited through the reception area.

When Melanie returned to her desk, the sky had darkened.

****

Melanie watched the clouds roll in and out of the harbor. It would not be the greatest or the worst evening in Boston, but she had lots of work to do and much to look forward to. She retrieved a healthy snack from the break room and prepared for a long night at her desk.

The protein bar in her hand made her smirk. Someday she would dig into the real Adam Barnes.

An incoming text message sounded on her phone. An unknown number with the iconic 3-1-3 Detroit area code.

Can we have a chat?

Who is this?

Adam Barnes. New phone.

She looked across the horizon and saw a plane heading into Logan. Life was moving on. People went to and from ports of call. Her own worn but comfortable path needed no disruption.

My work in Detroit is finished. No need to talk.

She sent the reply and put the phone face down on the desk.

A Waverly Consultants Novel

Published by

An imprint of D L Gollnitz LLC

OTHER NOVELS BY D.L. GOLLNITZ

Follow the Husting family saga through a tangled web to Ronnie's final resurrection.

Set in Wilmington, Delaware, these companion novels follow the life of Veronica Husting from birth in 1945 through age 75. She is born into great wealth but is motherless, raised by estate staff and an absent father. Ronnie's character is shaped when she reveals her deepest secret and navigates her way to true happiness.

Books in suggested reading order:

The Hustings: A Family Web takes the reader through Ronnie's struggle to maintain her financial status through marriage to a movie mogul. After nearly losing everything in a tragic accident, she returns to her roots. Sharing family secrets could destroy the very thing she is trying to save.

The Hustings: Ronnie's Resurrection visits her recovery when Ronnie sees the present, past, and potential future during a visit to the afterlife. She is determined to correct the wrongs of the past by exposing the truth. Ronnie finds love, makes difficult decisions, and saves her daughter and grandchildren from disasters in their own lives.

Available at Amazon and
Most Online Booksellers
DLGollnitz.com

ABOUT THE AUTHOR

D.L. Gollnitz dedicated the greatest part of her career to coaching student writers in high school classrooms. She writes fiction that focuses on family secrets that shape relationships. It is her goal to write for entertainment and create characters with whom her readers can relate. She enjoys the shift from years of academic research and writing to creative endeavors.

A guiding principle of her writing follows what research tells us about developing readers. Young readers need to see themselves in the books they read. People who are in later chapters of life will enjoy finding mature characters in her novels.

Gollnitz lives in the Midwest with her husband but hails from New England. In her spare time, she creates quilts because every good book needs a blanket!

Learn more at DLGollnitz.com

ACKNOWLEDGMENTS

Writing is a collaborative endeavor, even if only one person is producing the text. Without the kindness of fellow authors, book club members, and friends, this story would have huge flaws beyond those that might still exist. My thanks to the very early readers who were honest and critical about structure and character, including Terry Odell, author of multiple mystery romance series; Therese Stacy, fellow Readers Class member; and Kyle Hall, former colleague and literary scholar. The real criticism received from these beta readers was invaluable. Finally, my thanks for the editing work of Mary Yakovets that led to a polished manuscript of this book for readers to enjoy.

www.ingramcontent.com/pod-product-compliance
Lightning Source LLC
Chambersburg PA
CBHW050142120726
47903CB00002B/457

* 9 7 9 8 9 9 8 5 2 3 2 1 2 *